The

APPARITION

Martin J. Roddini

Dedication

This book is dedicated to those who fought and battled so that I could be free, and to those who continue fighting even to this day.

This is a work of fiction. Unless otherwise indicated, all the names, characters, businesses, places, events and incidents in this book are either the product of the author's imagination or used in a fictitious manner. Any resemblance to actual persons, living or dead, or actual events is purely coincidental.

Also by Martin J. Roddini

Saving Kings

They Can Hear

The

APPARITION

Chapter One

The Accident

It seemed as though Danny and Chris had known each other for their entire lives. In fact, they met when they were in kindergarten, and that's almost their entire lives. They remained as best friends throughout their elementary school years and continued that relationship right through high school. They even played on the same school teams. Danny was a little better at football while Chris excelled at basketball. However, nothing caused any kind of schism between the two.

The two friends looked forward to attending college, and although they might be accepted into different schools, they knew that the bond they had would not be affected. Their educational focus changed dramatically, however, when New

York City was attacked on 9/11. After discussing their options, they decided that finishing college could wait, and that their country needed them more. Both of their families being heavily patriotic, and with parental approval, Dan and Chris signed up for military duty after just one year in college. They were not alone in this decision. Many young men put their lives on hold and felt the need to defend their country against the possibility of another catastrophic attack. These new soldiers were going to find the perpetrators of the September Eleventh slaughter, and they were going to make them pay.

When the time came for Danny and Chris to report to their recruiting area, they realized that they would probably not see each other for quite a while. It was not the army's way to assign friends to the same unit. This realization was more difficult for them since they were more like brothers than friends. Neither one had any siblings, so their relationship grew to a bond that was normally associated with family members. They were looking forward to serving their country, but they were doing it with the heavy heart of separation. They were confidants, friends, and more importantly a support staff for each other. They were now being forced to cast that aside for the greater good. Being the strong and patriotic individuals they were, they accepted their fate.

Danny was the first to be called to get onto the bus that would take him to his destination for basic training. Having bid each other "good luck," Danny boarded the bus and forced himself not to look back. He had to be strong and get used to the fact that other guys were going to take Chris' place. Other guys on whom he would depend to possibly save his life. He looked at the faces of the other recruits and wondered if his face also reflected the uneasiness of entering this new arena that would shape his future, at least for the next four years.

Chris waited for his name to be called and did not visually follow Danny as he approached the bus. He had the same idea as Danny. He had to be strong and face this new life. Looking after Danny as he left for the bus would not help him adapt. So, like Danny, Chris turned his back and faced the other recruits waiting to be called to defend their country. He heard the bus pull away, and although he wanted to bid another farewell, he just turned to the young man next to him and started a conversation. It was difficult, but he had to start somewhere and that somewhere and sometime was now. Danny did the same thing and refused to look out of the window. Instead, he introduced himself to the guy next to him and started a conversation. It seemed that they were both in the process of making new friends and putting everything else on the back burner.

The bus ride brought Danny to Fort Dix, Lakehurst, New Jersey where he would board an army transport plane that would take him to Fort Leonard Wood, Missouri where his basic training would begin. Since they were all "in the same boat," conversation came easy. The recruits exchanged home origins and some background specifics, but all mentioned why they were joining the military. Each one stated how he was going to "make them pay." They were outraged that anyone would dare attack their country, and they were going to make sure that it never happened again. The period immediately following the 9/11 attack was one of the biggest recruiting cycles the military had ever seen. Everyone was geared up to seek revenge on the terrorists who had the audacity to attack Americans on their own soil.

It was Chris' turn to board the army bus. He was glad to get called because the longer he stayed and waited for orders, the more he began to doubt his decision. It was going to be a major change in his life and change didn't always come easy. As he began to walk toward the bus, he felt a tap on his shoulder. Standing right behind him and waiting to board the bus was the captain of his high school basketball team. Tim Jenkins felt the same patriotic calling as Chris and Dan had. Although he signed up to fight for his country, he was visibly nervous about his choice. Chris was glad to see him, and Tim was noticeably relieved to have someone he knew with him. Chris realized how nervous Tim was, and although he was probably just as nervous as Tim, he tried to distract his former teammate with memories of the games they played. Tim responded well to the distraction, and before they knew it, they were on their way to places unknown.

Danny was engaged in conversation, but the thought of where Chris might be permeated his stream of consciousness. Danny knew that Chris was more "laid-back" than he was, so getting into the mix of things was going to be more difficult for Chris. Danny had always been there to support Chris, but this time Chris was on his own. Although Danny was somewhat worried about his friend, he was also not totally relaxed with the situation. He was going to be trained so that he could fight and kill in a foreign land. As everyone chimed in with their thoughts regarding the attack in New York City, Danny could see through their mask of confidence, that behind it was a lot of angst and nervous trepidation. No matter what they said, everyone was on edge. They were going to face the unknown. None of them could boast of past experience or actual knowledge of what awaited them. It was exciting but also nerve racking.

The same way that Danny was thinking of Chris, the reverse was also true. Chris, however, directed his attention to calming the nerves of his friend Tim. He felt that his efforts were working. He was distracting Tim and, in the process, warding off his own nerves. Just as things started to calm down, there was a loud shout from the front of the bus. It seemed that one of the recruits had changed his mind and wanted to get off the bus. The recruit sergeant tried to calm the recruit, but the new soldier would not hear of it. The sergeant, with the help of some of the other recruits, physically restrained the individual. This was the wrong way to start a military career. We all wondered what was going to happen to the panic-stricken "newbie" when we arrived at the destination. He had signed a contract with the United States Military and was subject to their orders. It was too late to decide differently.

The military bus carrying Dan and his new acquaintances was only about twenty miles from their first stop, Fort Dix. They were now all military personnel and the anticipation of "what comes next" flooded their conscious thought. The atmosphere in the bus had calmed to a tolerable anxiety level when everything turned upside down, literally turned upside down. A tractor trailer was passing the bus when suddenly it swerved into the bus and forced the bus off the road into a ravine. The truck driver had fallen asleep at the wheel and caused the bus to roll out of control and tumble end-over-end into the ravine. It turned over twice and was now engulfed in flames. The bus had become a fiery tomb for the soon-to-be soldiers. Stumbling out of the bus, and collapsing to the ground was one survivor, Danny Ferguson. He was injured and fell unconscious. It was far from an auspicious start to a military career, but Danny Ferguson was alive, just barely alive. The bus behind him turned into a death trap for the recruits. It exploded with such an impact that it tossed Danny's unconscious body into the air, inflicting more damage onto Danny's motionless frame.

Irony had played a significant role in Dan's survival. No one wanted to sit next to the emergency exit on the bus. Apparently, there is a superstition that it's bad luck to sit next to the emergency exit on a military vehicle. The small group of recruits situated in the area of the emergency exit drew straws to see who the unlucky guy would be to challenge fate and sit in the unlucky seat. Danny drew the small straw. It was this "unlucky" result that enabled Danny to push open the emergency door and crawl his way to safety.

However, he needed more than luck to survive the aftermath of the deadly accident. He was in critical condition, and his future was far from guaranteed. His fate remained in question.

Chapter Two

The Unsuccessful Fake

Chris Martin's ride on the army bus was transporting him to McQuire Air force base in Lakehurst, New Jersey. From there, he and the other recruits were going to board a military plane that would take them to Fort Sill, Oklahoma to start their ten weeks of basic training. Chris and the other recruits wondered if the panic-stricken individual who caused all the commotion on the bus would accompany them to their final destination. The majority opinion focused on the fact that none of the recruits would ever see him again. That was okay with most of the guys on the bus. They didn't need someone adding to the stress of the moment.

McQuire Air Force base and Fort Dix are one and the same complex. So, Chris' bus would follow the same route that Danny's bus had used. The two buses were about three hours apart. Other than the outburst that was quelled by the recruit sergeant, the ride had been a relatively smooth and calm one. However, the serenity was blown apart when the bus had to slow down for a police operation. Chris and his companions were now in bumper-to-bumper traffic. Traffic never sat well with anyone, but the individuals on the bus wanted to get on with their indoctrination. They didn't need anything else to add to the anxiety of the moment. However, that wasn't to be the case. They could see the emergency lights of the police vehicles up ahead, and now they heard the siren of an ambulance as it weaved its way past the bus and through the traffic. This told everyone that there was an accident with injuries. Never a good thing to see.

As their bus got even closer to the scene of the accident, the recruits saw multiple emergency vehicles, including additional ambulances, fire apparatus and oddly enough, military police vehicles. They ultimately realized that it wasn't odd for military vehicles to respond when an accident involved a military transport vehicle. When they came upon the site, the recruits saw the military bus, similar to the one that was transporting them, rolled over on its side. It was smoldering and looked like it had exploded. A deafening silence came over the bus riders as the realization hit them. The accident involved the bus that left right before they did. To Chris this realization came with an alarm that took his breath away. That was the bus that his friend, Dan, was on. Was Dan okay? Was he injured? Was he even alive?

Chirs wanted to know what happened to Dan. He couldn't control his emotions, and he yelled: "Stop the bus! Stop the bus!" The sergeant immediately responded to Chris and tried to calm him down. When words of compassion didn't work, the sergeant, in no uncertain terms, ordered Chris to stay in his seat and "shut up." Chris was blinded by the fact that his lifelong friend could have been badly hurt in the accident, so he continued to yell to stop the bus while attempting to explain to the sergeant the reason for his concern. Chris' pleas fell on deaf ears, and, once again, the sergeant ordered Chris to stay put and be quiet. Chris persisted. The only thing that saved him from a disciplinary action was the fact that the bus was now passing the accident scene and was resuming normal speed. With the sight of the smoldering bus behind them, Chris realized the futility of continuing his request. He sat back down and went into deep thought about his friend and quietly prayed that Danny was okay.

Chris decided that as soon as they arrived at their destination, he would inquire as to the condition of his friend, Danny. And wherever Danny was, Chris would go to the location and check on him. He was sure that after explaining how close the two of them were, the officer in charge would let him go to see Danny. Even though he was now in the army, he was sure that under the circumstances, the army would understand. If they didn't, he would make his own way to whatever hospital Danny was in, whether they liked it or not.

Unfortunately, Chris Martin was totally unaware of how the military operated. He was in for a very rude awakening. Whatever Danny needed would be taken care of under military province. They did not need the help of anyone else. Not only did they not want or need the help, but they would make certain that nothing interfered with their planned procedures. Disobeying this tenet of military protocol could very easily result in charges being levied against the violator. Chris labored under the thought that the military would understand the close friendship, and that Danny would want to see Chris. He had better rethink the situation. The military was a strict and sometimes cold parent who knew what was best for its charges. Nothing was going to change that.

As the bus arrived at McQuire, Chris was one of the first recruits to stand at the ready to exit the bus. However, the recruit sergeant was in charge, and he ordered everyone to remain seated until he called their name. This was just another unnecessary delay, as far as Chris was concerned. He knew that he was already on the bad side of the sergeant, so he used his better judgement and waited for his name to be called before he exited the bus. The sergeant directed everyone into a four-deep, side-by-side formation and ordered them to march to a transport plane that was apparently waiting on the tarmac for them to board. This new set of orders did not allow Chris to inquire about his friend, nor did it give him a chance to find out where Dan had been taken. He had to do something. He decided that he would feign an injury to his foot after a calculated fall. This would at least give him time to find out if Dan had been injured and to what degree. He could even find out where Dan had been taken. He might also be privy to the possible devasting news that Dan didn't make it. But he strove to keep his thoughts on the positive side.

As he walked behind his fellow recruits, he intentionally stepped on the back of the foot of the person in front of him. With an obvious yell, he fell to the floor holding his ankle. He moaned in pain as the sergeant came to see what had happened.

"What are you yelling about? What did you do?

"Hey Sarge, I mis-stepped and accidentally landed on the foot of the person in front of me. My ankle is killing me. I might have broken it."

The sergeant bent down to look at the injury and after moving Chris' foot from side-to-side, accompanied with fake howls from Chris, he called two of the other recruits to assist Chris as they proceeded to the plane.

"There is no indication of any break. The most you have done is possibly twisted your ankle. We'll have it looked at when we arrive at Fort Sill." Sarcastically, the sergeant continued: "See if you can tolerate the excruciating pain until then." He directed his next comments to the two recruits who were there to assist: "Get him up and don't fall behind. This is an exercise in teamwork, and you should thank your injured buddy for the opportunity to participate." With a wry smile, the sergeant went to the front of the formation and ordered the group to continue to the plane.

Chris' plan had failed. He was quickly learning the army way. He had no recourse but to board the plane with everyone else and inquire about his friend when the plane finally landed at Fort Sill. He would not be able to see his friend, but maybe he would be able to speak with him. At the very least, he would find out what happened to him.

During the flight, the recruits started talking about the accident that they had seen. They wondered how many people got hurt, and if any of the recruits on that bus died from their injuries. The conversation put Chris on edge. He didn't know what happened; he didn't know how many were injured, and he didn't know if anyone died as a result of the accident. Those were all the concerns that Chris had internalized, but for him, it was different. He had a best friend on that bus, a friend who was more like a brother than anything else. They didn't realize how personal the situation was for Chris. Sure, they were all concerned about their fellow recruits, but no one could be more negatively affected than he. He could possibly lose a life-long friend. All the group did was to continue to speculate as to what had happened and how many could possibly be injured or even dead.

The recruit sergeant decided that this type of continued conversation was not good for the overall morale or attitude of newly indoctrinated soldiers. He came back to the rear of the plane where the recruits were huddled in whispers and addressed them: "To allay some of your fears and to afford you the opportunity of knowing some of the real facts, let me tell you what I know. And then I want the conversation about the accident to cease. It serves no purpose to dwell on a negative when we have to approach each day with a positive attitude."

The recruits waited with bated breath. In his military demeanor and in a cold and detached manner, the sergeant told the recruits what had happened, and informed them that it was a catastrophic event with only one survivor. He further added that in the service, they were going to witness a lot of injury and death. This should be considered as just one of those times.

Chris could not believe how the sergeant's announcement was given in such a routine matter-of-fact way. Although he heard the entire statement, Chris focused on the fact that there was one survivor. He prayed with all his heart that the one survivor was Danny. He also realized the odds.

Chapter Three

The Invitation

Danny Ferguson was in critical condition and was rushed to a nearby hospital. He suffered from numerous bruises and possibly broken bones, but the major concern was the burns that ravaged his body. He was conscious but in such pain that, at times, he knew he had just passed out. Danny was in the specialized burn ward of Lakehurst General Hospital. Lucky for him, Lakehurst was a burn trauma center. The doctors there had seen all kinds of burn victims, and Danny was right up there among the worst. He wondered about the rest of the recruits who were on the bus with him. Were they as bad as he? Did some escape with just minor injuries? Did some not make it? He didn't want to think about the last question, and he hoped that he was the worst of the crew.

The doctors had given Danny some medication to deaden the pain, but it was so severe that the medicine really wasn't helping that much. During the time that the pain subsided just a little, he thought about his friend, Chris, and wondered if he knew about the accident. Danny also wondered where Chris was at this point in his journey. He knew that if Chris was told about the accident that a team of wild horses couldn't hold him back from visiting or at least contacting his injured friend. Danny really wanted to see Chris because he knew that his injuries were severe, and he wasn't sure that he would ultimately survive. The way he felt and the pain that he was experiencing caused him to think that not only would he not be an active soldier, but that his time on this earth might very well be limited.

During one of his conscious periods, his thoughts about his friend and about his own demise were interrupted by what seemed like a melodic voice asking him how he felt. When he opened his eyes, which had been scorched by the fire, he saw what he believed to be the prettiest girl he had ever seen. It was no coincidence that the angelic-like voice came from this individual.

"Hello, Danny. My name is Melody. I am your nurse, and I will be taking care of you while you are here in the burn unit. Is there anything that I can do to make you more comfortable?"

"No thank you, Melody. Just seeing you has reduced the pain."

"I bet you say that to all the nurses, but if I can reduce the pain and suffering for you, then I am glad."

"Melody, there is something that you can do for me. My friend, Chris, was also on a military bus heading for basic training. His final destination is Fort Sill, Oklahoma. I was wondering if there was any way that you could possibly notify him or get the military to tell him about the accident. We are really close friends, and I'm sure he would want to know that I am alive and kicking, at least for the moment. We enlisted together but got separated at the recruit center. I would really appreciate it."

"I will try my best, Danny. Sometimes with the military, there is a lot of red tape, but I know some people at the base, and maybe they can help. Let me see what I can do."

"Thanks very much, Melody. I hope you can do it soon because I don't know how much longer I'll be around."

"That is not an option, Danny, and I don't want to hear that type of talk. Sure, you have some severe injuries, but we have the best doctors here at Lakehurst. You'll be around for quite a while and long enough to take me for a cup of coffee. So hopefully now, you have something to strive for."

"If I could, I would jump out of this bed right now to collect on that cup of coffee. Let the doctors know that a lot is riding on their medical expertise, not the least of which is our coffee date."

Nurse Melody Johnson smiled in confirmation and left Danny to his world of thoughts again. He felt that he wasn't a bad looking guy, but he wondered what he looked like now. He was certain that his face suffered damage, and the healing process would leave scars. He laughed to himself as he thought what Chris would say: "Hey, anything would be an improvement." Those were the kinds of friendly jabs that were a tenet of their friendship, but they would risk it all to make sure that the other was safe. He hoped that Melody could work her magic and get a message to Chris. Besides Chris knowing about him, Danny was curious about how Chris was doing on his own. Chris was a likeable guy and could make friends easily, but he was kind of "laid-back" and wouldn't initiate a friendship unless it hit him square in the face. That was Danny's value to Chris. He would get things started and maintain the open line of communication. However, Danny had confidence in Chris and knew that he would survive the impending turmoil of basic training.

As Danny thought about many things, a nagging theme permeated his consciousness. If he ever got out of the hospital, he would not be able to serve his country as he wanted. He was almost sure that his military career had ended as quickly as it had begun. That saddened him. He wanted to be one of the many who would make the villains of 9/11 pay for their actions. Now, he would have to stand by and watch others as they tracked down and punished the terrorists. Well, at least his best friend would be a part of the action. He took some solace in that.

His thoughts went back to his conversation with Melody. In his opinion, she was a "knock-out." He was sure that she could go out with any guy that she wanted, and here she was arranging a date with him. He hoped it wasn't purely out of pity; he couldn't take that. But why else would she offer herself up to a probably disfigured, injured, military failure. He was sure that she was earnest in her desire to see him fully recover but was the coffee date a part of the inducement for recovery? Who was he kidding? Of course it was. It couldn't be anything else. The exhilarating feeling that he had when she first mentioned the coffee get-together was gone.

The more he thought about it, the more disillusioned he felt. If and when he did recover, she might not even keep the date. He didn't want to rush to a quick judgement, but it was hard to imagine anything else. He had started the ball rolling when he told her that just the sight of her made him feel better. What else could she say in return? Her main focus was to assist in facilitating a patient's recovery, and for a short while, she did just that. Once again, he thought about what Chris would say: "Of all the men that she could choose from, she chose you. Yeah, when hell freezes over!" His friend, Chris, would be one hundred percent correct.

Chris and the other recruits were in a military transport on their way to Fort Sill, Oklahoma. This type of transportation is a far cry from the commercial airlines that most people are used to. To boot, they were flying in the midst of what the pilot said was the worst turbulence that he had seen in quite a while. The bouncing up and down and from side-to-side finally took its toll on a number of the other recruits. They were vomiting from air sickness amongst the unforgiving yells of the recruit sergeant. It had not hit Chris yet; but he felt an uneasiness in his stomach. He wanted to show the sergeant that he was one of the strong ones. There were only about five recruits who had not dumped the contents of their stomach on the floor of the plane. The sergeant was beside himself as he walked to the rear of the plane where Chris was sitting. He came up to Chris and commented: "You're green around the gills, but I'm glad to see that you're toughing it out. Maybe, I misjudged you."

"Thank you, Ser…," and Chris Martin projectile vomited all over the sergeant's uniform. It is hard enough to control the nausea when you are just dealing with the turbulence, but when others around you are vomiting, the sight and the smell of the partially digested stomach contents has a very strong influence over whether you are going to join the hurling party or not. To the aggravated dismay of the recruit sergeant, Private Chris Martin had just joined the party and sent a wet and chunky invitation to the sergeant.

Chapter Four

The Message

Needless to say, when the plane arrived, the sick and weary recruits were escorted to the exercise field where they had to indulge in pushups until the sergeant came back to them with a clean uniform. It was not a warm and cozy welcome for the recruits to the military life. It was more like a stressful, exhausting, and smelly invitation to army discipline that focused on building character and stamina. Whether it did that or not is still in question.

Following their "don't be a baby and man-up" exercise drill, Private Martin, along with the rest of the vomit-coated "newbies," made a bee line to the showers. The consensus of opinion was that the shower was even better than sex. One could hear the sighs of relief emanating from the locker room. There were a lot of doubts in the minds of the recruits as to whether this was the best way to serve their country, and it had only been the first day. Could things get any worse? Yes, they could and most certainly in basic training they would. However, the entire scene had brought the whole unit together. They were already a team. They experienced the same things, and they helped each other overcome the painful recourse the sergeant had imposed on them. It was one way to emphasize teamwork, but it sure was a drastic measure.

At 5:00 am the next morning, the recruits were treated to the angelic sounds of the sergeant's baritone voice barking out orders to be on the exercise field in fifteen minutes. Most of the recruits got into their work fatigues with their eyes closed and yawning in unison. They had not fully recovered from yesterday's ordeal, and here they were rushing into formation so that they could exercise, under the sergeant's tutelage, to the point of exhaustion. For some reason, the soon-to-be soldiers were under the erroneous opinion that they would ease into the strenuous road ahead. Apparently, they couldn't have been more wrong. Their first day was a grueling and exhausting introduction to road running and exercise conditioning. Instead of the future days getting better, they were informed that from here on they would be running with full packs on their backs. Not exactly what they were looking forward to. However, there was nothing they could do about it, and they were not given a choice. Welcome to basic training.

The days got longer and longer for Chris, and he continued to think about his friend, Danny. He was unable to find out what had happened to him. Was he injured? Was he hospitalized? Was he the lone survivor? As the days passed, however, Chris became more and more negative about Danny's condition. He had to find out. Chris was deep in thought in the barracks when he was summoned to the squad lieutenant's office. It was never a good thing when the squad lieutenant wanted to see you. So, with cautious trepidation, Private Chris Martin proceeded to the lieutenant's office.

"Private Chris Martin reporting as ordered, sir."

"Stand 'at ease,' Martin. First of all, what do you think about basic training, so far?"

Chris was disarmed by the informal question, and he really didn't know how to answer. If he stated that it was horrible, and that the sergeant was into distress and torture, he would be considered a 'wuss', and not a team player. Maybe, someone who shouldn't be in the military. If he said everything was just great, the lieutenant would know that he was lying. That wouldn't be good. So, Chris took the easy way out: "It was what I expected, sir."

"Do you know a recruit named, Dan Ferguson?"

"Yes, sir. I do." Chris was so enthused to hear Dan's name that he had a problem maintaining his composure.

"Well, he must have some connections in the military because I was told to give you an update on his condition. This is not the usual route for this type of communication. It's my understanding that the two of you are close friends, and that you enlisted together. Well, let me get to the point. You probably saw the bus accident as you were approaching McQuire Air Force Base. Your friend, Dan, was on that bus, and he was the only one who survived the accident. The bus caught fire and then exploded. Dan apparently was situated in the emergency exit seat on the bus. He was able to get out before the bus exploded, killing everyone on board. He seems to be one lucky guy."

Chris took a deep breath of relief and pushed a little further: "May I ask, sir, if you know how he is doing?"

"Private Dan Ferguson is in critical condition in the burn unit of Lakehurst General Hospital. Apparently, he made contact with someone who thought that his recovery would get a positive boost if he was able to let you know that he was alive and being treated for his injuries. On a personal note, Chris, his injuries are severe, and he is not yet out of the woods. However, he is alive."

Chris took this news as good and bad. It was good that Danny had survived, but the fact that he was in critical condition in a burn unit was not exactly something to cheer about. Chris decided to push the envelope just a little further: "Lieutenant, is there a possibility that I could contact him – speak to him in some way?"

"At present, that possibility doesn't exist. Doctors have insisted that he has no calls nor visitors. If the time comes when that order is lifted, I will let you know. For now, count your blessings that he is still alive. That is all. Return to your barracks."

"Yes, sir. And thank you for giving me the message. I really appreciate it."

"Understand, Martin. I had no choice whether or not to convey the message. I was ordered to do so. Understand also that I am not a fan of being ordered to take care of recruits' personal lives and concerns. You're dismissed."

Chris left the lieutenant's office with mixed emotions. His quest to find out about his friend was over. But that wasn't enough. He wanted to speak with Danny to possibly boost his spirits. However, the way that the lieutenant left off did not leave too many doors open. The lieutenant seemed annoyed that he had to convey a message that he was ordered to deliver. Chris also wondered how Danny was able to convince the brass that he needed to contact his friend. According to the way things seemed to work, it was a shock that Danny was able to get a massage out. Chris hoped that he hadn't made an enemy out of the lieutenant. He could see that the lieutenant was visibly upset by being ordered to do something for one of his recruits, but as Chris thought more about it, he didn't care about how upset anyone was. He had found out about his friend and that's all that mattered. Chris was going to soon find out that knowledge about his friend's condition wasn't all that mattered.

Chapter Five

The Last Straw

For the last two weeks, Sergeant Harmon Brown, the recruit sergeant, had been verbally jumping all over the recruits, but it seemed that he had a particular vendetta against Private Tim Jenkins. The sergeant was relentless in his verbal attacks on Tim. It was obvious to the rest of the recruits that Sergeant Brown did not like this private. Chris Martin was particularly concerned about this development. He knew how nervous Tim Jenkins was about the whole idea of going through basic training. It was going to be tough enough for Tim to get through the training without this additional harassment. Chris was truly worried about Tim.

One night as the recruits were in the barracks attempting to get some well needed sleep, he thought he heard sobs coming from Tim Jenkin's bed area. Chris got up and went to see if his friend was okay. To Chris' surprise, Tim Jenkins was actually trying to stifle the sounds of his crying. Tim Jenkins was apparently distraught over his decision to enlist. As quietly as he could, Chris tried to comfort Tim, but it was difficult to allay some of the fears that Tim had. Private Jenkins was glad to have someone to talk to about his problems. Chris Martin was not prepared, however, to hear what Tim had to say. Apparently, Jenkins was gay and had approached one of the other recruits. The recruit wanted no part of Tim Jenkins, and it seemed as though Tim had totally misjudged the situation. Worse than that, however, was the fact that the recruit went to Sergeant Brown and told him what had occurred. Now, it was beginning to make sense why the sergeant was so focused on making Tim's life miserable.

Chris tried to reason with Tim and explained that his time and place of approach was not the best. He also tried to explain that it would be best if he could show the sergeant that he was man-enough to endure whatever basic training threw his way. Chris spoke to Tim for a good fifteen minutes but felt like all of his suggestions fell on deaf ears. Tim Jenkins was inconsolable. Chris was able to stop Tim's flow of tears and told him that they would speak again in the morning after roll call. Tim agreed, and Chris went back to his bunk totally disturbed by the chain of events that Tim had relayed to him. Something had to be done because Chris was pretty sure, that no matter what he said, Tim was not going to be able to continue under the present circumstances. He was worried about his former high school teammate.

With just a few hours of sleep, Chris awakened again to the loud bellowing of the recruit sergeant. Chris was sluggish as he got into his fatigues and rushed out to roll call formation. As Sergeant Brown listened to the recruits calling out their presence, there was an obvious gap in the numbers. Private Tim Jenkins was not in formation. Sergeant Brown was livid. Knowing that Tim Jenkins and Chris Martin had previously known each other, the sergeant ordered Chris to get his "good-for-nothing" friend out of bed and into formation. Chris immediately broke ranks and ran to get his friend who was already in a world of trouble, and he didn't need anything else to make things worse.

Chris ran directly to Tim's bunk figuring that Tim didn't get much sleep last night and had overslept. To Chris' surprise, his friend, Tim, was not in his bunk. Chris called out after Tim but got no response. Chris started searching around the barracks and figured that maybe Tim was in the bathroom, so he went into the latrine and came upon a sight that he would never forget. Private Tim Jenkins, Chris Martin's high school teammate, was hanging from a ceiling beam in the latrine. Chris hesitated and then went over to Tim and lifted his body to reduce the pull on the rope that Tim had used for strangulation. Chris yelled at the top of his lungs for help. Sergeant Brown, hearing Chris' desperate yells, ordered all of the recruits, save two, to remain in formation while he responded with the two recruits to Chris' pleas. The two recruits, seeing Chris straining to relieve the pressure on Tim's neck, immediately assisted while the sergeant took out a knife and cut the rope. Tim's limp body fell into the arms of his fellow recruits.

After administering CPR for approximately five minutes and following the life-saving efforts of the emergency response team, Private Tim Jenkins was declared "dead." Chris Martin was devastated, and the more he thought about the situation the more his anger grew toward Sergeant Brown. As the squad lieutenant and the recruit sergeant were addressing the recruits regarding the unfortunate death of Private Jenkins, Chris Martin could no longer control his emotions and before he knew it, he was standing and yelling: "Lieutenant, the man standing next to you is the one responsible for Tim's death. He never let up on Tim. He drove Tim to do what he did. Tim would still be here if it weren't for the constant harassment by the sergeant."

"Private Martin, you are out of line. Your allegations hold no weight at all. I will let your comments slide because of the emotional connection you had with Private Jenkins, but if you continue, I will charge you with insubordination and have you drummed out of the military."

Chris, apparently not heeding what the lieutenant was saying, began to verbally strike back when he was smothered by the recruits next to him. They were trying to save him from a situation from which he would never recover. They succeeded in stopping Chris from self-destruction. The lieutenant ended his comments, and the sergeant dismissed the group. Chris wrestled himself free from the hold that the other recruits had on him. He was livid and began to address his fellow recruits: "Let me set the record straight. Yes, Tim Jenkins was gay. He approached another individual in this group, and unfortunately, that individual let Sergeant Brown know about the incident. The sergeant apparently has a strong dislike for gay men, and he proceeded to make everyday a hell for Tim. We all saw what was taking place; we just didn't know the specific reason. Now, we do. How can we just stand by and let that guy get away with murder? Yeah, in my opinion, Private Tim Jenkins would still be here if Sergeant Brown hadn't ridden him to death. I, for one, will not just let this slide into oblivion and let that prejudice Neanderthal get away with driving someone to take his own life. If we all stand together, we can make a difference. Don't let Tim Jenkins die in vain."

Unfortunately for Chris, he was more impassioned than the majority of his squad members. Although everyone seemed to nod and agree with him, no one openly stood up and said that they would become part of Chris' protest group. They were all starting out on their military careers, and it was a big risk to go up against the establishment. No one wanted to take that risk. Chris didn't give up: "Where is the camaraderie that we are supposed to have? I thought we were a team – all of us being teammates. What happened to all the macho that everyone was talking about? You are going to have to live with your decision, and I wouldn't want to be you, burdened with a guilty conscience for the rest of my life." He stared at all of them and then just walked away.

Chris was not going to let Sergeant Brown get off free. He had to figure out a way to make him pay for Tim's death. He realized that he couldn't openly protest by himself, and he apparently couldn't count on the support of his fellow squad members. So, the only avenue left to him was one of clandestine activity. He decided that whatever he planned on doing would be without the knowledge of his comrades. He couldn't depend on their loyalty when and if they were put under pressure. So, Private Chris Martin was going to become the lone wolf.

Lieutenant Bill Harley and Sergeant Harmon Brown had known each other for a long time. They were career soldiers and shared active duty in many of the same places. When the lieutenant and the sergeant arrived back at the lieutenant's office, Bill Harley addressed his friend, Sergeant Brown: "Okay Harmon, what happened? Is there any truth to what Private Martin is saying?"

"Yes, sir. Tim Jenkins was an out and out faggot. He approached one of the other recruits and propositioned him for sex. Apparently, Jenkins misread the other recruit who reacted by almost choking Jenkins to death. The other recruit, Private Aaron Obutu, came to me and told me what had occurred. He was afraid that Jenkins was going to report that Obutu tried to choke him. That was the reason that he came to me, but it gave me insight as to what type of individual Jenkins was."

"So, because you found out that Jenkins was a homosexual, you decided to make his life a living hell. Is that right, sarge?"

"One hundred percent, lieutenant."

"Well good for you. We don't want that kind of ilk in our ranks. Good job!"

"My pleasure, lieutenant. There might be a possibility that Martin might come to see you to plead his case. I don't think he's going to just roll over and die."

"You mean like his friend Tim. Don't you worry about me. Martin may find himself in the brig if he persists. And I don't think the rest of the panty asses in his squad will give him any support. He will be out on his own."

"I will keep you posted, lieutenant."

"You'd better, if you know what's good for you, and keep up the good work."

The sergeant left the lieutenant's office with a broad smile on his face. And from a distance, Chris saw that smile, and he thought to himself: "You can smile now, but it's not going to be there for long. I promise you that you will know that you did the wrong thing. Smile while you can!"

Chapter Six

An Experimental Option

Nurse Melody Johnson had been visiting with Danny throughout the day. She is a good nurse and very attentive to Danny's needs. Danny had suffered a setback with his recovery treatment as an infection began to appear in certain parts of his body. His raw flesh was susceptible to infection, and unfortunately, this vulnerability was being realized as the days went on. The doctors saw this new development as a major stumbling block to Danny Ferguson's survival. He was getting weaker by the moment, and he was slipping in and out of consciousness due to the severity of the pain and medication, or just from the general condition of his health.

"Hi Danny. You know I am a nurse who has to take care of all of my patients, not just you. But for some reason, I find myself constantly coming over to your bed. How are you feeling today?"

"You know. Better now, Melody, that you are here."

"I bet you say that to all the nurses who come in to see you." This greeting and the return comment had become a ritual between Melody and Dan, and they both would smile right after it.

"Melody, I appreciate your getting a message to Chris. I am sure he was glad to hear that I'm still around. I envy him because he will be able to serve the country in a way that I most likely will never be able to. I hope he is doing well and not getting himself into any trouble. Probably not. He's not that type of guy. But thanks again."

"No problem, Danny. I was glad to help, but I am not going to convey any future messages. You are going to have to do that yourself. That means that you have to get your rear end in gear and fight to get better as soon as possible."

"I'll try my best. In fact, I am feeling better already."

Melody smiled and saw how much effort it took for Danny just to speak. In her mind, he wasn't doing well. In speaking with the doctors, she had been told that the burns plus the aggravating condition of infection was taking its toll on Danny's ability to fight for his survival. In Melody's opinion, the doctors were not giving Danny good odds to beat his condition. Of course, she didn't give the patient any hint of what she was thinking, but she was devastated to think that this good-looking, very amiable young man might not make it. On her part, she was going to do all she could to help him, whether that help came in the form of professional medical aid or just personal spirit lifting.

Nurse Johnson bid him her usual good-bye: "Stay in bed and rest. You have to be in good shape when we go out." Melody smiled and left. Only when she was totally out of Danny's sight did she yield to her emotions. With tears in her eyes, she proceeded to assist the rest of her patients. Although her mind and thoughts were with Danny, she made certain that her other charges didn't suffer from her ongoing concerns about Private Danny Ferguson.

Danny's burns were so severe that he was wrapped in a medical material that resembled household wax paper. This was the only way that the doctors could keep the burns covered without having the complication of bandages sticking to the skin. Unfortunately, even with the unique covering, infection found its way into Danny's body. The doctors were at Danny's bedside now supervising the change of his medicinal coverings. This procedure was not without pain. Although the wax paper-like covering reduced the amount of skin removal, there was still some ripping of Danny's skin. He took it like a trooper and refused to yell out in pain. He was so weak that if he did utter his suffering, it would be more of a whisper than a yell. However, the pain was so bad that he felt himself fighting not to pass out. Following the rebandaging procedure, the doctors wanted to speak to Danny about a new experimental treatment for patients with severe burns.

"Hey Danny, I am Dr. Flemings. I am sorry for all the discomfort we have to put you through, but as you know, that's the only way we can cover your burns and give them a chance at healing. Speaking with the other doctors who are also involved with your treatment, we came to the conclusion that you might very well be a candidate for a new experimental treatment that has helped in burn recovery. It is still in the experimental stages, but at this point, it might be one of the only remedies that may help."

In his whispered tones Danny spoke: "Doc, are your saying that if I don't opt for this experimental procedure that my chances of getting better are zero to none, and what does this treatment consist of, anyway?"

"Danny, I am not saying that you have no chance of getting better without this experimental procedure, but without it, I believe your chances are gravely reduced. And if you opt to agree to the procedure, we have to start it as soon as possible."

"I understand, Doc. Just give me a little time to think about it. Experimental meaning that no one is sure that it will work, and no one is sure about the side effects of the treatment. Is that right, or could you tell me what some of the side effects might be?"

"From my understanding, the side effects have ranged anywhere from headaches to convulsions to, in the extreme, partial paralysis. It is not a proven remedy, by any means, and it is a calculated risk, but at this point, it might be your best bet."

"Thanks, Doc. It doesn't sound like the most inviting alternative, but as I said, I need a little time to think things over."

Dr. Flemings nodded an "okay" to Danny and left him to his own thoughts. It was a difficult time for Danny. As he weighed his options, he felt that if he took a chance with the experimental procedure, it was like jumping from the frying pan into the fire. But he also read between the lines regarding Doctor Flemings evaluation of his present state of health. It seemed to Danny that if he stayed the present route, he would be more than likely signing his death certificate. Surprisingly, he wasn't so concerned about that because he felt like he had already died. In fact, dying might be a relief. He definitely did not like the possibility of the critical side-effects from the experimental procedure, and there was no guarantee that it would even work.

Danny's thoughts were interrupted by the soft tones and smiling face of Nurse Melody Johnson. He was more than glad to see her. He now had someone with whom he could discuss his options. He explained to Melody about the experimental option that Dr. Flemings had offered. However, he quickly followed it up with the possible side effects of such a procedure. Melody listened without interruption, and when Danny had finished, she told him that she was aware of the procedure, and that in some cases it had helped. Danny asked about the other cases: "What did you hear about some of the other cases where the results weren't exactly positive?"

"Danny, I'm not going to lie to you. I've heard some really bad complications after the treatment with the experimental procedure. To be bluntly honest, I have heard that in some patients, it hastened their demise."

"Thanks, Melody. You know my condition. What do you think I should do?" Danny had a tough time even getting his words out.

"No Danny, I am not going to make that decision for you. You know how you feel. You can judge the odds. It is something that only you can decide. But understand that no matter what you choose, I will always be here to support you. I want that cup of coffee!" With that, Melody smiled and said good-bye.

"Thanks, Melody. If things go right, I will even throw in a Danish."

Danny didn't know if she heard the last part of his sentence because she seemed to exit in a quicker manner than usual. He was left to his own thoughts and decision making. He wished that there was a way that the decision could be made for him, but there wasn't. He closed his eyes as his pain increased, and he tried to further analyze the pros and cons of his present situation.

About an hour after her visit with Danny, as Melody was engaged with other patients, she heard the chilling loudspeaker announcement of a "Code Red, room 354. Code Red." That was Danny Feguson's room. She saw the emergency medical team running past her to the designated room. Melody quickly finished what she was doing and responded right behind the medical team. All of the hospital staff were trained in "code red" procedures, and Melody knew that someone had gone into cardiac arrest. Room 354 housed four hospital beds. As she ran, she selfishly hoped that it was not bed #2, Danny Ferguson's bed.

When Melody arrived on the scene, the alarm at bed #2 was still signaling. The emergency team was quickly at work trying to revive the patient who was suffering from cardiac arrest. She was not part of the team, at this point, so she stayed in the background just in case they needed additional help. The doctors used the emergency cardiac shock equipment in an effort to restart Danny's heart. Melody heard the resounding "clear" command of the attending doctor as he employed the shock pads. She heard it once. She heard it twice, and she heard it the final third time. Suddenly, there was deafening silence as all of the life-saving efforts ceased.

Nurse Melody Johnson witnessed Danny Ferguson's wish come true. He no longer had to make a decision. Fate did that for him. Private Danny Ferguson expired at an age when most of us haven't even begun to live. Danny Ferguson was twenty years old.

Chapter Seven

The Trip to Oklahoma

Because of the failure of his squad to support his ideas, Chris kept a cool distance from everyone. On his mind was the question of how he would get back at Sergeant Brown. He spent most of his free time thinking and walking alone. This one evening when night was just falling, his walking meditation routine was interrupted by a surprising tap on his shoulder. He turned around quickly and was confronted by Private Aaron Obutu, the recruit who squealed on Tim. He had no liking for Obutu and was ready for a physical confrontation. Why else would this guy be approaching him? Surprisingly, he was disarmed by Obutu as the squealer asked to speak with him: "Sorry to interrupt, but do you have a minute to talk?"

"Yeah Aaron, what do you want to talk about? I'm doing some serious thinking, and I have to stay focused."

"I want to set you straight about what happened between Tim and me. You have the wrong idea."

"Do I? Tim approached you, and you became so offended by what he did that you ran to Sergeant Brown to let him know that we had a gay recruit in the squad."

"Hold on Chris, that's why I want to talk to you. I didn't go to the sergeant just to let him know that Tim Jenkins was gay. You're right when you say that I was offended by Tim's approach. In fact, I was so offended that I interpreted it as an attack on my manhood. My macho kicked in, and I grabbed Tim by the throat and started choking him. When I finally came to my senses, I stopped my assault and realized that If Tim reported this incident, I would be in a world of trouble. I was afraid that Jenkins would go to the sergeant, so I went to him first. To cover myself, I explained what had happened, and the sergeant said that he would take care of it. I didn't realize, at that time, that the sergeant would begin a harassment crusade against Tim. I didn't go to Brown to jam up Tim; I went to cover my own actions. I am truly sorry about how things worked out. I never wanted anything to happen to Jenkins, but that night I just acted instinctively."

Chris Martin just listened attentively and tried to make sense of what Aaron Obutu just told him. He was actually taken aback by what his fellow recruit had said. After a long stint of silence, and after Chris fully mentally digested Obutu's comments, Chris nodded that he understood, and that he appreciated Aaron's effort to set things right. Chris looked at Obutu and said: "Thank you for letting me know the details, but unfortunately, whether it was intended or not, my friend, Tim Jenkins, is dead."

"I know, and I couldn't be more sorry. I am also here to tell you that if you need help with any plan that you might be developing, that you can count on me."

Chris was even more surprised, and he was ecstatic that he had an ally. He thanked Aaron for coming to him, and he let Obutu know that he appreciated his support. Private Obutu responded with an even bigger surprise: "I know that you probably don't trust many of our squad members, but I have befriended two individuals who I believe can be trusted. We are from the same town, and we have already spoken about helping you out. I can vouch for them."

"Thanks Aaron. I can definitely use some support, and if you are sure about your two friends, I can use all the help that I can get."

"Count us in, Chris. Let me know when you want to speak with them, and I will arrange it. I don't have to warn you that no one else in the squad should know anything about a plan. I am certain that some of them would take that knowledge right to the commanding officer. We would all, then, forfeit our futures."

"You took the words right out of mouth. The less people who know, the better the chance of success. I am putting together some specific ideas, and I'll let you know when we should meet. Thanks again for coming to me. It means a lot." With that, Private Aaron Obutu and Private Chris Martin went their separate ways.

It had been a good meeting with Aaron, and Chris was somewhat relieved that he would have some help in exacting his revenge. A revenge that he felt was more than justified. Although he had a lot to think about regarding his plan of action, other thoughts, however, came flooding into his mind. He hadn't heard from Danny, nor received any third-party message from the lieutenant. He really hoped that if he did get a message that it was not through the official conduit of the lieutenant's office. Chris realized that it was difficult to send or receive messages during basic training, but since the situation was a unique one, he thought that maybe there might be an exception to the rule.

Chris had no idea that his friend, Danny, had passed. He was hoping for the best, and he considered that the old axiom of "no news is good news" might apply. Chris was sure that if Danny hadn't pulled through as a result of his injuries, the military would have notified his best friend. Chris Martin wasn't really up on military protocol. He lived in a world of "wishful thinking." In addition to developing a plan of action against Sergeant Brown, his mind wrestled with ideas on how he could find out about the condition of his friend. So far, he had come up with nothing.

Nurse Melody Johnson knew how close Danny was to his friend, Chris, so she decided that Chris should know that Danny had died. She did not want to use the same communication channel that she used before, and she didn't think that letting Chris Martin know via an impersonal message was the right thing to do. She had vacation time coming to her, so she decided that she would visit a nursing friend of hers who just happened to be stationed at the hospital at Fort Sill, Oklahoma. She called her friend and made arrangements to visit her. While she was there visiting, she just might run into Private Chris Martin. She would make it happen. Reluctantly, she would let Chris know the sad news about Danny Ferguson's death. She felt that delivering the news personally would reduce the pain that Chris would feel at the loss of his friend. Additionally, she would be there to answer the many questions that Chris would undoubtedly have about Danny's last moments.

Melody wasted no time in making the arrangements to fly out to Fort Sill. The flight would take approximately two hours. That gave Melody plenty of time to think about how she was going to break the news to Chris. There was no easy way to tell someone about a relative or close friend dying. But there were definite things to avoid in breaking the news. She went over her approach at least a dozen times and finally settled on how she was going to tell Chris Marttin that his best friend, Danny Ferguson, had passed away. Being caring and sympathetic to the needs and feelings of others, she was not going to relate anything about the severity of Dan's burns, nor how much medication he had to take to reduce the constant pain. She was going to emphasize the point of how severe injuries could lead to a body shutting down. She will tell Chris that the situation was too much for Danny's body to take, and that he closed his eyes and passed peacefully.

When she arrived at the airport in Oklahoma, her friend and colleague, Nurse Holly Fisher, was there to greet her. They hadn't seen each other in quite a while, so the reunion was heartwarming. They had a lot to catch up on since nursing school, and they both could not wait to hear what the other had to say. They went from the airport directly to a small restaurant in town. It was a favorite location for Holly, and the staff knew her by her first name. They spoke throughout drinks and dinner, and then Melody told Holly one of the main reasons for her visit: "I had a patient named Danny Ferguson who was injured and burned in a terrible auto accident involving a military bus. He was heading to Fort Leonard Wood to start his basic training." Holly interrupted with a puzzled look on her face: "Melody, you used the past tense. What happened?"

"Three days ago, Danny Ferguson passed away. He had severe burns all over his body and there were indications that he had broken bones. His treatment had been progressing when he developed an infection. That was his downfall. With everything else his body had to deal with, the introduction of an infection was just too much for him to handle. He was in constant pain and could only speak in whispered tones. That's how weak he was. I got to know him pretty well, and he told me about his best friend who enlisted with him. His friend was sent to Fort Sill to start his basic training. Before he died, Danny asked me to contact his friend and to let him know that Danny survived the accident and that he was being treated at Lakehurst General. I did that for him."

"So, what do you need to do now, Melody? Don't tell me that you came all the way down here to tell one of the recruits that his best friend died."

"That's exactly what I am going to do. He deserves to hear it from me in person than coldly over the phone or through a military message."

"Melody, what's the Private's name? I am sure I can help."

"His name is Private Chris Martin, but that's all the information that I have."

"Chris Martin? We just had an incident involving Chris Martin and a recruit named Tim Jenkins. It seems that they were high school teammates, and Tim had a run-in with one of the other recruits in his company. As the story goes, Tim Jenkins was gay, and as a result of his homosexuality, he was harassed to the point that Chris found Tim hanging from a beam in the latrine of the barracks. Chris seemed to take it pretty bad, and he mouthed off to his sergeant and Lieutenant. If it wasn't for some of the other guys in his company who stopped him from yelling at the commanding officer, he might very well be in the brig and charged with insubordination. If that is the same Chris Martin, you really have a problem on your hands."

"I'm sure, Holly, that it's the same guy. How many Chris Martins could there be?"

"Melody, I don't know if he could take more devastating news. He hasn't recovered well from the Tim Jenkins event."

"I don't want to make things more difficult for him, but he has a right to know that his best friend has died. It is wrong to keep it from him. I will stay for a while and be the crutch that he may have to lean on. And I know that I can count on you to help."

"Absolutely, Melody. However, I have heard that Chris is blaming his sergeant for driving Tim to suicide. According to him, after the sergeant found out that Tim was gay, Sergeant Brown was relentless in his dealings with Tim. Jenkins turned to the lieutenant for some relief, but according to Chris, his pleas fell on deaf ears."

"Holly, I'm sure that once I start speaking with Chris, and he gets over the shock that Danny has died, he will tell me the whole story about Tim. If he is right, and I can help him with his commitment to making both the sergeant and the lieutenant accountable for Tim's suicide, I will. I still have some connections that outrank both the lieutenant and the sergeant. If I see that Chris' story is credible; I will run it by them."

"Melody, there's just one last thing that you should know."

"What's that, Holly?"

"The lieutenant and I are planning to get married!"

Chapter Eight

A Voice

Holly Fisher still lived alone and off base. She was a civilian nurse working in a military hospital. She insisted that her friend, Melody, stay with her in her apartment. In her rush to get to Fort Sill, Melody hadn't made any other sleeping arrangements, so she graciously accepted her friend's offer. The situation, however, had gotten a little sticky after Holly's revelation regarding her relationship with the company lieutenant. Throughout the subsequent conversations, the association between Nurse Holly Fisher and Lieutenant Bill Harley had definitely become the elephant in the room. Melody Johnson had a lot to think about.

It had been a long day, so Melody decided to retire early in the evening. She was tired and there were many things to consider. Unfortunately, and although she was very tired, sleep did not come easy. Her mind was in overdrive thinking about Chris Martin and how she was going to tell him about his friend. She also had the complication of her friend's relationship with the lieutenant. She did not want to upset the apple cart, but she felt that the sergeant and the lieutenant, if they had been involved with Tim Jenkins as described, should be held accountable for their actions.

Just as Melody was slipping into the throes of slumber, she was awakened by a voice in the room. As she opened her eyes, she thought she saw the outline of a faint figure talking to her from across the room. She blinked her eyes a number of times and shook her head in an effort to wake herself from what she thought was surely a dream, but the figure still remained. She sat up in bed, but strangely enough, she wasn't frightened. The voice she heard was a familiar one, and its tone was soft and calming. Still unsure if this was all part of a dream, she listened as the blurry figure told her that he was a friend and not to be alarmed. The male whispery voice continued to speak and told her that it would be best not to tell Chris Martin about his friend's death. The figure further informed her that, at this time, it would be more detrimental than helpful for Chris to know what happened. The voice said that there would be a better time to tell him, and this was not that time. As he finished speaking, the fog of the figure slowly disappeared and the room became quiet, once again. Melody, who had only been half awake, closed her eyes and drifted into the arms of sleep.

When Melody awoke the next morning, her head was spinning. In addition to the problems she had to face with Chris, Holly and the lieutenant, she was now hallucinating about a figure coming to her in the night. She believed the stress of her situation was taking its toll. She had to relax and collect herself. Melody decided that she was going to take the day off from her mental anguish and just enjoy the company of her good friend who she hadn't seen for a very long time.

Melody got dressed and went into the kitchen where she found a note from Holly: "Had to go to work this morning, but I am taking off this afternoon. Will see you about 1:00pm. Let's do something fun, and then we can talk about the other things that have to be addressed." As Melody read the note, she was gratified that Holly was thinking the same way as she. Having a good time and looking forward to her friend's company was just what the doctor ordered. Melody felt confident that things would work out, and she started to think about some fun things that they could do. And following an afternoon of good times, Melody decided that she would take her friend out to dinner wherever she wanted to go. That's the least that she could do.

When Holly came home from work, Melody was ready with a list of fun things. She listed everything from visiting the local museum to shopping at an exclusive complex of fashion shops. They both had a great time and discussed nothing but what they were going to do next, and where they would pick up lunch. As the day moved on to early evening, they were tired and bogged down with items they had purchased on their shopping spree. They headed towards home and arrived at Holly's apartment about 6:00pm. They took a breather before they freshened up for Melody's treat to dinner. Melody left the choice of restaurants up to Holly since she knew what was available, and because it was Melody's treat to anywhere.

Holly picked a restaurant that had a Mexican slant, and it was just the right place since they were both fond of Mexican food. The food was absolutely fantastic, and the drinks were outrageous. Everything was going along so well that neither one of them wanted to put a potential dampening effect on the evening, so no one brought up the elephant in the room. They both felt that tomorrow would be soon enough to discuss the plans that Holly had, and the concerns to which Melody had to face. Getting home later than they expected and having a couple of late-night drinks before bed, the friends said good night and headed to their bedrooms. They were both exhausted and probably a little intoxicated, but that just added to the ease of falling into a deep and restful sleep.

That's exactly what happened. They both just crawled out of their clothes and crawled into bed. Neither one was really a drinker, and they were not used to the effects of the alcohol. Melody was asleep almost before her head hit the pillow. Unfortunately, she did not stay asleep for the entire night. About 3:00 o'clock in the morning, Melody was awakened by the same voice she had heard the night before – a voice and a figure that she thought was just a figment of her imagination. That same misty figure was speaking to her again; and again, she was not frightened but amazed at what she was seeing and hearing: *"Melody. I am your friend, do not be afraid. I appreciate all that you have done, but I need you to listen to me and not mention anything to Chris. There will be a right time to tell him, but this is not that time. I know him very well, and I can tell you that, at this time, he cannot handle any more bad news."*

"I don't know if you are real or if I am hallucinating. Who are you?"

"Melody, I am real, and I am a friend. I would never do anything to hurt you or Chris. I am not a figment of your imagination, and I will come to you at different times, but I need your cooperation now. I also think that it's a good idea to keep our meetings just between the two of us. You know how people can be about these things."

Melody still couldn't believe that she was actually speaking to what she believed to be an apparition. Because of the misty, fog-like aura that accompanied the figure, she could not make out who it resembled, but the voice sounded very familiar to her.

"How do you know how Chris would react? What's your connection to him, and what's your connection to me?"

"The answers to those questions would be a lot for you to handle right now. However, in time you will come to know who I am, and the connection that I have with both of you. For now, I need you to trust me. We only want the best for Chris." With the

figure's last comment, the fog disappeared, and the voice was gone.

Melody just sat up in bed shaking her head. She spoke to herself: "Am I crazy? I am listening to a fog-figure and asking it questions. And here I am talking to myself. Something is definitely not right. I know I had a lot to drink tonight, but I didn't have many drinks last night, and the voice came then too. Whatever it is, it couldn't be more right. If I mentioned to anyone that I am speaking with a foggy apparition, they would look at me in that funny way that says, 'You're losing it.' Maybe I am losing it. It bothered me when Danny Ferguson died, and I am so focused on getting the information to Chris Martin that everything else seems to be going by the wayside. I'd better get some sleep and deal with whatever is going on in the morning when I have a clearer head."

Outside Melody's bedroom door, Holly just stood there in shock as she heard her friend speaking to someone who wasn't there and then to herself. Holly was concerned for her friend, and like the "imaginary" figure said, Holly felt like Melody was going off the deep end. The problem was how she was going to broach the subject and not offend her friend. Holly was not going to take "no" for an answer. Melody had to seek professional help, and if she didn't voluntarily do it on her own, Holly would apply whatever pressure necessary to persuade her to see someone. That's what a friend would do.

Chapter Nine

An Angel of Mercy

Melody woke up early the next morning and was surprised to see that Holly was already awake. She put on her robe and went into the kitchen where Holly was already drinking her coffee. They exchanged morning salutations, but Melody felt a certain concern in Holly's voice. After pouring herself a cup of coffee, Melody inquired: "Hey Holly, is everything okay? You seem bothered by something. I hope I'm not becoming a pest."

"Absolutely not, Melody. I am enjoying your company, and I can't remember when I've had such a good time."

"That's good to hear, but something is bothering you. Please tell me what it is, and I am sure we can work it out."

59

Holly looked at her friend and commented: "It is nothing regarding me, Melody. It has to do with you. I am concerned about you."

"Holly, I really haven't made a decision about Chris Martin and some of the problems he says that he's having. We have so far avoided the topic, and maybe it's time to address it."

"Melody, it's more than that. You asked for it, so, here it is. I heard you last night in discussion with no one. I heard you speaking to someone who apparently wasn't there, and then I heard you talking to yourself. I believe that you are totally stressed out over things, and that maybe you need some professional help. You have to address your problems now before they become uncontrollable. We know that from our medical backgrounds, but sometimes we can't see the forest for the trees. Melody, you need help!"

"Holly, I am not going to deny that I was speaking last night. In fact, I can't, especially since you heard me. And yes, I was talking to myself, but what I am going to tell you now sounds ridiculous, but it has happened more than once, and no, I am not imagining it."

"Melody, what the hell are you talking about? You sound even more out of it now than last night."

"Okay, Holly. Hold onto your hat. Two nights ago, while I was trying to fall asleep, I thought I had a dream involving someone talking to me about Chris Martin. I know it sounds crazy, and I just attributed it to fatigue and a bad dream. Last night, at about three in the morning, I was awakened by that same voice and the same apparition of what I believe is the blurred figure of a young man. Holly, please don't roll your eyes. The figure pleaded with me not to tell Chris Martin that his best friend had died. It said that there would be a better time, a time when Chris could better handle the news."

"Okay, I am trying very hard not to judge your sanity. Let's say that I believe you had a ghostly visitor last night. Did this ghost or apparition identify itself? Did it tell you what interest it had in the whole situation? Did it tell you what connection it had to you or to Private Martin?"

"No, it only said that it was a friend, and that it would not want to hurt me or Chris Martin. It also said that it would be in contact with me in the future. The voice was a very soft and calming voice, and it sounded very familiar to me. After it disappeared, I fell back to sleep and decided that I would discuss the whole situation with you in the morning. You just beat me to the punch."

"Okay, let me get this straight. You are talking to a ghost-like figure who won't tell you who he is, and who is advising you not to tell Private Chris Martin that his friend, Danny Ferguson, has passed away. Is that really what you want me to believe?"

"Honestly Holly. I don't want you to be offended, but at this point, I really don't care what you believe. I know you think that it's absolutely ridiculous, but I know what I saw and heard. Deal with it!"

Holly was somewhat surprised the way Melody explained her supposedly paranormal experience. She did not want this incident to come between them, but it was quite difficult to accept that Melody's description was reality. Not too many people can claim that they had a visit from, for lack of a better name, a ghost. Not only one visit, but at least two, and a promise that there will be more. Although last night Holly had a strong conviction that her friend needed professional help, she was at a loss as to how to present her suggestion to Melody, and additionally, Melody was somewhat convincing in her explanation. Holly was beginning to have doubts about her original thoughts about Melody's para-normal experience. Could it be that something did appear? Her friend was so adamant about the experience, that it was difficult to just disregard it. Holly decided to play along.

"Melody, you know it is hard for a person to believe in ghosts. However, I would like to give you the benefit of the doubt; so, do you think I could be there when your unknown friend appears the next time?"

"I don't know when he will visit. How can I tell you to be there when I don't know when it will happen again? I don't need you to believe me, and I don't need you to think that I'm losing 'it' either. I just wanted to talk to someone about what had happened, and you were available. I thought that you could give me your opinion about whether or not I should tell Chris Martin about his friend. I am still hoping that we can calmly discuss the situation so that I can weigh my options."

"I'm sorry, Melody. I guess I rushed to judgement, but you have to realize that a story like yours is difficult for anyone to believe. However, in my humble opinion, you don't seem crazy or possessed, and I'd like to help out if I can."

Melody was ecstatic about her friend's decision to help. It was a relief to have Holly on her side, even if she didn't totally believe what had occurred.

She was a true friend. Maybe in time, Melody would be able to convince her even more that the appearance actually occurred. Now, she had to formulate a plan on how to proceed. Even if she decided not to relate the sad news to Chris Martin at this time, she wanted to at least meet the man who Danny Ferguson held as a best friend. She relayed to Holly her desire to meet Private Chris Martin. Holly thought for a while and asked if Melody could extend her stay. Melody told her that if it meant that she would be able to see or meet Cris Martin, she would put in for emergency vacation time. Holly asked her friend to give her a little time to see what she could do.

They both went about their business during the day and when evening came, Holly sat down with Melody and explained what she thought would be a good plan to meet Private Chris Martin: "This week begins the mid-basic training physicals for the recruits. I will be involved in assisting the doctors as they examine and evaluate the health of the recruits. There is a strong possibility that I may need additional help during the physicals, and who better to give that help than another certified registered nurse. I will run it pass the lieutenant and tell him that it is a necessary request."

"But Holly, aren't you forgetting that both the sergeant and the lieutenant had a run-in with Private Chris Martin? Do you really think that the lieutenant would want to do anything for him? Is there an easier way to see Chris without involving the lieutenant?"

"Who said that the lieutenant would be doing something for Chris Martin. He would be doing it for me, his girlfriend. He wouldn't be privy to our plan. During basic training, the recruits are guided by even stricter prohibitions than the regular enlisted personnel. It would not be easy to arrange a meeting with you and Chris. Let me try to persuade the lieutenant that with help, things will go a lot smoother. If he knows what's good for him, he will let me get the help that I need, if you know what I mean?"

"Okay Holly, we'll do it your way, but I am not going to leave until I meet or, at least, see Private Chris Martin. I have to find out what is so special about him that a paranormal entity is involved in his well-being."

"For now, let's just say that you are acting as an angel of mercy and relaying a message that his friend could no longer give. Hopefully, when that is done, this whole apparition thing will come to a close, and Chris Martin will find out about his friend through other means."

"Holly, I ultimately want to be the one to tell Chris. I knew Danny Ferguson, and I can be much more sympathetic than someone else. Also, my ghostly acquaintance will let me know when the time is right."

"Melody, you're making it so hard for me not to call the psych ward and have you committed."

Holly laughed. Melody did not.

Chapter Ten

Fate Was Kind

Holly Fisher approached the lieutenant with her request for additional help. Lieutenant Bill Harley was less than engaging when he spoke with Holly. He did not think that it was a good idea to be doing anything for or to Private Chris Martin. He told Holly that there were some complications involving the private, and he did not want to exacerbate the situation. He took a hard-core line on his stance, and no matter what Holly said, the lieutenant was not changing his mind. This did not sit very well with Holly, but she couldn't convince him otherwise. She left in a huff and promised that she would not forget his lack of cooperation. She now had to tell her friend that they needed a different approach if Melody was to meet or speak with Private Martin.

Melody was not happy when Holly told her that the meeting with Lieutenant Harley was a failure. Holly had implied that she could make it happen, and Melody could see the embarrassment and disappointment on Holly's face.

"Don't worry about it, Holly. We'll find another way. I am sure that we haven't even thought of the many possibilities that we have available to us. We will think of something."

"I can't believe that he refused me. There must be something heavy going on with Chris Martin. Bill knows that he is going to suffer because of his stance, and yet he wouldn't give in. That's not like him."

"Okay, Holly. How am I going to meet the elusive Private Chris Martin? Put your thinking cap on. This is your territory, and I am sure it's easier for you to come up with something than me. There's got to be a way without making it obvious."

"Give me a little time, Melody, and I will think of something. I want to do it now just to spite Bill, and of course, to help you out."

Private Chris Martin spent most of his free time in deep thought. He had to come up with a foolproof plan that would not be traced back to him. With the extra help that Aaron Obutu offered, the execution of the revenge plot should not be such a difficult task. What he had to do, however, was to create a plan that was simple but effective. Something that would be long-lasting and have the earmarks of a Chris Martin endeavor, but a plan that could not be proven to be his. He tried to find out what the sergeant's daily routine consisted of, and of course, what he did in his free time. Ideally, Chris would like to include, maybe to a lesser degree, Lieutenant Harley in his "get-back-at-you" devilish scheme. That would be the cherry on the cake. But for now, he didn't even have a plan to bring down the sergeant. He was sure, however, that by the time the ten weeks of basic training were completed, Private Chris Martin would have his justified revenge.

Chris found out that Sergeant Brown was married, and that his marriage was a rocky one. The scuttlebutt was that, to the sergeant's dismay, his wife was considering a separation. Apparently, there was a rumor that reached the sergeant's wife that he had been unfaithful. The sergeant had been working very hard to show his wife that there was no truth to the rumor. People who knew the sergeant said that he would be devastated if the marriage went by the wayside.

After taking his nightly walk, Chris decided that the sergeant's marriage was his Achilles heel. Chris Martin would focus on that part of the sergeant's life to render his revenge. Now, he could direct his attention to how he would exact his get-back plan. He was going to need some help in setting things up, and he needed someone with connections to the local bordello.

Chris also needed a financial backer or backers to help defray some of the costs that he would surely incur as he executed his extravagant plan. Chris did not mind spending or owing the money. It would be well worth it.

Chris spoke with Aaron and asked him to arrange a meeting with the other volunteers. Aaron said that it would not be a problem, and that he would arrange the meeting as soon as possible. Chris was well on his way to developing a fool-proof plot that the sergeant would not soon forget. However, he did have some misgivings about what he was going to do because it involved hurting another unintended person – Mrs. Harmon Brown. Unfortunately for her, what the sergeant had done outweighed Chris' regrets for the sergeant's wife. Private Martin was going to go ahead with the plan even if an innocent person got hurt, and the more Chris thought about it, it was probably the best thing for Brown's wife.

Following the rigors of another basic training day, Chris Martin asked Aaron Obutu to arrange a meeting with the other willing recruits. To ensure the best confidentiality as possible, Chris suggested a local restaurant-bar that a hospital staff member had recommended. Chris told the staff member that a few of the guys wanted to get together in the evening and relieve some of the stress from training. She was more than happy to suggest a local gin mill. Unbeknownst to him, it would be the same destination that both she and her friend, Melody, would surely support for their evening's get-away.

The match maker, Holly, was more than pleased with herself. She couldn't wait to tell Melody that fate had interjected and supplied them with an alternative to the original plan. This was even better since the informal meeting was interlaced with a social atmosphere. Who knew what could happen? It was possible that Chris Martin and Melody Johnson would hit it off, but Holly didn't want to get ahead of herself. She hadn't even told Melody what was on the evening's agenda. She was sure, however, that her friend would be more than happy to participate in a well-executed impromptu meeting. Holly had worked an early tour at the hospital, and when she arrived home, she found Melody floundering in a disappointing, and unhappy mood.

"Well, hello, Melody. Am I going to make your day? Wipe that sad look off your face. I have got some really good news for you. You will never believe who asked for my help today."

"Holly, I'm not in a very playful mood. I spent all day trying to figure out how I can meet with Chris without it being so obvious. I am racking my brain."

"Well, rack no more. We are going out tonight to a special restaurant. One that you will surely like."

"Thanks Holly, but I am really not in a going-out mood, tonight. I've got a lot of things to think about. I can't leave here without some kind of interaction with Chris Martin. That's the main reason why I came here, and I am no closer to that goal as I was yesterday or the day before that."

"Pick your head up and smile, girl. We are going to, at least, see Chris this evening."

"What are you talking about? Are you going to have him kidnapped?"

"No Melody, but I did arrange to have him and a few of his friends frequent a local restaurant-bar that I know of. I got talking to him in the hospital when he came there to ask a few questions. In our conversation, knowing that I've been here for a while, he asked me if I knew of a quiet place where he and his buddies could get together and reduce their stress levels. I recommended a place where you and I will be drinking and eating. It will be an unexpected surprise to run into him and his friends. I will just claim that I didn't know that he meant that he was going out this evening. The meeting will be the perfect opportunity to get to know the elusive Chris Martin. What's the saying: 'when one door closes, another one opens,' and this one opened really wide. Well, don't just stand there. What do you think?"

"Holly, you outdid yourself. I can't believe that I am not only going to meet him, but it will be in a social setting where we can speak about a lot of different things. Holly, I can't thank you enough. Maybe, in conversation, he might bring up his close friend who enlisted with him. I will be able to learn a lot. However, I am still not going to tell him that Danny Ferguson has died. My ghostly friend will let me know when the time is right, and I haven't heard from him, yet."

"Melody, you're still holding on to the ghost. Tell me you're not, please."

"I can't do that. There was a reason why I saw that figure and heard his voice. Who knows? Maybe by tonight, I'll get another visit when he will tell me that the time has come to let Chris know about his friend, but until that time I'm committed to abiding by what I was told."

"Okay, okay, I understand. You know, Chris Martin is not a bad looking guy. You never know how things might turn out. A social meeting could develop into who knows what."

"Holly, stop. He's younger than me, and my interest in him is just getting to know him a little better before I deliver the sad news. That's all. So, put your match-making magic wand back in your pocket. Now, let's get ready for tonight's extravaganza."

"Holly picked up a wine glass and toasted: "Here's to more than our expectations." They touched glasses and started to get ready for the evening's event.

Chapter Eleven

A Criminal Act

Chris Martin left with Aaron Obutu for the restaurant that the female staff member recommended. The other three recruits (Aaron had recruited one more) were going to leave together and meet up with Chris and Aaron a little later in the evening. If anyone was watching, there wasn't a group of four or five leaving at once. That would show some form of cohesiveness among the group, and Chris didn't want to give anyone that idea. Maybe he was being overcautious, but his feeling was that when you are dealing with snakes, you never know when they will bite.

The restaurant-bar was small but nice. It had a western theme to it, and the music reflected that atmosphere. There was no blaring music that drowned out a conversation. It was an ideal place to discuss the revenge plan with the entire group. There were people at some of the tables, but everyone just kept to themselves.

Shortly after Chris and Aaron arrived, the rest of the group joined them. Chris acknowledged everyone and thanked them for their interest in his plan. Following an order of drinks, Chris revealed what he had in mind. He told the rest of the volunteers that he wanted to attack Sergeant Brown where it would hurt most. They all agreed that it was the sergeant who drove Tim Jenkins to take his own life; they all agreed that he should pay for it. Chis then told them what he believed was Sergeant Brown's Achilles Heel. He went on to explain that he had heard that the sergeant was having some marital problems, and that the sergeant was very concerned that his wife might be thinking of leaving him. Chris told them that he heard that the sergeant was trying very hard to persuade his wife to stay. She had heard a rumor that her husband had been unfaithful. She threatened to leave, and that is why Sergeant Brown was trying so hard to mend fences.

The group paid strict attention to what Chris was saying, but they didn't fully understand what their role was going to be, nor were they totally aware of what Chris was implying: "I see a lot of puzzled looks on your faces. Let me explain just a little more, and you will know what I intend to do." Just as Chris was about to go into detail, the waiter came over to the table to get their food orders. So, Chris stopped talking about his idea and allowed the rest of the table to order some food. It was frustrating to stop in the middle of his diatribe, but they were there for dinner, so, he let the guys order their food. Maybe, it was best to continue after their thirst and hunger were satisfied. Then there would be no further interruptions. They all ordered, and they toasted to success.

Just as the group finished ordering their food, Holly Fisher and Melody Johnson walked into the restaurant. They were escorted to a table that was only two tables away from Chris Martin and his group. Although both Holly and Melody noticed the recruit group, they didn't acknowledge them, and apparently the two young ladies didn't garner any attention from Private Martin or the rest of his friends. As the night went on, however, Melody was going to make sure that Private Chris Martin met her, and that they spoke for a little while. As Melody peeked over Holly's shoulder, she realized that her friend was right in one respect. Chris Martin was a good-looking guy. She quickly dismissed that fact from her conscious thinking and refocused on why she was there.

Melody would have to get him alone before any meaningful conversation could take place. That was just a small problem that she had to solve, and she had already thought of a solution. The restaurant featured country music, and many of the songs were ballads. That means that there were songs that invited a slow dance. When would a guy refuse an invitation from a decent looking female to join her on the dance floor. It was rare. She was sure that Chris would not be the exception. With that in mind and basking in a feeling of confidence and success, Melody and Holly ordered their drinks.

The recruit group was finishing their meals and getting to the point of wanting to hear additional information about Chris Martin's plan. It had been a good idea to wait until dinner was over before Chris started again to explain in detail what he had in mind. They might be interrupted one more time when the waiter would inquire if anyone wanted dessert. Chris would wait for that to occur before he would continue. That moment came quickly, and instead of ordering dessert, Chris ordered another round of drinks for the table. The drinks came quickly, and Chris Martin held his glass high and toasted to Private Tim Jenkins. They all touched glasses and drank. It was time for Chris to begin. Finally, there would be no further interruptions.

Time had passed quickly for Holly and Melody. They had their drinks and were done with their dinner. They were just listening to the band as it entertained the clientele with mostly country music. Melody noticed that the recruits had finished with dinner and in lieu of dessert, they ordered another round of drinks. Melody told her friend that she would wait just a little while longer for the perfect slow dance to ask Chris to join her on the dance floor. That would be her one chance to get Chris alone and start a conversation that would yield the information that Melody was looking for.

Chris began his detailed explanation of the plan that would hopefully bring down Sergeant Harmon Brown. He began again by telling the group that he thought that the sergeant's marriage was on very shaky grounds. He told them that if the marriage were to dissolve, Sergeant Brown would be devastated. And Chris, for one, wanted to see the sergeant crushed. It was not a hard sell for the rest of the group because they were of the same mind as Chris. They all thought that Private Tim Jenkins would be alive if it weren't for the constant harassment barrage levied by Sergeant Brown.

"Since we know that Brown's wife was contemplating divorce because of the rumor of infidelity, what I want to do is to reinforce that rumor by showing the sergeant in a compromising sexual event where there would be no doubt that he strayed from the norm. What I need for this operation are connections to women who would be willing to, at least, demonstrate that a sexual encounter was going to take place."

Chris could see that there were questions arising in the minds of the rest of the group, and rightly so. He continued in an effort to clarify some of the concerns that some of the guys might have had: "We have to arrange for a motel room in advance. In that room, we will plant a clandestine camera that would record everything going on in the room."

Aaron spoke up: "I see two major problems, Chris. How are we going to get Brown into the room, and where are we going to get the girls who are willing to participate?"

"Aaron, that's where I was hoping that you and your friends could help out. I will take care of getting Brown to the room, but I need some women to make the plan complete. They won't have to do anything but saunter around the room in some sexy outfits. I will arrange the camera so that it will record the women playing with the sergeant who, for all intents and purposes, will look like he is drunk. Seeing just a small portion of the film will push Brown's wife over the edge. He will not be able to recover from what his wife will see, and what she imagined happened."

One of the other recruits chimed in and asked: "I am curious as to how you expect to get Sergeant Brown drunk and into a prearranged room. That sounds like wishful thinking to me."

"I am going to convince the sergeant that I was wrong for accusing him of having any part in Tim Jenkins' death. To show my sincerity, I am going to invite him out for drinks with some of the guys. I know that I will convince him because I have to."

"Do you really think that you will be able to get him that drunk that you'll get him into a motel room."

"No, I am not going to get him drunk, but if I spike one of his beers and let the temporary effects of a drug do its thing, we should have no trouble assisting him into our prearranged room." "How are you going to get the drug?"

"I haven't worked that out yet, but I'll figure something out."

Aaron looked concerned and commented: "Let me get this straight, Chris. You are saying that you are going to drug the sergeant, and then get him to the room. I'm sure you know that drugging someone is a criminal offense. Do you realize what happens if someone finds out? That's jail time not only for you but for all of us who acted in concert with you."

The rest of the group all nodded with concern. The plan now involved outright criminal behavior. Chris saw that he might be losing the group, but they were right. It would be dangerous for all of them. There was no way that he could lessen their concern. If they were caught, they would all face criminal charges. Chris continued: "You all are one hundred percent correct. If we get caught, it will be curtains for all of us. I understand if you don't want to do it. However, one way or the other I am going to make Brown pay for killing Tim Jenkins."

There was total silence at the table. Chris was almost positive that he lost the group. It was asking a lot from them, and yes, he understood. His thoughts were interrupted when Aaron spoke up: "Chris, you know that you are asking a lot of us. Our future is in jeopardy. We could easily all become criminals and serve time in jail. When do we start?"

Chris wasn't sure he heard Aaron correctly. Was Aaron indicating that the group was still on board? "Aaron, are you saying...?"

"Yeah, that's right, Chris. We are all saying that we want that prejudiced son of a bitch to pay for what he did. So, let's get started and divide the tasks."

Chris couldn't believe what he was hearing. He was sure that no one wanted to risk everything just for Chris' friend, Tim. But he was wrong, and he couldn't be happier. A heavy weight was lifted off his shoulders. Just as he was about to thank the rest of the guys for their decision, he was tapped on the arm. He turned around, and a very pretty young woman was asking him to dance to what she said was one of her favorite songs. Chris looked at the rest of his table, and they all urged him to accept the invitation.

Chris Martin got up to dance with Melody Johnson, and Melody had finally succeeded in her goal. What she didn't know was that in addition to the other guys edging him on, Chris had heard a familiar voice telling him to accept Melody's offer. But the voice was, apparently, only in his head. No one else apparently heard it. He looked around and just chalked it up to what he probably heard from others in conversation around him. He cleared his head and didn't realize that he had walked to the dance floor with the only other person who had also heard that familiar voice. Chris Martin and Melody Johnson had a lot more in common than either one knew.

Chapter Twelve

The Dance

Talk came easy between Melody Johnson and Chris Martin. The music was soft enough so that neither one had to shout to be heard. Melody found out that Chris and Danny Ferguson were more like brothers than friends. They had known each other for their entire lives, and they did mostly everything together including enlisting into the military. Melody realized that Chris was going to take the news of his friend's death very badly, and she now knew why the voice told her to wait until the time was right. However, she could not imagine when that time would be, because as soon as Melody mentioned that she was a nurse at Lakehurst General, Chris could not stop talking about his friend, Danny.

Melody skirted around the many questions that Chris had and was able to redirect Chris' attention to the training that he was going through. One song led into another as they continued to dance. Neither one wanted the music to end. It was during this extended period of musical harmony that Melody learned more about the Tim Jenkins incident. Since Chris had what he thought was a sympathetic ear, he laid out the entire scenario, even accusing the squad sergeant of his involvement in Tim's death. He relayed that, in his opinion, the sergeant should pay for what he did, and in Chris' words, "he will." Melody was somewhat alarmed by Chris' determination, and she wondered if this new soldier was planning something that might short circuit his military career. She could not continue to ask specific questions, however, without raising suspicion as to why she was so interested. So, she changed the subject for a while and allowed the evening to follow its natural course.

When they finally left the dance floor, Chris escorted Melody back to her table. That was when he recognized Holly: "Hello Holly, I didn't realize that you were sitting here all the while. This is a great place. Thank you for the recommendation and thank you for bringing your friend along."

"You're very welcome, Chris. I didn't realize that you were going out this evening with your friends. But it worked out well. You guys seemed very busy and deep in thought when I looked over to your table. Are you planning a coup or something?"

"No, not exactly a coup. We just want to make sure that we are all on the same page, and it is a way to get to know your fellow recruits without the disciplines of basic training interfering with the socialization process."

"Wow, Chris that was a mouthful. Speaking of basic training, how are you getting along?"

"Well Holly, if it weren't for our hard-nosed sergeant and the lieutenant who supports his every move, even if its outside the boundaries of military ethics, the training would be fine. Unfortunately, we have to deal with the sergeant's unorthodox moves every day, and with no recourse with a lieutenant who doesn't want to hear anything negative about his underling. Sometimes, it gets out of control, and we are strategizing on how we can combat what we believe to be unfair treatment. Hey, I am sorry for getting so serious and involving the two of you in our problems. Thanks again, Holly, for this place, and thank you, Melody, for allowing me to step on your toes."

As Chris took his leave, Holly and Melody started to analyze what Chris Martin had said. Holly wasn't happy hearing about the disdain that Chris' group had for the sergeant, but she was even more concerned that they seemed to feel the same way about the lieutenant – her lieutenant. Holly asked her friend what Chris had told her while they were dancing.

"Well Holly, let's say that the incident involving Private Tim Jenkins hit the squad really hard. They feel that Sergeant Brown pushed Jenkins to take his own life, and unfortunately, they have no faith in Bill Harley to make things right. I know that you are involved with the lieutenant, but I am just telling you what Chris had to say. I also got the indication that the group at Chris' table are willing to take action on their own. I don't know what that would be, but I saw committed determination from Chris. I am surprised that he went as far as he did in telling me that they would consider some kind of action. And this is all being done because they feel that the lieutenant lets the sergeant get away with everything. Chris implied that they had no other alternative than to take matters into their own hands."

When Chris arrived back at his table, he faced a flurry of questions worse than if he was being cross-examined in court. He put his hands up and tried to calm the onslaught of inquiries. When he calmed the wave, he explained that he and Melody had just exchanged introductory remarks. He further explained that Melody was a nurse in the same hospital where his friend, Danny, was being treated. Unfortunately, she couldn't shed any light on Danny's condition.

As Aaron listened, he became concerned about what Chris might have said. He waited for Chris to answer some of the other questions which mostly focused on how well Chris got along with the pretty woman. Aaron waited for his turn and then asked: "Did you speak to her about anything involving the squad or Tim Jenkins. Did you tell her that we weren't exactly happy with the sergeant or the lieutenant? Did you get into any discussion regarding the blame-game?"

Chris saw how pointed Aaron's questions were, and how concerned he was that Chris might have given a hint at retaliation. Chris shook his head and said: "No, I didn't give a strong indication, but I might have mentioned that we were not exactly happy with both the sergeant and the lieutenant. I did mention that we were all concerned about how Tim ended his life. But I don't think she took anything away from my comments."

"Chris, you don't think she took anything away from your comments, but how about her friend, Holly."

"Why would Holly care about what goes on in the squad? She doesn't even know us or Tim Jenkins."

There was silence at the table, a deafening silence. The others all looked at one another as if Chris was the only one who didn't know the obvious, and in fact, that was, apparently, the case. After what amounted to a pregnant pause, Aaron directed his comments to Chris again: "Let me tell you why Holly would probably be more interested in your comments than your paramour, Melody. Your friend, Holly, happens to be going out with Lieutenant Bill Harley, and the word is that they are going to get married. That's why she might be interested in your comments about our squad sergeant and lieutenant."

Chris looked stunned and couldn't believe what he was hearing. He tried to quickly review the conversation he had with Melody. Did he say more than he should have? Did he jeopardize the entire plan? Did he put his fellow recruits in harm's way? How could he have been so stupid? He looked at his fellow planners with a heavy heart. He didn't know what to say, and he waited for someone else to comment. No one did, so he started to speak: "I had no idea that Holly was, in any way, connected to the lieutenant. If I did, I would have made sure that I mentioned nothing about the squad, Tim Jenkins or our sergeant and lieutenant. I understand that I may have put us all in jeopardy. I am very sorry, and I don't blame anyone if they want to back out."

Aaron spoke for the group: "No one wants to back out, but you are going to have to make sure that neither Melody nor Holly mention anything to the sergeant or the lieutenant. I know that I am calling for a tall order, but that is the only way we can go ahead with anything. As it is right now, if anything is said to our bosses, we are in a world of trouble. You are going to have to meet with Melody again and stress that her confidentiality is paramount whether we do anything or not. Since you just met her, I don't know if you are going to be successful in your efforts. And then you have to depend on Melody to convince her friend, Holly, to keep her mouth shut. I highly doubt that she will do that. At this point, I think we have had it. We just have to hope that the hammer doesn't come down even now before we do anything at all." To add a little levity into a very serious condition, Aaron added; "I'm sure you will have no trouble in wanting to meet with Melody again. Just remember why you are meeting with her."

"Again, I can't tell you how sorry I am that I put us all in this precarious situation. I will try my hardest to convince Melody; however, if I feel that my plea falls on deaf ears, I will let you know immediately. To follow it even further, I will also let you know if Melody feels that she can convince Holly to remain quiet. As much as I can, I will not let anyone get hurt. Of course,

I can't guarantee that we will escape any blame, but you can be sure that I will confess to everything."

The recruits all rose at the same time and left the restaurant. No one said anything, but the silence said enough.

Chapter Thirteen

She Finally Believes

As Chris Martin was leaving the restaurant, he stopped at the table where Holly and Melody were sitting. He bent down to whisper in Melody's ear, and he asked if he could see her the following evening. Without hesitation, Melody agreed to meet with Chris again. She was unaware as to the reason why Chris wanted to meet, but she saw it as another opportunity for her to get to know Chris even better. She was surprised by the invitation, but more than welcomed the meeting. When he left, Holly asked what the secret was. Melody explained that she thought that Chris was shy, and that was why he whispered to her. She told Holly that Chris wanted to meet with her the following evening.

Holly was surprised that Chris entertained the idea of meeting Melody again and thought that there might be an ulterior motive as to why he wanted to share an evening with her. She reflected back to what Melody had told her and imagined that Chris was somewhat leery as to how much he revealed to Melody. It was no secret that the lieutenant and Holly were an item, and she was sure that, by this time, someone had to have told Chris what the relationship was. In Holly's mind, Chris was probably afraid that Melody would confide in Holly who ultimately would let the lieutenant know what was possibly going on. To Holly, that was probably the primary reason Chris wanted to meet Melody again, and she let her friend know what she was thinking.

"So, Holly, you don't think that he is attracted to me. You just think that he wants to convince me to keep my mouth shut and to possibly convince you to do the same." In a sarcastically humorous way, and couching her face in her hands, Melody continued: "Are you just jealous that I have a certain appeal that men, no matter what the age, can't resist?"

"Yeah, you guessed it. That's exactly what I was thinking. I am so jealous, and I can't hold back my feelings of envy. But seriously, you have to think that after he returned to the table, and they all discussed your elongated dance with Chris that they wanted to know what happened and what was said. If Chris told them exactly what transpired, I am sure that they were not happy with your conversation. Since we are friends, I am a threat to them because of my relationship with Bill. I could be wrong, but I would bet that tomorrow night you will hear the plea for confidentiality. Mark my words."

"You may be right Holly, but I hope it's more than that. I enjoyed his company, and he is mature beyond his years. I could do a lot worse!"

"Melody, listen to yourself. Are you trying to talk yourself into a possible relationship that you and I both know isn't in the cards? I don't care how nice he is, or what kind of company he is, or how handsome you think he might be; he is not the one for you. You're not thinking straight, and I'll let you off the hook by saying that it's probably the effect of the alcohol. You're better than that."

"Okay Holly let's say that you're right, and he wants my loyalty and trust. How does he think that I am going to convince you to keep his secret? If he knows that your boyfriend is the lieutenant, and you are my good friend, does he think that I would betray you?"

"I don't know what he thinks, but just prepare yourself for a conversation geared to elicit your cooperation."

Following their back-and-forth conversation, Holly and Melody left their table and exited the restaurant. To say that Melody was anxious about the following evening would be an understatement. She hoped that Chris would not focus on getting her cooperation, but Holly had made a lot of sense. Prior to the subsequent conversation with Holly, Melody had been flattered and looking forward to meeting with Chris again. Now, she was filled with apprehension and doubt as to Chris' real intention. As she continued to think about the upcoming date, she felt more and more that Holly was correct. She realized that Chris might really be afraid that her telling Holly about the conversation would result in the lieutenant and sergeant knowing that there might be a plan afoot to seek justice for Private Tim Jenkins' death.

As the recruits settled in for the night, the barracks were eerily quiet. They all had a lot of thinking to do. Their concerns were far from lost on Chris Martin. He knew that he had screwed up, and he was trying to think of a way to convince Melody not only to gain Holly's cooperation, but to convince her that he and the other recruits were correct in their thinking. Lieutenant Bill Harley and Sergeant Harmon Brown caused one of recruits to take his own life. Of course, the sergeant was more directly involved than the lieutenant, but the lieutenant by his lack of action was, in the minds of the other recruits, just as guilty.

Chris was up for most of the night, and just when he had exhausted all possibilities regarding the Melody situation, that familiar voice came to him. At first, he thought he was imagining it because he was dog tired, but he soon realized that it was the same voice that he had heard before. It was a calm and soothing voice, but one that only he heard. He sat up and looked around the barracks to see if anyone else was privy to this vocal visit, but most of his fellow recruits were already asleep or just about to nod off. No one appeared to hear anything but the other soldiers snoring. Again, it was just him and the voice.

"*Hello again, Chris. You are going down a path that may cause you problems that you will not be able to overcome. You are also involving others who may suffer from what you are planning to do. I am aware of how your friend, Tim, has died, but no matter what you plan, it will not bring him back. Be sure you want to risk everything to satisfy your revenge. It is noble that you care so much for the injustice that Tim suffered but are you willing to risk not only your future but that of the others who want to help you? You have to depend on someone you hardly know to keep silent about your plans, and additionally, her cooperation in convincing someone else to remain silent. That is a difficult proposition. I would recommend that you do not continue with this venture, but if you choose to continue, I will offer whatever support I can.*"

Chris listened attentively to what the voice in the fog was saying, but, as usual, he had many questions for this spirit-like visitor: "Who are you? How do you know so much about me and what is going on? Why are you appearing to me? Unless I know from where you come, I can't put any faith in what you say. For all I know, you are a hallucination created in the mind of a very tired and stressed individual. You may very well be my own conscience dictating to me."

There was no answer to Chris' questions. The fog had cleared, and only silence remained. Chris was starting to think that the stress of the whole situation was beginning to play on his mind. He was listening and speaking to an entity that was invisible, and he was the only one privy to its existence. That alone was enough to start questioning his own sanity. His mind had been working overtime, and he was at the mercy of sleep deprivation. If he was going to be able to continue, he had to start relaxing just a bit more and try to calm down.

Coincidentally, that same night, Melody also had a visit from her spirit-friend. She had just finished washing off her make-up and donning her nightwear. She got into bed and brought the covers up. Her head hit the pillow and that familiar voice filtered through her thoughts.

"Hello Melody. I understand that you have finally met up with Chris. I am glad that you followed my advice and delayed telling him about Danny's demise. I do really believe that, at this time, it would do more harm than good to give him the sad news. He is dealing with other problems right now and treading very dangerous waters. When you meet with him tomorrow night, he might very well ask for your help and loyalty, whether it is deserved or not. Chris Martin is a good man and has a devoted attitude toward justice. As you know, he is seeking justice for another of his friends who met an untimely death. I think that it would be the right thing to help him as much as you can. I would never ill-advise you, and I believe he is doing the right thing."

"I am asking you again. Who are you, and why are you so involved in my life? Why does it matter to you or anyone what I do with Private Chris Martin? How do you know about Danny Ferguson? Are you real or are you something that I just conjured up to justify what I am doing? I need to have some answers."

"No, Melody. I am not a figment of your imagination, but I am not of this world. I have evolved from your world into a *spiritual existence where I can see many things. You are not ready to know my true identity just as Chris is not ready to hear about Danny Ferguson. You must believe that I only have Chris' best interest at heart. Additionally, I am also looking out for you."*

"Well, if you are so interested in my well-being, maybe you can help me. Right now, my friend, Holly, believes that I am losing my mind. If you are such a benevolent entity, I need you to convince my friend that I am still sane. Can you do that?"

"Not only can I do it, but I will do it. As a sign of good faith and intention, I will wake Holly from her slumber and introduce myself to her. However, I will not enter into any discussion with her. I will only let her know that I am the one who has been visiting you, and I hope that it will be enough to convince her of your sanity. I am also hoping that with my visit, she will help you as much as she can in whatever you decide to do. I will be with you soon."

Shortly after the entity left, Melody heard Holly yelling from her bedroom: "Melody, Melody, come quickly, come quickly."

Melody ran from her room into Holly's bedroom: "Holly, what is it? Are you Okay?"

"Yeah, Melody. I am okay, and I guess you are too. Unless I was dreaming, I believe I had a visit from your misty friend. I was petrified, at first, but he spoke so softly and calmly that my fear simply melted away. Tell me that I wasn't dreaming; that I'm not crazy!"

"No Holly, you're not crazy. Welcome to my world."

Chapter Fourteen

An Undesirable Coincidence

It was a very long night for the two friends. They couldn't stop discussing the entity that visited both of them. They both now had heard from the voice, and Holly seemed engrossed with the possibility of a supernatural visitor. It's not something that everyone could say that they experienced. In fact, they both surmised that a visit like their's was rare. Although both Melody and Holly were amazed with what they saw and heard, they were not yet convinced that they should assist Private Martin, even if it was just their silence that they offered. The situation was more significant for Holly, of course, since she and the lieutenant had a special relationship. Would it be a betrayal for Holly not to let her boyfriend know if something was brewing?

The situation put the two friends in an unenviable position. They had to discuss what they were going to do and the ramifications of their actions.

As the sun rose and daylight peeked its head over the horizon, Holly and Melody were still discussing the "what-ifs" of their potential decision. They were both tired from staying up all night, so Holly called out sick to her job. They decided that it would be best for both of them to get some sleep before they made a final decision on what to do. Melody felt like Holly was still favoring her relationship with the lieutenant, while she was leaning toward helping Chris. The last thing that Melody wanted was a schism between her and her friend. Compromise might be the way to go, but what would the compromise be? Melody couldn't continue to ponder the issue as sleep wrapped its waiting arms around her. Holly had already given in to her body's desire for rest.

Chris Martin was still feeling the ill effects of the mistake that he had made. He was trying to figure out a way to let Melody know that her silence was necessary. Even more than that, he had to convince her that she had to convince her friend, Holly, that the same was required of her. That, he felt, might be the stumbling block. The other hurdle that he had to overcome was the fact that he hardly knew either one of them, and he was asking for their confidence and loyalty. If it were reversed, he didn't know if he would comply with such a request. But the damage was done, and he had to face the music. The evening's meeting was such an important one that it was all he could think about as he mindlessly participated in the day's training exercises.

Aaron Obutu and the others were very concerned about the situation. Chris could tell as he caught them constantly watching him throughout the day. He couldn't blame them. After all, he might have put them in harm's way even before they actually participated in any suspicious action. He owed them his best try, and he would bring out the big guns when he met with Melody – whatever that was!

It seemed that the sergeant was paying special attention to whatever Chris did. This could have been the result of an interaction between the lieutenant and his girlfriend, Holly. Chris did not know what she might have said to the lieutenant, but it was awfully odd that Sergeant Brown was constantly barking at no one else but him. If this were the case, his meeting with Melody was going to be even more difficult. He had to prepare for the worst because it sure looked like that was coming.

During the training break, Aaron, who knew that Chris was going to meet with Melody in the evening, came over to Chris and asked how he was going to broach the subject with Melody. Chris wanted to give Aaron a definitive answer, but, in reality, he still didn't know how he was going to approach the subject without totally turning Melody off. Aaron let Chris know that if, in his opinion, he succeeded with Melody, that he would still have the support of the group. However, Aaron warned Chris that he had to be sure that he convinced Melody, and that she was going to give it her best shot with Holly. Aaron further relayed his concerns as he told Chris that just letting Holly know that we were soliciting her silence would give her a strong indication that they were planning something. Aaron shook his head and said: "It's almost a no-win situation."

"I know how difficult it is going to be, Aaron, but I will not involve any of you if I am not absolutely certain that I have succeeded. I may even risk a meeting directly with Holly to explain why Private Jenkins' death negatively affected us all."

"Chris, you do realize if you meet with Holly, you would be walking into the lion's den. There will be no coming back from that if she goes to the lieutenant with the results of her conversation with you. No one would be able to help you then."

"If I have no other choice, and it comes down to my having to meet with Holly, so be it. I will have already revealed my concerns to Melody, so I will have been committed anyway. It's a risk that I may have to take."

The break was over and instead of feeling better about the situation, it was weighing like an anvil around Chris' neck. The importance of his persuasive powers was amplified after his quick talk with Aaron. However, when he and Aaron went back into the formation, he saw a thumbs up signal from the other three recruits who were intricately involved with him and his plan. He was gratified by the show of support, but it only put more pressure on him to succeed.

Holly and Melody both woke up at the same time in midafternoon. As soon as they reached the kitchen table, and even before a cup of coffee, the discussion from last night began again. Melody started using a different tact. She mentioned that her spiritual visitor told her that whatever decision she made that the entity would support it. She also mentioned that Chis Martin was venturing down a very dangerous path, but that his pursuit for justice was above board: "It seemed to me, Holly, that the voice wasn't encouraging Chris to react radically to his friend's death, but that if he and others wanted some sort of satisfaction for what they seemed to believe was a death influenced by the actions of Sergeant Brown and/or Lieutenant Harley, that we give whatever support we can. Maybe, I am reading into my interaction with the voice, but it sure seemed that it was prompting my cooperation with Chris."

"Melody, I know that even without this spiritual creature influencing your collaboration with Chris and his band of 'do-gooders,' you are leaning toward helping Chris. I can't tell you that right now I am of the same mind. You and whatever that fog entity is are asking me to turn my back on the person who I intend to marry. I don't know if I can do that."

"Even if he had a part in driving someone to take their own life? I don't even know if that is the person you should be looking to marry."

"Melody, you're jumping the gun. We really don't know what happened and what part the sergeant or Bill had, if any, in Tim Jenkins' death."

The conversation started to get a little heated, and Melody thought that the best thing that she could do, at this point, was to let Holly know that she agreed with the fact that neither one of them knew what had happened to cause Private Jenkins to take his own life. Melody tried to reinforce the fact that she would seriously question Chris about the situation before she would make any decision. She told her friend, Holly, that whatever she learned about the situation she would relate to her. This seemed to cool the heated waters a bit, and they started talking about what Melody should wear for her date which was only a few hours away.

Chris Martin was nervous about the meeting. He wasn't nervous because he was going out on a date with a pretty woman. In fact, that hadn't even entered into his mind. All he could concentrate on was how he was going to get into the subject of asking for her cooperation and ultimately, her help in convincing her friend, Holly, that silence was golden. Chris had suggested that they meet at the restaurant that Holly had originally recommended, but Melody wanted to try something new; so, she asked Holly for another restaurant recommendation. This particular restaurant was a little farther from the base, and Melody had to get specific directions.

In an effort to avoid curious eyes and the ensuing questions that were sure to follow, Chris met Melody outside of the confines of the base where she picked him up in Holly's car. The ride was longer than they both anticipated, and small talk wasn't so forthcoming. They were both nervous, but for different reasons. Finally, they reached the restaurant where they found out that it was ladies' night. Instead of the restaurant being a location that encouraged quiet and possibly intimate conversation, it was loud with a cacophony of voices. This was not the ideal place for either one of them to get a point across. It was a unanimous opinion, therefore, to relocate to an establishment that was more conducive to meaningful conversation.

Although they had no reservations, they decided to try a restaurant that they passed along the way. It was a small eatery, and it seemed to be a lot less crowded than the one they were originally going to. The restaurant was dark but appealing. There were only a few tables occupied, and it seemed like the perfect place for their exchange of ideas. Chris couldn't wait to get it off his chest, but he didn't want to seem rude or overanxious. The restaurant was so dimly lit that it was difficult to make out the people who were a table or so away. In Chris' opinion, it just facilitated the comments that he was planning. He almost felt that he could remain anonymous as he was speaking. Of course, it wasn't the case, but he welcomed the air of privacy.

They got their order of drinks, and they were about to let the waiter know what they wanted for dinner, when Chris felt the presence of someone standing right beside him.

"Well, hello, Private Martin. It's quite a coincidence running into you or is it that you just don't get enough of me all day long?" Then acknowledging Melody, the intruder asked: "And who do we have here? Who is this pretty young lady?"

"Melody Johnson meet Sergeant Harmon Brown."

Chapter Fifteen

The Restaurant Scene

Sergeant Brown left Chris' table and proceeded to the restroom. Chris Martin was shocked and surprised to have run into the sergeant. What are the odds? Well, no matter the odds, the unscheduled meeting took place. It definitely made Chris more apprehensive about what he was planning to discuss with Melody. His game plan was shattered, and he didn't know how to get back on track. Melody was looking at Chris waiting for him to say something, but Private Martin was at a loss for words. He tried to identify the other person seated at the sergeant's table, but the lighting was not good, and Chris didn't want to make it obvious.

When the sergeant returned from his bathroom visit, he just smiled as he passed the table where Chris and Melody were seated. It wasn't a smile conveying a friendship or warmth, but a sneering smile that said: "I'll be seeing you tomorrow, so, be ready."

Melody broke the silence and asked Chris if Sergeant Brown was his squad sergeant. Chris readily answered and used her question as an in-road into the discussion he originally wanted to have with her. He started: "Melody, I have to be straight with you. You probably realize that a group of us feel that Sergeant Brown and Lieutenant Harley were a major influence toward Tim Jenkins taking his life. Since we feel that going through the chain of command would not get us the satisfaction that we want, we have decided to do something about it ourselves. What I alluded to when last we spoke was just that. However, by implying our intentions, I put all of us in a very precarious position. I was unaware of your friend, Holly's, relationship with Lieutenant Harley, but the rest of the group enlightened me when we got back to the barracks. I am sure you discussed the conversation we had with Holly, and I am hoping for your cooperation."

"What kind of cooperation are you looking for, Chris? And what kind of retribution are you planning?"

"Let me answer the second question first. We haven't decided on a specific plan as of yet, but we are close to agreeing on some details. I am asking for your cooperation in remaining silent about what you know, and more so, I am asking that you convince Holly to do the same."

"Chris that is an awful lot for you to ask. I hardly know you, and you're asking me to trust in your opinion regarding Private Jenkins' death. In addition, you are asking me not to say anything regarding a possible plan that could potentially hurt, embarrass, or damage a man's reputation. No, not just a man, but two men. After I comply with that, you want me to convince my friend, Holly, not to repeat anything that she has heard, even though one of the men who most likely will be negatively impacted is the person she plans to marry. Chris, you seem like a nice, well-intentioned guy, but you are asking me to indirectly be a part of your plot and in so doing, drag my friend down with me. I don't think I can do that."

"I know that I am asking a lot, Melody, but Tim Jenkins should be alive today. What kind of individuals would harass someone and permit that harassment to continue until it drives a person to suicide? Is that the kind of person Holly would want to spend the rest of her life with? Maybe, she should know what the lieutenant is really like. I know that I am going out on a ledge here, and I am sure that my fellow recruits would not want me to possibly dig the squad into a deeper hole, but do you think it would help if I met with Holly? I can explain to her exactly what happened and why we are seeking some kind of justice."

"I don't know if that is the right thing to do, Chris. I don't even know right now where I stand on all this. Let me think about everything, and I will let you know."

"You do understand, Melody, that once you confide in Holly, she has the option of going directly to her boyfriend. Once that happens, me and the rest of the guys are all in a world of hurt."

"I realize that, and I will proceed with the utmost caution, weighing everything as I go. I have a friend that visits me every now and then, it might be able to shed more light on the situation and convince both me and Holly to cooperate."

"What do you mean 'it'?"

"Oh, did I say 'it'? I meant 'he'."

Chris was a little confused by Melody's mistake and wondered what she meant by "it." But that was the least of his problems. In addition to everything that was going on, he still had to face the sergeant in the morning when he was sure that the sergeant would not rest until he found out about the young lady who had been Chris' date.

The night progressed rather well after the serious conversation had been concluded, and Chris did not want to leave unit he saw who the sergeant was with. However, it was getting late, and he had to be up bright and early in the morning. He was disappointed in not identifying the sergeant's dining partner, but fate decided to grace Chris with an advantage. Just as he and Melody were about to get up from the table, Chris heard a movement from the direction of the table where the sergeant had been sitting. Chris motioned Melody to wait just a moment longer, and they both saw the sergeant leaving with his dinner partner. The sergeant and his blond female friend left making certain that their faces were turned in such a manner that they could not be identified. Of course, it was futile for the sergeant since he made it his business to introduce himself, but the woman who accompanied the sergeant could only be identified as having blond hair.

Chris was curious as to whom the blond female was. He secretly took a photo of the sergeant and his date as they left the restaurant, but all Chris really had was a female with blond hair. If it wasn't his wife, this would be real evidence as to the sergeant's infidelity. Chris took a wild shot and asked if Melody had any idea who the woman might be. Since she was just a visitor and staying for only a short time, she had no idea regarding the female's identity. Chris knew it was a long shot, but he didn't want to leave any stone unturned.

When they reached the base, Chris, once again, emphasized how important Melody's cooperation would be. But he also let her know that he would understand if things didn't go his way. Melody just smiled, and Chris left the car. As he entered the barracks, his group of comrades were anxiously awaiting to hear the results of the meeting. He let them know that Melody was attentive to their needs, but she had to give it some serious thought. He emphasized to them that the evening was actually a win since she did not come right out and say "no." When he told them that he happened to run into the sergeant, they started with a deluge of questions. Chris calmed them down and told them that the sergeant just came over to the table, and upon his insistence, Chris introduced Melody to the sergeant.

Chris also mentioned that the sergeant was with a blond woman.

"Does anyone know what color hair Sergeant Brown's wife has. If it wasn't his wife, that would be good to have in our back pocket. It would add support to our overall plan. And by the way, I took a picture of the sergeant and the blond as they left the restaurant, but they were smart enough to leave with their backs facing us."

Aaron spoke up: "We'll find out about the sergeant's wife, but, in your opinion, what do you think Melody will do?"

"I think if it was only Melody, we would be okay, but she has to deal with her friend and the fact that Holly and the lieutenant are an item. I really don't know if Melody will go against her friend if Holly offers strong resistance. I can only hope, but I did let her know that things can get awfully rough for us if either the lieutenant or the sergeant gets any wind about us or a plan that we might have."

"Did you elaborate on what we are thinking. Does she have any idea about our plan."

"No, I know you think I screwed up already, but give me a little credit. She doesn't know."

Melody parked Holly's car in the designated spot, but she didn't immediately exit the car. She was alone, and she tried to plan how she was going to approach her friend. She was confused, and she really hadn't wholeheartedly bought into the total cooperation scenario herself. But if she was going to solicit Holly's help, she had to be very convincing about her own cooperation. It was a rough decision, but she had to make it one way or the other. Melody exited the car and got ready to face her friend, who she was sure would be waiting up.

"Hi Holly, how are you doing? How was your evening?"

"Melody, it was fine until I got a phone call from Bill. He wanted to know why my friend, Melody, was going out with one of his recruits. He told me that the sergeant saw Private Martin with a young female, and Bill assumed correctly that it was you. Bill was not at all happy, especially after he had mentioned to me that Private Martin was a problem."

"Holly, are you telling me that lieutenant is going to dictate who I choose to date? What did you tell him?"

"Well, Melody, I didn't get a chance to tell him anything since he hung up on me!"

"Holly, we have to talk."

Chapter Sixteen

Finally, He's Identified

Both Melody and Holly decided to talk about everything in the morning. Holly was off from work, so they would have plenty of time to discuss the matter. In the solitude of her bedroom, Melody kept reviewing the evening's events. Chris' words kept repeating in her mind as she tried to make an informed decision. She hated to believe that someone who was so close to her friend, Holly, would be involved in harassing someone to death. However, Chris Martin had no reason to lie to her about Tim Jenkins' death. This was not going to be a restful night by any means. As she was taught a long time ago in school, she got a pad and pencil and put down the pros and cons as they influenced her decision. But even that did not make the decision process any easier, since there were an equal number of pros and cons on both sides.

Melody closed her eyes and concentrated as hard as she could to come up with a viable decision; however, her in-depth thinking process was interrupted by that familiar voice and the unidentifiable figure who had appeared to her at other times. She reacted, as usual, with a start, and only calmed down as her spirit-like friend continued to speak in that soft and disarming tone. The clouded figure directed its comments to the very thing that Melody was having trouble with, and she was amazed that this unknown spirit would be aware of what was bothering her. It seemed that it knew a lot about many things, but in particular, about her, Holly and Chris Martin.

"Hello, Melody. I am sorry if I surprised or frightened you again. I don't know how to make any other appearance. I guess I have to work on my entrance."

Melody thought to herself that with everything else, this entity or whatever it was, also had a sense of humor. She just shook her head in disbelief as the voice continued to speak: *"Melody, I am aware of how hard a decision it is for you to hurt anyone, but realize that whatever decision you make, someone will be negatively affected. In this situation, you cannot please everyone. In fact, in life and in most situations, you cannot please everyone, so this is just another one of those decisions where you have to see who will be hurt the least. I know we are just recently acquainted, but I believe that I know you well enough that you will follow your heart and make the right decision."*

"Hold on, whoever you are. You're telling me that I will make the right decision, but you will give me no clue as to what you believe is the right way to go." Melody shook her head with a realization: "I must be losing it, 'cause here I am asking a possible figment of my imagination to make a decision for me. Am I heading for the men in the white coats? I must be out of my mind."

Once again, Melody was amazed with the sarcasm and humor this spiritual entity had. It quickly vanished into thin air, the same way he or it appeared. Even though her exchange with her spirit friend was weird, she did feel better about the whole situation. It amazed her though how something as indescribable as "it" could have such an influence over her. However, she wasn't going to fight it. Maybe, with its help, she would be able to convince Holly to see things her way.

With at least certain things settled in her mind, Melody was able to drift off to sleep. She slept through the night, and for the most part, she was well rested when she awoke in the morning. She was up before Holly, so she put on the coffee and started to scramble some eggs. Maybe, it was the smell of freshly brewed coffee or the aroma of the bacon and eggs, but Holly came into the kitchen shortly after Melody had started to prepare breakfast. There was no big "hello" or "good morning," just a nod of the head. Melody surmised, by Holly's actions, that she was still put off by the way Bill had acted on the phone as a result of Melody's evening interactions with Chris Martin. *"Melody, we've already discussed this. You are not out of your mind, and I am as real as you want me to be. Reality is different for everyone, and I am part of your reality. So, let's drop the "out-of-my-mind" concept and concentrate on how you might affect others' lives."*

Melody was taken aback by the serious admonition that she had just received, and it jolted her back into her original decision-making process. Things were not any clearer, but for some reason, she now considered that helping Chris Martin and his comrades might be the right thing to do. He was trying to right a wrong and to make certain that it doesn't happen again. How could she stand in the way of such a noble effort? She could not and would not. Her decision was made, but now, the more difficult problem faced her. How was she going to convince Holly that supporting Chris and his friends was the right thing to do, even if it meant that her boyfriend might suffer from her decision?

"Well, whoever or whatever you are, and I don't know how you did it, but your appearance has influenced my decision. I am going to help Chris, and if that means that I just stay silent, then that's what I'll do. However, before you go and disappear into whatever world you frequent, I could sure use some help when I speak with Holly in the morning. As you probably know, since you seem to know everything, Holly wasn't exactly warm and fuzzy toward me when I came home tonight. I feel that it is going to be a tough sell for Holly not to warn her partner that something bad might be coming. So, if you're not doing anything in the morning, I'd appreciate it if you dropped around."

"Well, I'll check my appointments, and if I am not scheduled to appear and frighten anyone else, I will try to help you."

"Good morning, Holly. How about a cup of coffee? I 've also made some bacon and eggs, if you're hungry."

"I'll just take a cup of coffee, thanks. I'm not very hungry. Melody, I don't know if your staying here was the right move for me. Things are getting really strained between me and Bill. He was very upset about you and Chris Martin seeing each other. Your goal to meet Chris is slowly destroying my relationship with Bill. I don't want to lose him, especially over something that we don't even know to be true. It seems to me that you're putting all your eggs in Chris' basket, and you're not considering anything else."

"Holly, you couldn't be more wrong. I struggled with what seemed like forever, before I came to a decision. I carefully weighed the pros and cons regarding the entire situation, and I thought that I couldn't come to a reasonable conclusion until I got some unsolicited help. Not that 'it' made the decision for me, but after my brief discussion with 'it,' my head was much clearer, and I only saw one solution. Chris needs my help. No, let me correct that. Chris needs our help."

Holly was just about to comment to Melody when they both heard a weird noise coming from Holly's bedroom which was still dark. The blinds had not been opened, and the day was a cloudy overcast mess. They both hurried to the room where they found a misty cloud hovering at the end of Holly's bed. Both

Holly and Melody stopped in their tracks as the voice began to speak.

"Hello Holly, I am here, once again, to speak to you before you make any decision about your friend, Melody, and Private Chris Martin. Melody has decided to help Chris in any way that she can. Unfortunately, if you decided to do the same thing, your relationship with Lieutenant Bill Harley may be damaged. Before you think about anything, let me give you some facts that even Melody might not know."

"Hold on. I am listening to an entity that I don't even know exists. Before I listen to anything else you have to say, I want to know who or what you are. I know that you aren't imaginary because we both heard you and saw the cloud in which you exist, but why should I listen to something that doesn't even want to let me know where it comes from or what it is? This conversation, or whatever it is, is over unless I get some answers."

"I understand, Holly. I was hoping that my mere appearance would be enough to persuade you to, at least listen, but apparently, I was wrong. I am very close to your friend, Melody."

With that comment, Melody perked up and tried to make sense of what it was saying. She addressed the entity: "What do you mean that you are close to me? I don't know who or what you are, and I only know you through your eerie appearances. I don't believe that I am close to you at all."

"*Melody, you were and still are very close to me. You cared for me and visited me every day. You were the only light when the darkness of suffering wrapped its torturous arms around me. It was you who helped me get through the darkness and enter into a world of constant light. I always felt better when you were near.*"

Suddenly, like a flash of lightning, Melody thought she knew what or who the entity was: "I bet you say that to all the nurses. I can't believe that I am speaking with you, Danny. What is happening?"

"*Only good things, Melody. I have been given the opportunity to help out with certain people, and my closeness to Chris Martin just facilitated my coming to you. I have already appeared to Chris, but he is unsure as to who I really am. Now, I will also let him know. I know that it is difficult for you and Holly to actually accept that you are speaking with an other-worldly being, but consider me an apparition who just wants to help. You would be surprised at how many people experience this sort of thing, but no one ever speaks about it. So, although it may seem strange, it really isn't so unique.*"

"Danny, I can't believe it's you. Well, your spirit anyway. I guess I'm going to have to explain to my friend, Holly, that we were close."

Holly chimed in: "No, Melody. You don't have to explain anything to me. I am now a part of an insane scenario where you and I are speaking to the spirit of someone you were assigned to assist in the hospital. It's very natural. Nothing unusual about it. God help me!"

"*Holly, God is always there to help, and I am lucky enough to be an agent of that help. Since we are all on the same page now, let me tell you what has been going on with my friend, Chris Martin, and the bosses that head up his squad. I will tell you right out that Sergeant Harmon Brown torturously harassed Tim Jenkins about his sexual persuasion. It was this harassment that finally drove Tim to take his life. Unfortunately, Holly, your lieutenant friend not only failed to stop the harassment, but he encouraged the sergeant to continue with his 'good work'.*"

"I find this all hard to believe, but who am I to question a supernatural being who has chosen to appear to my friend, Melody, and who now is revealing such outrageous facts to me? I guess I should reconsider who I choose as my lifetime partner."

Melody embraced her friend, and together they hugged, laughed, and cried.

Chapter Seventeen

Friendly Advice

Private Chris Martin was waiting patiently to hear from Melody. Her cooperation and that of her friend, Holly, was of paramount importance if the execution of any plan was going to be successful. Aaron and the other recruits who were involved were also anxiously awaiting any news. They were also interested in whether or not Holly was going to speak to the lieutenant or already had. If that was the case, then they were all in hot water. No news is good news as the saying goes and, thus far, they hadn't heard anything, but the waiting was killing them.

Melody and Holly had apparently settled their differences, and they were on the same page when it came to helping Chris and the other recruits. Melody was waiting for a break in the basic training exercises to let Chris know that she and her friend were on board. Unfortunately, the break never came, and Melody was going to have to wait until evening to track down Chris. She was anxious to let him know that they were up for whatever Chris needed.

Chris was unaware, of course, of the positive turn of events, and he was counting the minutes until he could find out from Melody what had been decided. Because of his anxiety, the day never seemed to end, and the sergeant seemed to be making the exercise program even harder than usual. The day was miserable, and Chris wondered if he was the catalyst for the harder than usual drills. He also wondered if the other guys were blaming him for the sergeant's attitude. There was nothing he could do about it, so he just complied with the sergeant's directions.

Finally, the training day came to an end, and the recruits were dog-tired. All they wanted to do was to lie down and rest - all the recruits, but one. Chris was wired, and he needed to see Melody to find out what she decided. Chris made himself obviously available as he walked outside of the hospital hoping to get a shot at seeing Holly or Melody. He was tired, but he wasn't going to rest until he knew what Melody was going to do and furthermore, how she made out with her friend, Holly. Unfortunately, his waiting did not pay off. He wasn't able to see either one, and that bothered him. He had to know as soon as possible so that a flawless plan could be developed. Time was running out quickly.

Night was settling in, and Chris had not seen Melody. It bothered him that it was taking so long for Melody to make contact with him. He decided to rest for a while, and he laid down in his bunk. Most of the other recruits were already sleeping, or on their way to slumber city. He decided that he was just going to close his eyes for a little while but stay up to give Melody every opportunity to reach out to him. Chris underestimated how tired he really was, and he slipped into a deep, comfortable, well-needed sleep. He stayed asleep for a good four hours when he was awakened by that familiar voice which had appeared to him before. He groggily opened his eyes to see the blurry cloud and heard his name being called: *"Wake up, Chris. I've got some good news for you."*

"Couldn't you have waited 'till morning to tell me? I am bush tired. Whatever the news is, I'm sure that it's not so important as to deprive me of necessary sleep. Come back in the morning."

"No Chris, we have to discuss circumstances that can't wait until the morning, so wake up and pay attention. I know that you were waiting to see Melody, but she got tied up with other things. I have the news that you've been waiting for."

"Why didn't you say so? Well, what did Melody decide to do? Is she with me or against me? Tell me."

"Before I get to that, I want you to hear me out and maybe after digesting what I have to say, Melody's decision wouldn't matter."

"I don't understand. The most important thing to me right now is to know whether or not Melody, and for that matter, Holly are going to, at least, not expose us. So, get to the point, please. Let me know."

"For argument's sake, let's just say that Melody and Holly agreed to stand by whatever you are planning to do. If your plan succeeds, you will be getting back at the very least, Sergeant Brown. I believe that's your main goal. And you will have succeeded in turning his life into a turmoil of hurt and emotional stress. That's Great, but what about the collateral damage that you and your friends will cause? An innocent woman will suffer the consequences of a divorce that will tear her apart. Do you want your plan to succeed at the expense of an innocent person who might suffer hurt for a very long time? Is it worth it to you? I don't think your friend, Tim, would want that. As a matter of fact, I know that Tim Jenkins would tell you to let it go. You know, Chris, life has a way of righting the wrongs without any outside help. Please think it over. Don't do something that you may regret."

"Hey, whose side are you on? You're supposed to be a friend of mine. You sure don't sound like a cheerleader for the cause."

"Chris, you don't know how good a friend I am. One day, you will realize that you have no better friend than me."

"I have a good friend, and I don't think anyone could take his place, no matter what powers you may have. I wonder what he would say to do. Danny always knew what to do, and how to do it. I could sure use his help now."

"Chris, I have never lied to you, and I never will. Danny Ferguson would tell you to forget about revenge. It can only hurt you. In fact, I know for sure that Danny would be disappointed if you continued with your plan. I'm positive of that!"

"How could you be so sure; I don't even know who or what you are? And you're advising me as if you were Danny himself. Oh, how I wish he were here. I miss his friendship and his advice. Everything was so much clearer when he was around."

"Let's assume he is around, and he told you to give up on your conquest for revenge. What would you do?"

"I'd probably listen to him. I can't remember when he was wrong, or when he gave me bad advice."

The voice was quiet for a few seconds and apparently adjusted his tone: *"Well, consider me him, and forget about what you are planning to do."*

It worked, and in that instant, Chris thought he actually heard Danny's voice, and it moved him to rethink the whole situation. He knew, of course, that it couldn't be Danny since his friend was a patient in Lakehurst General. But for that moment, it sure sounded like him, and just the sound of his friend's voice pushed Chris to reconsider. It was as if Danny himself was giving him advice.

After just a moment or two, Chris spoke to his spirit-friend: "I don't know how you did it, but it felt like Danny himself was giving me advice. And I always listened to Danny. Maybe, this crusade wasn't the right thing. I am going to tell the rest of the gang that, in due time, both the sergeant and the lieutenant will get what they deserve. By the way, even though their decision doesn't matter anymore, what did Melody and Holly decide."

"You're right, Chris. It doesn't matter anymore, so why belabor the issue. You've made the right decision, and you can face both of them without having a guilty conscience."

"Before you go, I still don't really know who or what you are. You come in and out of my life like a winged messenger. No one else knows about you, but you seem to be there for me whenever I need it. I should at least know who you are."

"Chris, you said it before. I am your good friend," and he was gone.

Chapter Eighteen

Fate Steps In

Chris slept through the rest of the night. It was a much more relaxed sleep than he had been getting; his mind was free, and he was not plagued with worry and indecision. However, he did want to see Melody to let her know that there was no plan to seek satisfaction with regards to either the sergeant or the lieutenant. He hoped that she would come around sometime during the day. It was Sunday, and the recruits had the day off. This is supposed to be their recovery day, and a day where they can take care of their individual personal needs. It would be the best time for Chris to meet Melody, but he didn't know where she was. He was anxious to let her know that she no longer had to strain over the decision-making process.

Chris decided to head over toward the hospital where he hoped that he might meet up with Melody, or, at least, see Holly to find out where her friend might be. Once again, fate smiled on Chris Martin. As he approached the base hospital, he saw Melody approaching from the opposite direction. Everything seemed right with the world. He saw her before she saw him, so she just continued toward the hospital entrance. He hurried his approach and got to Melody before she entered: "Hi Melody, I am glad I caught up with you.
I have some good news for a change."

"Hi Chris, I also have some good news, but you go first."

"Well, I had a debate with, let's say, my conscience, and after agonizing over what to do, I decided that first: it wasn't worth the risk, secondly: doing something to get back at the sergeant might hurt innocent people, and I didn't want to do that, and thirdly: I don't think Tim would want us to do something harmful in his name. A good friend told me that life has a way of righting the wrongs that come our way, and that it didn't need any outside help. My friend is usually right about things."

"Wow, Chris. That surely takes the steam out of my announcement. Both Holly and I decided to give you whatever cooperation you needed, but I am glad that it won't be necessary now. I believe it is the better way to go, and I don't believe that your friend, Tim, would have wanted you to do something that would hurt others. Holly and I also had the benefit of a good friend's advice. He didn't pressure us either way, but he shed light on a very dark situation. I am very happy you will avoid the possibility of retaliation."

"Can I assume then that Holly is not going to mention anything to the lieutenant about what we were thinking of doing?"

"Chis, Holly and the lieutenant aren't exactly on the best of terms right now, and 'yes,' she has agreed to say nothing. I am sure, however, that she will be relieved to know that her cooperation is no longer needed. She did struggle, as I did, to make the right decision, but now it is all moot. I couldn't be happier that you trashed your original idea."

"Melody, I guess you'll be heading back to Jersey now. I hope I'm not being too up front when I say this, but is there a possibility that we can keep in touch? I find it very easy to talk to you, and I feel that we have some kind of connection. I know that sounds corny, but I really think we do."

"I would like that, Chris. By all means, we should keep in touch. I know that you will probably be assigned to somewhere in the Middle East, but they get mail there too. As soon as you get your assignment, let me know the address where I can send my letters."

"I'll do that, but before I get my station assignment, I will be going to Advanced Individual Training (A.I.T.). I am not sure where that will be."

"No problem. Wherever it is, just let me know, and I will write to you there."

As they were speaking, an ambulance and fire apparatus with sirens blaring and emergency lights employed raced past them. Melody and Chris looked in the direction that the emergency vehicles were heading, and they could see a large plume of black smoke rising toward the sky. Everyone in the area just stopped and looked at the emergency response. The dark smoke wasn't that far from where Chris and Melody were standing, so they decided to head toward the scene of the emergency. They were joined by a whole cadre of people wanting to know what happened.

As they arrived on the scene, they saw numerous firefighters and emergency workers trying to control flames that were originating from the base gas station. Chris started talking to one of the other onlookers who apparently had more information about the incident. The curiosity seeker told them that he had heard that one of the drivers, the fuel truck operator, lost control of his fuel truck and crashed into an army jeep that went out of control and slammed into the gas pumps at the gas station. He didn't know if anyone was hurt or how many people were involved in the accident.

Melody's experience and background as a nurse forged her into action. She ran to the medical officers who responded and asked if she could help. The emergency medical team at the scene told her that they had everything under control and thanked her for volunteering. Most ambulance crews are territorial and do not want outside help. So, Melody was expecting a negative response to her offer. She was close enough now, however, to see emergency responders assisting at least three people who were injured in the accident. The scene was a volatile one since there was the danger of explosion from the exposed gas tanks. The firefighters were engaged in controlling the potential for explosion while the medical crews were carefully extracting the injured parties from the scene. From Melody's vantage point, she could see that at least two of the injured individuals were soldiers in uniform. They seemed to be badly injured and suffering from burns. She didn't get a good luck at their faces since she was being pushed out of the way by the military police officers who also arrived to help.

A large crowd had gathered, and as usual, there were all kinds of being circulated among the onlookers. It went from a drunk non-facts driver incident to an unconscious, heart attack victim. No one actually knew what had happened or who was hurt nor the extent of their injuries. This would come out at a later time. For now, it would have to suffice that there were three people involved in an automobile accident, two of which could be identified as military personnel.

As both Chris and Melody continued to watch the efforts of the emergency response teams, Melody felt a tap on her shoulder. Holly had just arrived to see what had happened: "Melody, I just got on my break when someone said that there had been a bad accident at the gas station. Tell me what happened."

"We really don't know much, Holly. I saw that two of the injured persons were in uniform, and they seemed to be badly hurt and also suffering from burns. I don't know about the third individual. It looks like there were only three people involved in the accident. The fire fighters are focusing their efforts on eliminating the possibility of an explosion since gas tanks are involved. That's why we were pushed all the way back from the scene."

"Do you know how it happened? You know what caused the accident?"

Chris interjected: "There's all kinds of rumors circulating, but no one really knows for sure why it happened. I guess we'll find out later on in the day what caused the crash. Holly, you'll be able to find out who was injured since they are being taken directly to the base hospital. I hope the guys aren't injured badly."

"I'll get back to the hospital now and see what I can find out. These types of accidents are so disturbing, especially when burns are involved. If I find out anything, I'll let you know. It's bad for anyone to be involved in an accident, but I hope that it's not someone we know. Let me get back. Talk to you soon."

Chris and Melody just stayed a while longer, and then they went back toward the hospital entrance where they first met.

"Thanks Melody, for trusting in me, and please thank Holly. It's gratifying to know that both of you had my back. I feel relieved on two fronts: one, I don't have to do something that I might have regretted for the rest of my life; and two, I was able to convince the two of you that I had a just cause. That means an awful lot to me."

"I have to tell you, Chris, I and Holly struggled for a long time in making a decision, and without the help of my other friend, I don't know if the two of us would have reached the same conclusion. But that's behind us now, and we can all take a sigh of relief."

As they spoke, they saw additional fire apparatus responding to the accident scene. One of the trucks had the words "foam retardant" labeled on its side. It was a truck that dealt mainly with gas and oil-fueled fires where water would only add to the spreading of the flames. The foam acted as a retardant, and it was surely needed at this accident scene.

They said their "good-byes," and with a kiss on Chris' cheek, Melody turned to enter the hospital. She was going to thank her friend, Holly, once more, for everything that she had done for her. Melody's leaving saddened both of them, but they promised to see each other again soon.

Melody had just exited the hospital and was her way to gather her things for her departure to the airport when she heard what sounded like desperate cries coming from behind her. The voice calling her name was a familiar one. Holly was yelling and running as fast as she could toward Melody. Holly grabbed onto her friend, and in-between desperate sobs she said: "Melody, I just found out that the two soldiers who were involved in the accident are Harmon Brown and Bill Harley. They are badly hurt. Oh my God, Melody, what do I do?"

As Melody attempted to comfort her friend, something that Chris had said resounded loudly in her head: "Life has a way of righting the wrongs without any outside help." Fate had stepped in and became judge, jury, and executioner!

Chapter Nineteen

An Overwhelming Guilt

Holly Fisher was beside herself. In addition to her concern for the health of her boyfriend, she felt an enormous amount of guilt over even considering to be a part of any plan aimed at hurting him. Unfortunately, she blamed Chris Martin and her good friend, Melody, for "convincing" her to cooperate. Holly was under a lot of stress and was having a difficult time dealing with her feelings of guilt. Melody understood that and just let Holly get things off her chest. Melody offered no response to the accusations directed at her, but it was difficult to hear her friend so desperate and condemning.

After what seemed like an eternity, Melody was able to calm her friend and started to try to talk some sense into her. Although Holly was not as accusatory as she was just a few moments ago, she was still not willing to release herself from the anvil of guilt hanging from her neck. She just kept repeating that it was karma for her decision to go against her boyfriend. The result was that he would suffer the consequences of his alleged actions and she would be impacted by the dissolution of what could have been a lasting relationship. It had been their plan to eventually solidify their relationship with a marriage ceremony that now would probably never take place.

When Chris got back to the barracks, everyone was talking about the accident. As soon as the recruits realized that Chris had entered, however, a hush came over the entire space. Of course, Chris realized this and asked why everyone became so close-mouthed. Aaron was the first to respond to Chris: "Hey, Chris. You know that there was a bad accident a little while ago at the base gas station, right?"

"Yeah, I was at the scene with Melody. It looked really bad, and I heard that two of the injured were uniformed soldiers. So, why all the silence and drama?"

"Chris, the two uniformed soldiers were Lieutenant Bill Harley and Sergeant Harmon Brown. It is rumored that not only are they at risk, but surely, their military careers are over. The other man who was involved in the accident apparently died of a fatal heart attack. That was the reason for the crash in the first place."

Chris was stunned. He just stood there in disbelief. He looked at the other recruits who were staring at him. When he finally came out of his shock induced trance, he looked at them and said: "You're all looking at me as if I had something to do with what happened. What's the matter with you? Do you think that I wanted them to get seriously injured? Believe me, I get no satisfaction out of what happened. I don't want anyone to get hurt. Sure, you all know that I detested both of them for what they did to Tim Jenkins, but I certainly didn't want something like this to happen. Get real!"

"Chris, we know that you had nothing to do with it, but to many of the other guys, it certainly seems like you brought on some kind of karma. I know it sounds absurd, but it sure is a strange coincidence."

"Aaron, that's exactly what it is, a strange coincidence. It is nothing more. You all have to come to your senses. You're acting like I put some kind of voodoo curse on the two of them. If I had that kind of power, I wouldn't be in this shithole with the rest of you. Think about it. I really can't believe that I even have to explain any of this to you. Rest easy, I can't put a curse on any of you."

With his last remarks landing with focused emphasis, the recruits laughed uneasily and seemed to realize the absurdity of their thinking and began to attend to their own personal needs. The conversation ceased about the accident and the two bosses who were injured. There was just general discussion about everyday matters. Aaron approached Chris: "I was just wondering, Chris. You said that you were with Melody at the accident scene. Did she say anything about whether Holly mentioned anything to the lieutenant about our proposed plan? We could still get disciplined because we were plotting an action even though nothing actually happened."

"Rest easy. Aaron. Melody mentioned that both her and Holly had decided to cooperate with us. They were not going to mention anything to anyone. So, we are off the hook."

"But you know, Chris. Now that something awful has happened especially to the Lieutenant, I hope that guilt doesn't drive her to ask the lieutenant for his forgiveness for her even thinking about betraying his trust. Woman are funny that way, and the guilt that she is probably carrying could bring her to her knees. It might not be a bad idea to check in with Melody just to make sure nothing has changed."

"I don't have a problem with that, Aaron, but Melody was leaving for New Jersey today. I don't know if I can catch her before she goes, but I'll try."

Chris left the barracks and headed toward the hospital where he thought that Melody might be consoling her friend. When he got to the entrance, he hesitated, thinking that he might be the last person that Holly would want to see. If she was suffering pangs of heavy guilt, his appearance might trigger an event that would not be advantageous to anyone. He decided to just hang around the hospital in the hope that if Melody stayed because of her friend's situation, that at one point, she might leave the hospital. But as far as he knew, she was still scheduled to fly back to New Jersey. He wasn't sure how badly Holly might have taken the news about the lieutenant's accident, and if Melody might change her flight to be with her friend. Everything was up in the air, but he thought it best not to risk a personal visit. So, he waited for the possibility that Melody might leave the hospital either to catch her flight or to make new arrangements. Because of the circumstances, he had no other choice. However, he owed it to the rest of the recruits to find out for sure if they were in the clear. He understood their angst, and he wanted to know for himself too, but waiting was tedious and boring.

When Chris left the barracks, Aaron had a chance to address the rest of the guys. He let them know that Chris was trying to meet up with Melody to find out, for sure, that everything was all right. He also emphasized to the group that Chris was a stand-up guy who wouldn't let them down. A few of the recruits still mumbled about how coincidental the accident was with a plan to destroy the lieutenant and the sergeant. They couldn't get it out of their heads that possibly something greater than them was at work. Whether they believed it or not, they heard that such strange oddities like voodoo and karma, according to some people, could affect one's normal existence. They just wanted to make sure that after what could have been defined by some as a karma-influenced accident, they were not going to be impacted by the resultant aftermath. Aaron understood, but he mentioned to them again that they could do nothing but just wait for Chris to return with the information.

Chris had waited for over an hour already, and he still had no idea if Melody was at the hospital. He was getting close to risking it all and going inside when he noticed two nurses exiting the hospital. With as much diplomacy as he could muster, he inquired about Holly. They told him that she was in the hospital, but not working at her regular station. They mentioned that she was assisting in the emergency room. Chris thanked them and decided to venture into the hospital toward the emergency room. When he arrived there, he saw a number of ranking officers standing outside of the emergency room entrance. They seemed to be in heavy conversation, so Chris avoided them at all costs. He stayed in the rear of the waiting room and from the corner of his eye, he saw a young woman sitting by herself dabbing her eyes. As he got closer, he realized that he had found Melody.

Without bringing attention to himself, he cautiously approached Melody. She looked up with tears in her eyes and seemed surprised to see Chris. She got up and hugged him trying to console herself. He didn't want any attention to be focused on them, so he gently moved her to the chair. Chris held her hand and waited for her to regain her composure. When she did, she started to tell him about how Holly had reacted to the news. Unfortunately, it wasn't what Chris wanted to hear. She mentioned how Holly had accused her of being part of the betrayal that Holly felt. Melody also said that Holly blamed Chris for what happened and that now, because of him, her life would be changed forever.

"You realize, Chris, that Holly was speaking out of a desperate attack of guilt. She couldn't get over the fact that what she believed was karma had played a significant role in the disastrous event at the gas station. She did calm down after a while, and she's now in the emergency room with Bill."

"Melody, how are you doing? I know you were on your way to pack for the airport. Has that changed? Did you reschedule?"

"I cancelled my flight as soon as I heard that Bill was involved in the accident. I knew that Holly was going to be devastated, and I wanted to be here for her."

"You're a good friend, Melody. So, I assume you'll be staying for a little while."

"I called work and told them that I needed an extended leave. I explained the circumstances, and they agreed to let me stay for another two weeks, but I will have to go back then."

"Is Holly going to be okay with your staying with her for another two weeks? According to what you told me, she was pretty upset with you."

"She did calm down, and I'm sure that she'll be okay with my staying. In fact, she will probably want some company. I feel very bad for her, and I don't want to leave her while she is hurting so badly."

"I understand, Melody, that the lieutenant and the sergeant were both badly burned. Do you know how they are doing?"

"No, but I do know that Sergeant Brown was in worse condition than Lieutenant Harley."

Just as Melody finished speaking, the inner door of the emergency room opened and a masked doctor came out. He asked for the ranking officer. As the captain came forward, the doctor asked to speak with him privately. When they were out of earshot from the rest of the officers who were waiting to find out the condition of the two soldiers, the doctor addressed the ranking officer: "I'm sorry captain, we couldn't save the sergeant. His injuries and burns were too severe, and he never regained consciousness."

Sergeant Harmon Brown had expired.

Chapter Twenty

On Pins and Needles

Chris Martin and Melody Johnson learned that Sergeant Harmon Brown had died. Melody was worried for her friend, Holly, who was sure to find out that the sergeant died. Holly had to be an emotional mess. When Chris and Melody learned of the sergeant's death, all they could do was to stare at each other in silent disbelief. The immediate thought that came to both of them revolved around the possibility of the lieutenant suffering the same fate. What would they do if Bill Harley died? How would they be able to console Holly?

The waiting room was buzzing with the news of the sergeant's death. Many of the officers who were present had known Harmon Brown for a long time. He had come through mobilizations in the Middle East without so much as a scratch, and here he was in a peaceful environment succumbing to the injuries sustained in an auto accident on an army base. Fate has a strange way of dictating one's future.

There was enough guilt to go around. Both Melody and Chris were engulfed in its realm even though any plan for revenge had been trashed. They continued to sit in the waiting room not commenting to one another. Finally, Melody broke the uncomfortable silence: "Chris, what do we do now? I feel very anxious for Holly, and I want to be here for her, but I don't know what to do."

"Melody, I guess we'll just have to wait until she comes out of the emergency room, but I don't know if my staying here waiting with you is the right thing to do. She might not want to see me at all, and I don't want to cause her any more grief."

"You might be right, Chris. I don't even know how she is going to react toward me. It might be best if you leave, and I will contact you later on."

"Okay, Melody. I'll be around. Please let me know how things are going as soon as you can."

Melody just nodded her head, and Chris got up from his seat and exited the hospital. There were so many things going through his mind, and he was anxious about all of them. To his chagrin, the time was never right for him to ask about Holly's commitment to silence. He wanted to ask Melody a number of different times, but something or someone always interrupted, and he had to put his inquiry on the back burner. The rest of the guys weren't going to be happy not having a definitive answer, but there was nothing that he could do about it. Also, he didn't want to turn Melody off by asking a question that totally seemed self-serving. He was hoping to broach the subject when Melody contacted him later on in the day. It might be easier then.

As Chris walked back to the barracks, his mind was working overtime in an effort to come up with something that would be satisfactory to the rest of the recruits. After debating the issue over and over again, he decided to be straight with them and let them know that he would try again later when Melody contacts him. They wouldn't be happy, but there was nothing that he could do about it.

Even though it was a Sunday, and the recruits had a day off, no one left the base. In fact, it seemed as though no one left the barracks. Chris knew that they were on pins and needles, but he wasn't expecting such a large welcoming committee. The interested group had expanded from the original three. He entered the barracks, and the guys just congregated around him anxious to hear that they were in the clear. Unfortunately, he was going to disappoint them: "Well, I'm glad to see that you all missed me." His humorous sarcasm didn't sit well with the group, so he came right to the point: "I was able to meet with Melody. I found her sitting in the waiting area outside of the emergency room. You have to understand that she was very concerned about her friend, Holly. We spoke for a while, and I was about to ask her if she thought that Holly would be so overwrought with guilt and grief that she might weaken her resolve and let the lieutenant know what we intended to do. But just as I was about to speak, the emergency room doors opened, and a doctor addressed the brass who were there. The doctor informed the captain that Sergeant Harmon Brown didn't make it."

Apparently, the news of the sergeant's demise had not yet reached the enlisted personnel. Chris' remarks brought looks of disbelief and shock. A number of questions simultaneously flew out at him: "Sergeant Brown is dead. Is that what you are telling us?"

"Yeah, that's right. Apparently, his injuries and the amount of burn damage was so severe that he couldn't survive. He died a little while ago, and before you ask, the lieutenant is still alive and fighting for his life."

Aaron spoke up: "How did Melody react to the news of the sergeant's death? Maybe, we can gear Holly's reaction by what Melody did."

"Of course, Melody was shocked and saddened by the news, but she seemed even more concerned about her friend. She remained silent for a long time before she told me that she wanted to remain there for a while longer to help Holly get through this rough period. She never mentioned anything about us or any plan. So, there's no way to gather any information about how Holly is going to react. We'll just have to wait. I'm sure that I'll get the opportunity to bring up the subject when I speak to her later. I'll let you all know as soon as I know."

The recruits weren't exactly happy with the news that Chris had, or the lack of news, but there was nothing they could do about it. It wasn't totally negative, however, since Chris was going to have another opportunity to speak with Melody and possibly find out where Holly's head was. He had to find out soon because graduation from basic training was only a few days away, and no one wanted any surprises at graduation. Especially, if that surprise amounted to disciplinary procedures that would impact the future of those soldiers who had been assigned to the same company as Chris Martin.

Holly finally left the emergency room, and Melody was there to greet her. Her eyes were red, and she looked very worn. Melody felt terrible for her friend, took her hand and brought Holly close to her so she could hug her. Holly melted into Melody's arms, and they both cried. Melody walked with Holly as they headed to Holly's apartment. When they reached their destination, Melody told her friend that she was able to stay with her for, at least, another two weeks. Holly seemed overjoyed and grateful that Melody could stay. She was surprised, but pleasantly surprised: "Oh, thank you, Melody. I can sure use the company, and I know I'll need someone to talk to. Are you sure it's okay with work?"

"Absolutely. I called as soon as we found out about the accident. They gave me two more weeks, but I don't know if I can get any more than that."

"That's fine, Melody. Hopefully, Bill will be getting better as the days go on, and I can get back to a regular routine. Two weeks is fine. Unfortunately, at this point everything is up in the air. No one knows if Bill suffered any permanent damage, that is – physical damage. I'm sure that emotionally, he is a wreck. The continuation of his military career, of course, is in jeopardy, and any plans for marriage are surely on hold. It's unbelievable that in one instant, a person's life is changed forever. I know I have to be strong for Bill, but it's not easy. My future hinged on Bill's future; so, I am looking at the upcoming days, months, and even years as a time of flux. I don't know where we're going from here."

"Have faith, Holly. You are too good of a person for things not to work out. You'll see. Before you know it, you'll be living a life that you deserve with the man that you deserve to be with. Sure, it might be rough in the beginning because you will have to deal with Bill's disappointment, and probably some of his recovery, but that too will pass. Holly, I want you to know that I will always be here for you. We have shared too much for me not to be that crutch of support that you may need from time to time."

"Thanks, Melody. I wish that I could be as positive as you are about future days, but there are so many hurdles that we have to clear before we are able to see through the fog of pain and hardship. Bill has suffered a lot of damage, and the pain from the burns is sometimes overwhelming. As I looked at him, I thought about the situation with Chris Martin. The thought that I was going to be a part, even in a small way, of a plan that would potentially hurt Bill, disturbs me. I can't believe that I was going to do that. Bill deserves better than that. I know that basic training will end in a couple of days, so my confessing to Bill at this point would really have no impact on him or the recruits. If he was in better shape, I would have to let him know everything that I know."

Melody was taken aback by what she had just heard. She attributed it to the present circumstances, and the guilt that Holly felt as she looked at her boyfriend. She didn't want to respond to Holly's remarks, but Bill Harley was still the same guy who supported what Sergeant Brown had done to Tim Jenkins. His personality hadn't changed with the change in his physical appearance, but Melody wasn't about to offer any comments that would make things worse. The fact that, no matter the reason, Holly was not going to betray Chris and the other recruits was enough for her.

Following some coffee and snacks, Holly told Melody that she was going to lay down for a while before she went back to the hospital. Melody agreed and told her that it was a good idea. Holly needed rest if she was going to help Bill. This brief rest period gave Melody a chance to contact Chris, who she was sure was worried about Holly's commitment to confidentiality.

Since she would only be gone for a short while, she borrowed Holly' s car and headed toward the base and ultimately to Chris Martin's barracks. Melody took a cup of coffee with her and planned to drink it on the way. When the car in front of her unexpectedly jammed on its brakes, Melody's attempt to avoid an accident was thwarted by hot coffee spilling on her legs. The coffee distraction brought her to the point where she was unable to stop her car in time. Rushing to see Private Martin, Melody had neglected to fasten her seatbelt which now resulted in her head coming in direct contact with the windshield. Melody Johnson was bleeding and unconscious at the scene.

Chapter Twenty-One

What Else Could Go Wrong

Chris was beginning to get worried. It was getting late in the day, and he had not heard anything from Melody. The guys in his company were also getting antsy. He thought that Melody would, at least, come around the barracks to let him know that she was on base. There was no word from her, and no one had seen her. Chris decided to walk to the base hospital again to possibly find out if Melody or Holly were there. At this point, he would even risk seeing Holly to find out where Melody was. Maybe, Melody was having a hard time with Holly. Because there was a guilt factor involved, Holly may have insisted on telling her boyfriend about her potential involvement. If that was the case, Melody was going to have a tough time convincing her friend to remain silent. So many possibilities were racing through Chris' head that he was feeling the beginnings of a major headache. He had to remain cool. He sat on a bench right outside of the hospital and tried to calm down.

He was there for no longer than ten minutes when he heard that familiar voice which usually comes to him at night. The voice whispered something that Chris could not understand. Of course, no one else heard the voice but him, so he asked it to repeat the message. If anyone was watching, they would assume that Private Chris Martin was talking to himself since there was no visual representation attached to the voice. There was no fog, no mist, just a whispered voice that only Chris alone was able to hear.

"I can't understand what you are saying. You have to say it again. I can hardly hear you. What did you say?"

"To find Melody Johnson, you must get to Lawton Indian Hospital. She will be there."

"Did you say Lawton Indian Hospital? I don't understand. Why would she be there?"

The voice was gone. There was no answer to Chris' questions. He had never heard of Lawton Indian Hospital and had no idea where it was or why Melody would be there. However, his spirit friend always seemed to be on the mark, so Chris wasn't going to doubt him now. The first thing he had to do was to find out where the heck Lawton Indian Hospital was, and then, he needed a way to get there. Someone who was familiar with the area would have probably heard of Lawton

Indian Hospital and would probably know where it was. Chris wasn't thinking straight. All he had to do was to go into the base hospital and ask anyone in there where this Indian Hospital was. He was sure that they would know about another hospital in the area.

Chris walked into the base hospital and asked the first person he saw about the Indian Hospital. The name plate read, "Dr. Jason Chance."

"Excuse me, Doc. Could I ask you a quick question?"

"You surely can as long as it is a quick one. I'm running late to teach a class at another hospital. So, go ahead."

"Have you ever heard of Lawton Indian Hospital? I've never heard of it, and I don't even know if such a place exists."

"It certainly does exist, soldier. We have an ongoing relationship with the medical team there, and we often meet with them to discuss medical resources that might be available to both our staffs. In fact, I am on my way there now. Why do you ask?"

"Well, Doc, I am supposed to meet someone there, and I am at a loss to know where it is or how I am going to get there."

"It's only about a 4-mile drive from here, and I can give you a lift there, if you want to take a "chance." The doctor smiled and pointed to his name plate. Chris got the pun but didn't expect that kind of reaction from the doctor. A doctor with a sense of humor. That was rare. The doctor continued: "I can get you there, but you will have to find your own way back."

"Thanks, Doc. That's great. By the way, I am Private Chris Martin."

"Good to meet you, Private. Follow me to my car and we'll be on our way."

Chris couldn't believe his good fortune. Not only did he find someone who knew about the Indian Hospital, but he also found a way to get there. Chris was more than confident now that things were going to turn out just fine.

The car ride was only about seven minutes, and before he knew it, Chris was being dropped off in front of Lawton Indian Hospital. Dr. Chance went on to park his car, and Chris went into the hospital. It was a small modern, three-story building that offered approximately thirty patient beds. Chris went directly to the main desk station and asked the receptionist if Nurse Melody Johnson was available. Chris was surprised by the answer that there was no Nurse Johnson at the facility. Chris then resorted to describing Melody and got the same response. He was confused. The voice had not been wrong in the past, and it seemed certain that Melody would be at this hospital. At a loss for what to do next, he exited the hospital and sat on a bench just outside of the entrance. Chris didn't want to just leave because he felt that the voice was sure that Melody was there.

As Chris remained on the bench, two nurses passed him on the way into the hospital. He heard some of their conversation, and he thought he heard Melody's name mentioned. He bolted up and approached the two nurses: "Excuse me, I am sorry to bother you, but I thought I heard you mention the name, 'Melody'."

One of the nurses acknowledged Chris, and responded: "Yes, that's right. We were just commenting about how a name like 'Melody Johnson' seemed like it should belong to an actress in Hollywood."

Chis couldn't contain his enthusiasm and asked where they had heard that name. The nurses inquired as to Chris' interest in the name and the person to whom it belonged. He was able to convince them that he was a close friend, and that he was worried about her. He was taken by surprise when they told him that Melody Johnson was a patient at the hospital.

"Melody Johnson is a patient here? When did that happen? Do you know the reason why she is here? Do you know her condition?"

The nurses directed Chris to the patient information desk where he inquired about the patient, Melody Johnson. He had a tough time convincing the nurse on duty that he needed to see her. Just at that time, Dr. Jason Chance passed by the desk. Chris caught up to him and asked if he could intervene and facilitate his visit with Melody. For the second time on the same day, Dr. Jason Chance came to Chris' rescue. The doctor vouched for Chris, and he was escorted to Melody's room. Chris quickly learned that Melody was suffering from a concussion. She was unconscious with a deep laceration to her head and with the possibility of broken ribs. Dr Chance helped as much as he could, and left Chris at Melody's bedside.

Chris was alarmed when he saw Melody and even more concerned when Dr. Chance had told him the extent of her injuries. He wanted to find out what happened, and how Melody wound up there. He looked down the hallway and saw a uniformed police officer apparently completing some paperwork. On a pure hunch, Chris approached the officer and asked if he was involved with a report regarding Melody Johnson. The officer was reluctant to discuss anything, but when Chris identified himself as a soldier at Fort Sill, the officer softened his stance and related to Chris that his "girlfriend" had been in an automobile accident.

While Chris was visiting Melody at Lawton Indian Hospital, Holly was awakening from her rest period. She looked around and Melody was missing. She searched further for a possible note or message. She found none. That wasn't like Melody to just disappear without any indication of where she might be going. Holly figured that her friend had just stepped out for a moment and that she would probably be back shortly. In the meantime, Holly took a shower and got dressed in preparation for her return to the hospital to see Bill.

Just as Holly finished dressing, the apartment doorbell rang. Holly immediately assumed that it was Melody who forgot to take the keys to get back in. When she opened the door, she was surprised to see a uniformed police officer from the Lawton Police Department standing at the door. Reacting as everyone does when they see a police officer at the door, Holly nervously asked if everything was okay. The officer responded by giving Holly a description of her automobile and the corresponding license plate number. He then asked if that was her car. Of course, she answered that it was and quickly asked why the officer was inquiring: "Yes officer, that is my car. Is there a problem? Has someone hit my car?"

"Yes Mam. Your vehicle was involved in an automobile accident in Lawton Township on U.S. Route 44."

"What do you mean my car was involved in an accident. Who was driving my car?" Right after she uttered those words, it came to her that Melody probably borrowed her car: "Was Melody Johnson driving my car?"

"Yes Mam. Miss Johnson was driving your car when she rear-ended the car in front of her. She was taken to Lawton Indian Hospital, and your car has been towed to our auto impound area. You will have to have it towed to a repair shop."

Holly was trying to comprehend everything that the police officer was saying, but there was so much information all at once that she was having trouble understanding. She was mentally digesting as much as she could and was not saying anything. The officer asked her if she had any questions, and that brought her into the moment. She immediately asked how Melody was doing.

"Miss Johnson was unconscious at the scene and was brought by ambulance to Lawton Indian Hospital. I have no further information about her condition. Please sign this report that you were notified about the accident, and you will be able to pick up a copy of the vehicle accident report tomorrow at the station house."

Holly signed the notification form and thanked the officer as he left the apartment. Things were getting convoluted now. Her boyfriend was in bad shape in the base hospital; her friend was unconscious at some Indian Hospital; her damaged car was at the police impound, and she had no way of getting to a car rental location. What else could go wrong? Just then the phone rang, and the landlord informed her that her lease was not being renewed.

Holly had twenty days to vacate her apartment. So now, she had no means of transportation, was soon to be homeless, and was the apparent health caretaker for both her boyfriend and her girlfriend. She looked around in a dazed manner and decided never to ask the "what else?" question again.

Chapter Twenty-Two

The Foiled Escape

Of course, Chris was concerned about Melody's well-being, but he could not get the thought out of his mind about how his barracks' buddies were going to react when he told them that he couldn't find out whether or not Holly was going to remain silent. But it was out of his hands. He was genuinely concerned about Melody, especially since she hit her head hard enough to suffer a concussion. That was no laughing matter. He stayed with Melody for the rest of the day and night.

When Chris was about to leave to find a way back to the base, he noticed a familiar face running up to the hospital entrance. The young woman stopped suddenly in her tracks as she recognized the person who was standing in front of her. They exchanged stares until finally Chris broke the silence: "Hello Holly. I just visited Melody. She has some bruises and possibly some broken ribs, but more importantly, she suffered a concussion and is unconscious."

"What? Melody is unconscious? How bad was the accident? What are the doctors saying, and how did you know that she was here?"

"A friend of mind heard about the accident, and he mentioned that Melody was taken to this hospital. I was able to bum a ride with a doctor who happened to be coming this way. In fact, he helped me get in to see her, and told me about her injuries. I have been here for quite a while, and I was about to search for a way to get back to the base. Let me take you to her room."

"Thanks, Chris. If you stay a while longer, I can give you a lift back to the base in my rented car. I was told that my car was in the police pound, and that I have to get it towed to a repair shop. My insurance company already okayed a rental."

Chris went with Holly to Melody's room. He decided that since this unexpected meeting with Holly went better than expected, he would wait with Holly and accept her ride back to the base. Holly was teary-eyed when she first saw her friend lying in the hospital bed. She felt so bad for her, but also for herself. The two people she most cared about were in hospital beds in two different hospitals suffering from God knows what.

Shortly after Holly and Chris entered Melody's room, the hospital doctor who was treating Melody came into the room. Both Holly and Chris were glad to see the doctor because they wanted an update on their friend's condition. The doctor greeted both of them and was cordial in response to their questions. He mentioned that Melody had a confirmed concussion, and that x-rays indicated two fractured ribs. The doctor felt that Melody would regain consciousness in a relatively short time, but that she would be in pain from the fractured ribs. It was a "no-brainer" that he wanted her to stay in the hospital until she regained consciousness and until the staff had a chance to observe her condition. They thanked the doctor for updating them both but were advised that they would have to wait until tomorrow to visit the patient again. Although they both wanted to stay a bit longer, they complied with the doctor's directions. Holly, as well as Chris, kissed their friend goodbye and left the hospital room heading for the exit.

There was very little conversation on the way out of the hospital, and the silence continued on the ride back to the base. Chris eventually broke the silence: "I really appreciate your giving me a ride back to the base, Holly. I came to see Melody as soon as I heard that she was there, and I gave no thought as to how I was going to get back. I was just in a hurry to find out how she was doing. Speaking of being in a hurry, you must have your hands full now with both your boyfriend and girlfriend in the hospital. How is the lieutenant doing?"

"He's definitely not in the best shape. He is going to have a long road to recovery, but I believe he will recover. He's also going to have some permanent scarring and definitely pain that he will have to deal with, but I think that he's mostly concerned with the idea that he will no longer be able to remain in the military. I guess you're glad to hear that."

Chris was taken aback by Holly's last comment, and hesitated before answering: "Holly, I really don't want anyone to get hurt or be in pain, but you have to realize that, as far as I know, Lieutenant Harley agreed with the actions of Sergeant Brown and was going to do nothing to step in and stop it. I just can't accept that. All the recruits in my company are of the same opinion that my friend, Private Tim Jenkins, would be alive if it weren't for the harassment by Sergeant Brown. The sergeant, unfortunately, has passed, but I am certain that nothing would have been done to him if he had survived. And yes, Holly, we were going to seek some revenge for his actions."

Chris knew that he was taking a substantial risk in being so blunt with Holly, but he couldn't hold back. It also gave him an opportunity to gauge Holly's intentions regarding a confession to the lieutenant. He waited in the deafening silence for Holly to respond. It took a while, but Holly turned to Chris and said: "You know, Chris, Melody told me all about you and your friends. She supported you and asked for my cooperation. Before the accident involving Bill and Sergeant Brown, I was willing to stay silent about your plans; however, in my heart of hearts, I knew it was a betrayal not to let Bill know. When I saw how Bill and Harmon were injured, the guilt of my betrayal became overwhelming, and I decided to free myself of it and tell Bill everything. As of the present, though, I haven't done that, and I really don't know why. That does not mean, however, that at some point, I won't confess. I am aware of how you feel about Tim Jenkins' death, but I am not sure that you have all the facts. My main concern now is to get Bill well."

"Let me be very frank about the situation, Holly. Graduation from basic training is scheduled for only a few days from now. We are all worried that something can come down before or at graduation dictating our punishment for even thinking about seeking revenge, and I have to let you know that I take blame for the whole idea. I pushed the others to join me, so if anyone should be disciplined, it should be me."

Holly was surprised with Chris' integrity, and his sincerity persuaded her to delay any action that would interfere with the basic training graduation. However, she hadn't made any permanent decision about never telling the lieutenant.

"Chris, I can tell you that I will not mention anything to Bill prior to your graduation, but I cannot guarantee that, at one point, I may explain what my role might have been in a deceptive plan to seek revenge. Melody was convinced that your cause was justified, and it is mostly because of my friendship with her that I will remain silent, for now. Especially with Melody lying unconscious in a hospital bed, would I want to disappoint her. She fought very hard for my cooperation, and I don't want to turn my back on her while she can't even discuss the situation further with me."

They arrived back at the base, and Chris thanked Holly for the ride and for her apparent cooperation regarding graduation.

But the cloud of uncertainty remained floating above the recruits' heads. The possibility of disciplinary action could follow all of them as each found out their Military Occupational Specialty Code (MOS) and attended Advanced Individual Training School (AIT). Chris was hopeful that his MOS and AIT would take him a distance from Fort Sill as he was relying on the axiom of "out of sight, out of mind" to come into play. If he was gone, neither the lieutenant nor Holly would be constantly reminded about what almost took place, and what the ramifications of the planned conspiracy might have been.

Basic Training Graduation finally came, and this was the time that Chris would escape the imminent threat of discipline as he left Fort Sill for destinations far removed from the grave mistake that he almost made. Though fate had proved to be an ally on other occasions, it had played a nasty trick on him this time. Private First-Class Chris Martin's MOS sent him to U.S. Army Field Artillery School. Where was the AIT school located? Field Artillery School was located in Oklahoma, and more specifically, at Fort Sill, Oklahoma. Chris' futile attempt at escape saw him remaining as a thorn in the side of a potentially dangerous lieutenant and a one-time indecisive collaborator. The only positive remnant was the fact that he would remain close to Melody Johnson, at least for a little while longer. Ironically, however, this lone ally remained unconscious in a hospital bed at Lawton Indian Hospital. Fate owed him one!

Chapter Twenty-Three

A Moral Purging

Graduation finally came, and the recruits sighed a breath of relief. It seemed like they escaped any disciplinary action. Most of them would be leaving Fort Sill for destinations dictated by their MOS. They would be going for advanced training at different military installations throughout the United States. However, Private First-Class Chris Martin apparently drew the short straw as he was to remain at Fort Sill for his advanced training.

Holly Fisher attended the graduation ceremony and congratulated Chris on his accomplishment. She and Chris spent a little time in discussion. Chris asked Holly how the lieutenant was doing and mentioned that he was going to visit Melody as soon as he could break away from the rest of his squad. Holly informed him that she was also going to the Indian Hospital, and that there was a possibility that after four days there, maybe Melody could be released. She had regained consciousness and was dealing well with the fractured ribs. The doctor had mentioned that if Melody felt okay, he would release her. Holly told Chris that if he waited until she spent some time with Bill, she could give him a ride to see Melody. In fact, she mentioned that she could use the help getting Melody into the car at the hospital and out of it when they got home. Chris eagerly accepted her invitation and was glad that he could help with Melody.

Melody Johnson could not wait to get out of the hospital. She now realized how her patients felt when they had to remain in the hospital. She was on the other side of the fence experiencing a patient's anxiety. She knew that Holly was planning to visit, and she hoped that it would be sooner rather than later. Melody felt terrible about damaging Holly's car. After everything Holly was going through with Bill, Melody felt that she just added to her friend's stress factor. She had no idea that the landlord had told Holly that he was not renewing the lease, and that he wanted her out by the end of the month which was in twenty days. That news would make Melody feel even worse about the accident.

Lieutenant Bill Harley was conscious but under the influence of powerful pain killers. So, his speech was somewhat garbled and hard to understand. Holly listened carefully, and she heard him ask about Sergeant Brown. Bill had been in serious condition, and the news about the sergeant would have only served to hinder his recovery instead of helping it. However, Bill was in better condition now, not in great condition, but in a better state than he had been. So, Holly, after conferring with the doctor, told her boyfriend the bad news. Bill took the news to heart and shook his head in despair. He then asked Holly what the doctor had said about his own condition. He wanted to know the prognosis. Was he going to fully recover? Was he going to always have pain? Was there a possibility that he would have a permanent disability? Did she know if he was going to be able to remain in the military? He bombarded Holly with one question after the other, not giving her a chance to give an answer to any one of them. Luckily for her, the doctor arrived at the bedside: "Hello, Holly. Hello, Lieutenant. How are you feeling? Are you ready to get up and leave or are you going to spend the rest of your military career lying on your back?"

"Well Doc, I can only say that I feel like I faced off with an 18-wheeler and lost."

"Well, you're close, lieutenant. It wasn't an 18-wheeler, but it was definitely a large trailer. And you didn't lose the fight. The truck was damaged beyond repair, and you are on your way to recovery."

"I'm glad you brought that up, Doc. I asked my girlfriend, but she wouldn't answer. How bad are my injuries? Will I have a permanent condition, and will I be able to continue with my military career?"

"Let me put it this way, Lieutenant. You will definitely have some scarring, and your healing will take a while. It is not up to me, however, whether you are able to continue in the military. That decision will be made by the Commanding Officers' Review Board. I will have some input, but the final decision is not mine."

"Hey Doc, if I didn't know better, I would say that you are avoiding the issue. I am sure you have some idea as to whether I would be able to continue or not."

During the whole exchange, Holly just sat there saying nothing, but knowing that it was more likely that Lieutenant Bill Harley's military career was over. She had previously heard the doctors discussing Bill's case, and from what she gathered, the injuries that Bill suffered would prevent him from carrying out the duties of a ranking officer. That being the case, she was not going to be the one to tell him that his time in the military was coming to an end.

"No Lieutenant, I am not going to speculate. It is much too early for me to make any informed decision. In my opinion, it all depends on how well your recovery goes. Forget about anything else, and focus your energy on recovery. In the days to come, the attending team will be in a better position to make an evaluation. Now, do you need any additional pain relief or is it tolerable?"

"I'm okay for now, Doc. Thanks."

"Don't be a hero, Lieutenant. Pain retards healing. So, if you need something, you should let me know."

"No, really, Doc. I'm okay."

Holly came closer to the bed and tried to reinforce what the doctor had said. She emphasized that Bill had to focus on his recovery and not think about anything but that. But she knew that he was not capable of putting other concerns aside. She knew him well, and the uncertainty of whether or not he would continue in the military was something that he could not put on the back burner.

"Holly, I realize how close I came to dying, and it forces one to think of his mortality. It could have been me instead of Harmon who is laying in a casket. The near-death scenario also influences one to attempt to get things off one's chest. I have not always been the person who I should have been, and something occurred recently that I have to confess to someone. It involves Private Tim Jenkins."

Holly wasn't sure that she wanted to hear what Bill was about to say so she hushed him and said: "Bill, there's plenty of time to talk about work-related things, but now you should rest and concentrate on getting better."

"No Holly. I have to tell someone, and you are the closest one to me. I knew that Sergeant Brown was harassing Private Tim Jenkins, and by not stopping the sergeant, I encouraged his behavior. Also. I believe that the constant harassment that the private endured was a major factor in his taking his own life. In fact, you should know, Holly, that I congratulated Sergeant Brown on a "job well done." My conscience is bothering me, and I need to free myself of this guilt as well as morally readjusting my outlook on life."

Holly had a tough time hearing what her boyfriend had to say. It was brutal reality to hear Lieutenant Bill Harley admit to a lack of proper action which ultimately led to the death of an army recruit. Although his confession was a step in the right direction to repairing his moral compass, Holly looked at her boyfriend as having reaped the "rewards" accurately associated with his prejudiced attitude. She looked at Bill now with a jaundiced eye and felt something toward him that she had never felt before – pity. And again, although he confessed his horrible actions, a certain disdain permeated Holly's emotional anxiety. As she mentally digested Bill's comments, the revelations that her friend, Melody, had presented about Chris Martin and his fellow recruits, flooded into her stream of consciousness. They were not wrong. They were justified in seeking some satisfaction for the untimely and premature death of their fellow squad member.

As Holly continued to ponder Lieutenant Harley's comments, she also felt the weight of the guilt that she had been carrying slowly melt away. If there was any guilt that should have been levied, it should have been directed toward the deceased Harmon Brown and the recovering Bill Harley. Holly felt an emotional schism evolving as a result of the situation, and she decided that she had spent enough time with Lieutenant Bill Harley. Chris Martin was patiently waiting outside for her, and at this point, she realized that she would rather be in his company than that of the person lying in front of her.

Private First-Class Chris Martin waited patiently on a bench directly outside of the hospital entrance. As Holly exited the hospital, she motioned to Chris that she was ready to drive to see Melody: "Are you ready to go, Chris?"

"Sure Holly, I am waiting on you. How was your visit and how is the lieutenant doing?"

"Well, it seems that the lieutenant is having a moral rebirth. He mentioned some things to me that I will not repeat but that have influenced me to look at him in a different light, and that light is glaring. His physical recovery is improving, but it is an extremely slow process. I am glad that his moral judgment has gotten back on track at a much quicker rate than expected, and I'll leave it at that."

Chris was a little confused over Holly's comments, but she seemed more friendly to Chris than she had previously been. Whatever went on during her visit with Lieutenant Harley seemed to have had a positive effect on the relationship between her and Chris. So, he wasn't going to belabor the issue, and he just accepted what he deemed to be an advantageous situation for him.

"Okay, Holly. Let's get Melody out of that Indian Camp. I am sure she's chomping at the bit to escape. I wonder if she will want to stay with you for a little while longer until she feels better. I am sure you wouldn't mind having her around for a short-extended stay."

"I wouldn't mind it at all, Chris, if I had a place for us to stay. I was just notified by my landlord that he is not going to renew my lease. He wants me out by the end of the month."

"Gee, I'm sorry to hear that. It seems that when it rains, it pours."

"It's not pouring, Chris. I am in the center of a thunderstorm, and the flooding is creating irreparable damage!"

Chapter Twenty-Four

A Major Decision

On the way to Lawton Indian Hospital, Holly and Chris commiserated about the dictates of life. It was a heavy venting session, and one which was a catharsis for both. Whatever had occurred during Holly's visit with the lieutenant apparently broke down the barriers of doubt to which Holly had been attached. She was much more open about recent events that had been affecting her relationship with both Melody and Chris. By the time they reached the hospital, the friction that had existed, for all intents and purposes, was no longer there. It was a much more friendly interaction, and one that Chris thoroughly enjoyed.

When they arrived at Melody's bedside, she was up and ready to go. The doctor had given her the discharge papers and the instructions for her continuing recovery. Melody still had pain from the fractured ribs, so she moved slowly. Following their initial "hellos," Holly and Chris helped Melody to the car. She couldn't get out of the hospital fast enough. Getting her into the car was a very delicate process because of the ribs, but Melody just bit her lip and suffered through the stabbing pain. Once in the car, the pain subsided, and they all entered into a "catch-up" conversation.

As Melody listened to Holly explain some of the details of her visit with her boyfriend, she noticed that there was something wrong. As far as Melody was concerned, Holly just wasn't herself. Holly was upset with Bill Harley, but, in Melody's opinion, it was more than that.

"Holly, you're not yourself. Besides Bill, there is something else bothering you. What is it? I hope you're not upset with the fact that I might stay a little longer, and if you have to put out any money for the repairs to the car, I will pay for it. I am so sorry about the car and the accident. Please tell me what's bothering you." Chris knew exactly what was on Holly's mind, but he felt that it wasn't his place to say anything. So, he just sat in the car and said nothing.

"You're right Melody. Something else is bothering me. I am not concerned about the repairs to my car. I am sure that the insurance company will take care of the expenses, and I absolutely would have no problem with your staying with me for as long as you want."

"Holly, you used the term "would have," so you do have a problem now with my staying. Although I contacted my job and told them to put me on extended sick leave, I can make arrangements to leave as soon as possible and convalesce at my apartment."

"Melody let me finish. It has nothing to do with how long you want to stay. It has to do with where you will stay. My landlord recently informed that he is not going to renew my lease, and I have until the end of the month to move out. That's only about twenty days from right now. So, I do have a problem with your staying because I don't know where that will be."

"I am so sorry to hear that, Holly. Boy, if you didn't have bad luck, you'd have no luck at all. How can I help?"

Chris, who had been listening all the while, saw his chance to join in: "Holly, I can also help. Just let me know what you need and consider it done."

Melody was somewhat surprised when she heard Chris' offer, especially since, in her mind, he was shipping out: "Chris when and where are you going to be stationed? It's a nice gesture, but I doubt you'll be traveling from your new assignment back and forth to Fort Sill just to help Holly."

"Well as luck would have it, my new assignment takes me to no other place than Fort Sill, Oklahoma."

"What do you mean, Chris?

"My Military Occupational Specialty is Field Artillery, and the Advanced Individual Training school for Field Artillery is located at Fort Sill. So, I will be staying around for a while, and I will be available to help Holly."

Melody smiled with approval. She was more than happy with this positive twist of fate. He was not only going to be around to help out, but she was going to be able to see more of him than expected. The more she met with Chris, the more she liked it. She was feeling things that she hadn't felt before, and it was strangely exciting. She wondered, however, if the feelings were reciprocal.

Chris continued with his comments: "I know this might be premature, but a couple of my former squad members said that they had heard that Mrs. Harmon Brown was not going to remain in the area. Her husband's body was being transported to her home state of Connecticut for burial, and the word is that she is planning to move back to Connecticut where most of her family resides. She apparently wants to leave as soon as possible. It might not be a bad idea, Holly, to let it be known that you are in the market for an apartment."

"That's a great idea, Chris. I know that they lived not far from the base, and I imagine that it is really a nice place. My only concern is what the monthly damage will be. I hope it is not so heavy that I couldn't afford it. I am going to make some subtle inquiries, and hopefully, my landlord's dictum will be a blessing in disguise."

When they arrived at Holly's apartment, Chris helped Melody out of the car and into Holly's flat. There were some moans and groans as Melody aggravated the area housing the fractured ribs, but the move was quick, and the pain didn't last long. As soon as she settled into a comfortable chair, she was able to catch her breath. She thanked both her friends for their help and felt embarrassed at the thought of needing so much help. Chris stayed for short time before he mentioned that he had to take care of some preliminaries associated with his attendance at the advanced training sessions. He said good-bye to Holly and reiterated that he was available to help with her move.

He then kissed Melody on the cheek and wished her a quick recovery. He told her that if it was okay, he would check on her later or, at the latest, by the following day. Melody looked at Holly for approval, which she gave, and Melody mentioned that she would be looking forward to his visit.

When the two friends were alone, Holly sat next to Melody and confided in her: "You're right, Melody. There is something else also bothering me. My visit with Bill, to say the least, was informative. However, it was also unnerving and devastating, and frankly unbelievable." Tears started to well up in Holly's eyes.

"What is it, Holly? You really look upset. What happened?"

Holly took some time to compose herself, and then she continued: "Bill did some soul searching, and he realized that he could have been the one who was no longer around. He mentioned that his near-death experience forced him to look at his life through a different prism. He also said that he needed to get some things off his chest, and that I was the one who was closest to him. He confided in me and revealed some things that I am having a very hard time accepting."

"Holly, take your time and catch your breath, I am sure it is not that bad. We will work things out together. Don't worry."

"It's not that simple, Melody. When I tell you, I know what your reaction is going to be. I almost didn't want to tell you because of that, but I have to confide in someone, and who better than my good friend. Before you say anything, let me finish the entire story, and then you can condemn and criticize, but hopefully offer some suggestion on how to move forward."

"I am all ears, Holly."

"Well, Bill confessed to me how sorry he was about Private Tim Jenkins' death. He mentioned that he knew that Harmon Brown was continuously harassing Tim because he knew that Tim was gay. Apparently, one of the other recruits came to the sergeant and said that he had been propositioned by Tim for sexual favors. The sergeant let the other recruit know that it would be taken care of. Instead of Bill ordering the sergeant to desist from further harassment, he encouraged the sergeant to continue, and according to Bill, he told the sergeant that it was a 'job well-done.' Melody, he told me that Private Tim Jenkins was driven to take his own life mainly because he couldn't tolerate the constant harassment by the sergeant, and that he had nowhere else to go for relief. Bill said that he should have been that relief, but he only encouraged the sergeant's actions. Bill said that he was drowning in a sea of guilt, and that he had to confess to someone."

By the time Holly finished relating the details of her discussion with Bill, she was sobbing with grief and disappointment. Melody couldn't believe what she was hearing, and she wanted to get up and hug her friend in a consoling manner, but the effort caused pain that restricted her movement. So, after telling Holly that everything was going to be okay, and that they were going to work things out together, she asked Holly the inevitable question: "Holly, what do you want to do? Are you able to deal with the flaws in Bill's character that we can assume he now realizes he has? Are you able to put his past actions aside and help him cope with the ramifications of what he has done? Do you love him enough to balance his confession with the results of his actions? Holly, these are questions that only you can answer, but his confession allows us to fully understand why Chris Martin and the other recruits were so determined to seek justice for Tim Jenkins."

"Melody, I don't want you to make a decision for me, but if you were in my place, what would you do?"

"Holly, I can't answer that question because I am not in love with Bill. Emotions play a significant role in any decision that you make. I do not have the same feelings you have, so my decision cannot be influenced by them, and it is unfair to you to offer a purely objective evaluation."

"So, you are implying that a purely objective decision would see me separating myself from such an individual, and possibly notifying his superiors about the incident."

"I don't know if I would go that far, but an objective onlooker would say that you should go as far away from him as possible. I think that his personal guilt is punishment enough, so officially notifying Army personnel, in my opinion, is not necessary. You don't have to make a decision right this minute. Why don't you think about it some more, and we can discuss it further. I think the important thing for you right now is to find a place to live, and Chris' suggestion about Harmon's wife's apartment might be a good place to start." "You're right, Melody. I am going to make sure that the sergeant's wife knows that I am interested in moving into her place, and hopefully, once I get that settled, I will deal with whether or not I want to continue in a relationship with someone who has indirectly caused the death of another human being."

Melody was taken aback by the sharp tone and content of Holly's statement. In Melody's mind, Holly had already made her decision.

Chapter Twenty-Five

The Apartment Swap

Chris had an entire week off before he had to report to his advanced training school, but he had to complete a number of forms before he could attend. So, when he left Holly's apartment, he went to collect the paperwork and started filling in the blanks. He originally intended to either go back home or attempt to get in contact with his friend, Danny. However, with the complications of Melody getting hurt and Holly needing his help to move, he decided that he would see Danny and go back home in between the time he finished advanced training and traveling to his permanent station, which he believed would most certainly be somewhere in the Middle East.

As Chris maneuvered through Fort Sill, he ran into a few of his recruit friends. He was glad to see them because he could now tell them that they had nothing to worry about. There would be no disciplinary action in their future, at least not related to anything in which Chris had been involved. He felt good about that, and he was sure that they would feel just as good. He learned that a few of his friends were going to attend the same advanced training as he, and that made the next assignment all the more palatable. He really would have liked to continue his training with Aaron also being there, but Aaron's advanced training brought him to a Fort that was halfway across the country. Aaron had been a good friend, and Chris felt that Aaron was the kind of guy that could be trusted with anything. He had helped Chris when Chris had needed it most and, at a risk that could have negatively affected his future in the military. He was a stand-up guy, and Chris was going to miss him.

It took quite a while to complete the hordes of paperwork, and the time passed quickly for Chris. By the time he looked at his watch, it was too late to go by Holly's to visit Melody. So, he was resigned to the fact that his visit would have to wait until the next day. He was disappointed, but he didn't want to seem overanxious either. Maybe waiting until tomorrow was the better thing to do. Of course, he was concerned about Melody's health, but it was more than that. He actually missed seeing her. He wondered if she felt the same way. He realized that she was somewhat older than he, but he knew instances where that had worked out. In fact, he knew a very personal instance. His mom was older than his dad. They were happy, and it surely worked out for them. But he didn't want to get ahead of himself. For now, it was just a comfortable relationship, and one that might come to an end as he would most likely be going to the Middle East. He was tired, and he headed for the barracks to get some well-deserved shut eye.

Holly had taken Chris' advice and was trying to figure out how she should approach Harmon Brown's wife. It was Sunday, and she knew that Mrs. Brown would probably be at home getting things together for her move. Holly knew that the quicker she let Mrs. Brown know that she was interested in the apartment, the better her chances were of succeeding. However, she felt bad leaving Melody alone since she wasn't able to move about easily. Holly had discussed the possibility of getting the Brown apartment, and Melody was all for the idea. Melody also saw how anxious Holly was about notifying Mrs. Brown that she was interested in the apartment. Melody told her friend to stop her pacing and go to see Mrs. Brown: "Go Holly. I will be fine. I am not going anywhere, and I am comfortable sitting here. Chris said that he might be coming by anyway. Don't worry about me. Take care of the things you need to address. That's more important, and furthermore, it's in my best interest that you get the apartment. If I stay for a while longer, I'll, at least, have someplace to rest my head. Otherwise, we might be sharing a park bench." They both laughed, and Holly got ready to go.

Holly was unsure of how to broach the subject with Mrs. Brown, but it didn't matter since Mrs. Brown opened her door just as Holly was about to knock: "Well hello there. Aren't you

Bill Harley's girlfriend? I recognize you from the photo he showed us. I was just about to check the mailbox since I didn't check it yesterday with all that is going on. What can I do for you?"

Holly was totally disarmed. This was not how she planned to start her conversation with Mrs. Brown, but here she was: "First of all, I am very sorry to hear about Sergeant Brown. I am sure it has been very difficult for you. If there is anything I can do, please don't hesitate to ask."

"Thank you, Holly. It is Holly, isn't it?"

"Yes, and I was hoping to speak with you. I just received some bad news from my landlord that my lease is not being renewed. I have to get out by the end of the month." Holly didn't want to boldly just get into the topic, but before she knew it, she had blurted it out.

"You must have heard then that I was moving back to Connecticut. Wow, news travels fast around here! I will probably be out of the apartment by the end of the month, and frankly, I would rather see the apartment rented to someone I know than to a total stranger. I know the landlord rather well, so I will put in a good word for you."

"Do you think that you would be able to persuade him to rent it to me?"

"Holly, I can guarantee that both he and his blond wife will welcome you with open arms."

By Mrs. Brown's tone, Holly wondered how well she really knew the landlord, but that was none of her concern. If she was able to get the apartment, she could care less about anything else. Holly was elated and thanked Mrs. Brown for her help. Mrs. Brown said that she would contact Holly as the time came closer. They exchanged phone numbers and Holly left. She couldn't wait to get back to her apartment to tell Melody the good news. Things were looking up.

Chris didn't realize how tired he really was. He started reading some information about the advanced training, and before he knew it, his eyes closed, and he surrendered to the throes of sleep. However, his sleep was interrupted, once again, by that voice and the blurred, fuzzy figure: *"Hey Chris. Wake up. We have got some things we have to talk about."* Chris was groggy with sleep, and the last thing he wanted to do was to discuss anything with this undefined entity. He was tired and just wanted to go back to sleep.

"Come on, Chris. Get the sleep out of your eyes and pay attention. I see that your interest in Melody goes beyond your concern for her health and recovery. Do you really think that it is a good idea to become involved with someone who is older than you, and with someone you will be leaving behind as you are stationed over in the Middle East? That doesn't seem like it is a prudent thing to do. You don't know how long you will be there, and from my experience, long distance relationships rarely work."

Now, Chris was wide awake: "What the heck do you know about long distance relationships, or for that matter about any kind of relationship? Who are you to tell me what is prudent or not? I appreciate your past help, but I think you are way out of bounds on this."

"Chris you may be thinking with your heart instead of your head. Try to introduce some logic into your thinking. Your emotions are clouding your thoughts. First of all, you don't even know if the feelings that you have are reciprocal; secondly, you expect to solidify those feelings in the 4-8 weeks of field artillery training. You do realize that you will be at Fort Sill, Oklahoma for the training while Melody Johnson will be back in Lakehurst, New Jersey. Even if you wanted to visit her on a weekend, those passes are few and far between and are usually only given in the final phase of the training. Additionally, it's my understanding that the unit decides who gets a pass for weekend liberty, and that pass is designated for on-base liberty. So, you would have to wait 'till the very final phase of training to possibly get a weekend pass to travel to New Jersey. So far, do you really think that this planned relationship will be a successful one?"

Chris realized the pitfalls that a possible relationship with Melody would present, but, as the voice indicated, his heart overruled his head. He didn't want to think about it anymore, and very abruptly dismissed his visitor as he went back to sleep. What he didn't know was that his otherworldly friend was trying to save him from possible future pain and heartbreak. The familiar voice knew of a potential tragedy that could easily befall Nurse Melody Johnson.

Chapter Twenty-Six

An Unexpected Setback

Holly rushed home so she could tell Melody the good news. The whole conversation with Mrs. Brown went a lot better than she could have imagined. Not only had Holly found an apartment on such quick notice, but she found one that was bigger and better than the one she rented now, and, according to Mrs. Brown, it would be within her budget. The good news about the apartment, at least temporarily, overshadowed the unnerving recent conversation she had with her boyfriend. Her mind was focused on getting things ready for the move. That was a good thing. The situation with Bill was filled with disappointment and doubt. And a decision that she had to make was difficult and could possibly be life changing. So, pushing the boyfriend scene to the back of her mind and replacing it with the excitement of a beneficial move was a welcomed position.

As Holly opened the door to her apartment, she was already calling out her friend's name. It was hard to control the excitement that she was feeling and couldn't wait to share her good fortune with Melody: "Melody, Melody, you're never going to guess what happened." Even with Holly shouting her name, Melody didn't answer. Holly hurried to the living room where she had left Melody sitting on a sofa chair. However, to Holly's horror, Melody was out of the chair and lying face down on the living room floor. Holly's shock caused her to hesitate and shout out Melody's name, once again. She quickly came to her senses and crouched down next to her friend. Holly could not wake her, and she realized that Melody might have reinjured her head, complicating recovery from her concussion. Holly reached for the phone and dialed the emergency medical number. Melody needed an ambulance and immediate medical treatment. Because of her nursing training, and the fact that she had worked on the ward where patients suffered from neurological maladies, Holly knew that impacting one concussion on top of another could easily result in a serious medical condition called Second Impact Syndrome (SIS) or even death.

Holly waited with Melody as the ambulance arrived, and she was emotionally torn to see her friend in such a helpless and possibly serious condition. She was able, however, to arrange to have Melody brought to the base hospital for diagnosis and treatment. At least there, she could keep a watchful eye on test results and potential treatment. Holly followed the ambulance to Fort Sill and was right behind the gurney as Melody was wheeled into the emergency room. She explained to the attending doctor that her friend had been recovering from a previous concussion, and that there was a possibility that she might have suffered another one.

The doctors immediately sent Melody for a CT scan of the brain in an effort to see if there was any brain swelling present. Holly waited patiently for the results. In most cases, a patient wouldn't get the results for a few days, but because this was an emergency and because Holly was there to move things along, the doctor told her that he could probably get the results in about an hour. Even that was too long for Holly, but that was the absolute best that she could hope for. In the midst of being so happy about how the apartment hunt went, Holly was now thrown into a spiral of worry and despair. There were so many negative possibilities with head trauma ranging from headaches to disability and even, in some cases, to resultant death. That was the double-edged sword of being a professional in the medical field. You knew most or all of the possibilities for treatment, but you also knew the levels of suffering and disability when treatment didn't offer total recovery. Holly was in that compromised position right now, but there was nowhere else that she'd rather be.

As Holly awaited the results of the tests, she wondered if she should contact Chris. She wasn't sure if it was the right thing, however, since it was late, and she was uncertain if Chris had retired early for the evening. He had seemed tired and had gone through some grueling training. She also realized that her notifying him was for her own benefit and not so much for Melody's. Holly felt alone and also felt that she could have used some company. However, after giving it some more careful thought, she decided to contact Chris when she knew more about Melody's condition. Tomorrow would be soon enough to weigh him down with negative news. She went back to waiting alone.

Every minute seemed like an hour, and Holly was getting more and more anxious as she waited for the doctor to talk to her. Finally, the emergency room doors opened, and the doctor came out to speak with Holly: "Well, Holly, I don't have the best news for you, but as you know things can change rapidly in these types of cases. It seems from the tests that your friend reinjured her head which caused another concussion. I believe she is suffering from Second Impact Syndrome, you know, SIS. The tests show that she has some brain swelling which we are going to treat with corticosteroids.
Hopefully that will help with the inflammation to the brain."

"Doctor, what if it doesn't? What's next?"

"We have the option, as you are probably aware, of following up with a Mengy Injection, a combination of Glycerin and Mannitol. Hopefully the Mannitol will act as a diuretic and draw water out of the brain tissue while the Glycerin will help with the inflammation. Even with all of that, you have to understand that Melody could suffer anywhere from mild to moderate traumatic brain damage."

Holly couldn't believe what she was hearing. She had to hold on to the chair support not to collapse. The doctor saw Holly's reaction and quickly guided her to the chair.

"Holly, take some deep breaths and keep your head down. You have to think positively about this. Will Melody come out of this totally unscathed? Probably not, but she could experience such a minor disability that it could easily go unnoticed by the untrained eye. Let's hope for the best, and you have to be strong for her."

Holly listened carefully and what she heard was the fact that Melody was likely to escape any life-changing conditions. Everything else that was said did not register. She was only hanging on to the positive. How Melody was going to ultimately recover was still to be seen. Holly wished that she could rely on another person to share the hardship that might be coming her way, but even Chris was not going to be available for any length of time. When his eight weeks of advanced training was completed, she was sure that he would be sent to a station in the Middle East. Well, for now she did have him to help out, at least at nights. Hopefully, by the end of Chris' training, Melody would be well on her way to recovery. She wanted to believe that, but she wondered if that was just wishful thinking.

Since he had the entire week off, Chris slept in the next morning. He was used to getting up early as a result of the basic training schedule, but he forced himself to stay in bed and get some additional sleep. He woke with a start when his cell started ringing. He groggily picked it up and answered as best he could.

"Hello Chris, this is Holly. I am sorry if I interrupted anything, but I have to speak with you. Is there a possibility that you could come to the hospital about noon when I have my lunch break? It's important."

"Sure Holly. Is everything okay? You sound down and worried."

"No, Chris. Everything is not okay, but I will explain when I see you. Meet you at noon."

Chris was wide awake now and was worried about what Holly was going to tell him. Maybe she was concerned about getting Sergeant Brown's apartment, or maybe she already tried and failed. But she seemed more worried than not getting an apartment. Maybe something happened with the lieutenant, but why would she want to speak to him about that? He was probably the last person who she would speak to regarding anything about the lieutenant. He racked his brain but couldn't come up with something that was so important that she wanted to tell him in person. And then it hit him! Holly had decided to report the whole situation involving Private Tim Jenkins. That had to be it. She wanted to tell him so that he could be prepared when he is questioned about a conspiracy to seek revenge on both Sergeant Harmon Brown and Lieutenant Bill Harley. He started to worry that his future in the military was uncertain. He was even more worried that his squad buddies might also be the recipients of damaging discipline. He had already told them that they were in the clear. How could he now tell them that their army life was in jeopardy? He hurriedly got dressed and prepared to go to meet Holly, something that he was dreading.

Holly met him at the entrance to the hospital and thanked him for coming. Chris had an apprehensive look on his face and quickly told Holly that he was available if she needed any help.

"Thank you, Chris, but it's more than my needing help."

Chris was even more apprehensive now: "Tell me. Holly. What do you need?"

"Chris, I need a miracle. Melody had an accident, and she suffered another concussion."

"Holly, what does that mean? Is she okay? What did the doctor say?"

"She has been diagnosed with cerebral edema. She has a swelling of the brain. It could be very dangerous, but right now the doctor has said that she has mild to moderate swelling. It is a serious condition, but, at present, not critical."

"I can't believe it. How did it happen, Holly?"

I don't know, but when I came home from seeing Mrs. Brown, I found Melody face down on the living room floor. I called the ambulance and was able to get her into the base hospital. She already had a CT scan of her brain and that showed the swelling. That's where we're at."

"Holly, tell me the truth. Is there a possibility that she could die from what she has?"

"Chris, it all depends on how she reacts to treatment. But yes, Melody could suffer complications and die. As I said, we need a miracle and a good reaction to treatment. Without that, Melody could very well leave this earth. I am so sorry to break the news to you."

"I appreciate your telling me straight out. I would have welcomed any other news than what you've told me, but unfortunately, that's not the case. It seems that a black cloud has settled over our heads, and we can't get out from under."

"Chris, it is not a black cloud. It is life!"

Chapter Twenty-Seven

A Disappointing Visit

Chris stayed with Holly for her whole lunch break, and then he went to visit Melody. She was still unconscious, but the doctors told him that it was only a temporary condition. It was still up in the air, however, as to what damage, if any, Melody had suffered. It was confirmed that she had some brain swelling, but it remained uncertain as to how long the swelling would last or to what degree the swelling would affect her cognitive abilities. Chris couldn't believe he was looking at Melody, the same person who was so vibrant and alive just a week ago. In the blink of an eye, fate can dictate a tragedy whose effects could last a lifetime.

Sitting by himself and pondering so many things, he started to focus on the last visit by his unknown spirit friend. He started thinking that maybe he could ask this friend if it could intercede, and maybe help with Melody's recovery. This blurry entity seemed to know many things, and it often gave Chris helpful advice. Yeah, tonight he would call upon the voice to appear so that he could ask for its help. He was feeling good about the possibility of helping Melody. For a change, the entity wouldn't surprise him with an unexpected visit. He would request the voice to appear. He had never done it before, but it was worth a try. He had no other alternatives, and if his friend was truly a supernatural being, it could surely help with Melody's recovery.

Following her eight-hour shift, Holly stopped in to see her friend. Chris was still there and welcomed Holly's company. She stayed for a short while, and then suggested that Chris take a break and go with her for a bite to eat. After staying by her bedside for a good portion of the day, Chris was still reluctant to leave Melody. However, Holly insisted, and Chris finally agreed to leave with her. But before leaving, Chris rose and kissed Melody's forehead telling her that he would return in a short time.

Because of Holly's relationship with the lieutenant, Chris was not totally at ease being in her company. Holly picked up on this and, with small talk, tried to make Chris feel more comfortable. She knew that he was up tight about her relationship with Bill Harley, so she decided to address the elephant in the room. She explained the whole conversation that she had with her boyfriend and told Chris that she hadn't yet decided whether she was going to continue seeing him. Chris was quite surprised to hear how Holly reacted to the lieutenant's remarks. However, he was incredibly pleased with how Holly felt about the whole situation with Sergeant Brown and her boyfriend. It more or less cemented his conclusion that nothing was going to come of the potential scheme that he and his fellow recruits had been planning. It was a relief to hear her words, and it was even more of a comfort that he didn't have to alarm his friends again about the possibility of discipline. His joy was only dampened by the recurring thought about Melody, and what could possibly happen to her.

Dinner was uneventful with talk about the new apartment, Melody's recovery, and, of course, Holly's relationship with Lieutenant Bill Harley. However, the only steadfast conclusion that resulted was the fact that Holly, and now Melody would be moving into a bigger and better place. Although Chris enjoyed dinner and Holly's company, he was anxious because he wanted to get back to Melody and be there when she opened her eyes. He wanted to be the first person she saw. His anxiety did not go unnoticed by Holly who began to realize more and more that Chris not only cared about her friend's health, but he cared about her feelings too – feelings that he hoped were nothing less than loving. Holly let Chris know that she had to go back to her apartment to start preparing for the big move. Chris understood and told her that he was going back to the hospital for a while before he retired for the night.

He thanked her for dinner and her company. They parted ways, and Chris hurried to the hospital.

When Chris arrived at Melody's bedside again, he was both glad and disappointed at the same time. He was happy that he returned before Melody regained consciousness because he could still be the first person she saw, but he was also disappointed that she remained in such a state. As he gazed upon her, strong feelings that he had never felt before permeated his emotional awareness. He really cared for this individual and couldn't imagine not being able to see her. The thought of being shipped out to some foreign station bothered him to no end. He only had eight weeks to cement a relationship that he hoped would last forever. Ironically, he wasn't even sure that Melody was amenable to such a relationship, but he was going to give it his best shot in trying to convince her.

As he continued his watchful stance, the words of his spirit-friend reluctantly came to his mind. Not only was Chris going to disregard what his otherworldly apparition previously thought was good and helpful advice, but he was going to implore it to do whatever it could to help with Melody and her recovery. Chris wasn't even sure that he could contact this entity, but he would attempt to do it this evening. He knew, however, that even if he was able to garner an appearance by the voice, it was going to be a hard sell to not only explain that he was not following its advice, but that he wanted it to help him save Melody from any future suffering. Talk about moxie, but he didn't care. He wasn't going to leave any stone unturned in his attempt to find a way to facilitate Melody's total recovery.

Chris stayed for longer than he had planned and was surprised to see Holly return for a quick good night to her friend.

"Chris, I can't believe that you're still here. You have to leave and get some rest. Before you know it, you'll be coming down with something, and I can't handle anyone else getting sick."

"Right back at you, Holly. You're running around like a chicken without a head, and you're telling me to slow down. Between apartment hunting and the move, tending to your boyfriend and trying to take care of Melody, you have to be exhausted. So, maybe you should practice what you preach."

"You're right. We both have to slow down, but there will be time enough for that when things get back to normal. I am going to stay for just a little while, and you should be on your way."

"Okay, Holly. You convinced me, but I will be back here first thing in the morning."

"I am sure you will, Chris. Good night."

Chris stood up and went closer to Melody and kissed her forehead. The tenderness of Chris' approach reinforced Holly's assumption about his feelings toward Melody. Chris reluctantly left Melody for the night but was anxious to get to the barracks and attempt to gain the attention of that blurred, foggy figure who comes to visit whenever it wants. This time, however, the visit was going to be initiated by Chris. He had to make contact to ask for the help that he was sure Melody would need.

It was quite unusual for a visitor to be able to stay with a patient and remain long past visiting hours. Chris was sure that the liberty given to Chris was a result of Holly's employment there. He didn't care how he got it; he was just glad that he was able to stay for as long as he did.

It wasn't easy staying awake in the barracks, especially since he was dog tired after a long day of emotional ups and downs. He fought his fatigue because he had to stay awake and attempt to contact his spirit friend. Ironically, he had no idea how to begin contact since the apparition was the one who had always initiated the visit. Chris tried meditating and mentally calling out to the voice; he tried whispering for its attention by calling to it as his "spirit friend;" he even pounded on his bed as an attention getter. Nothing seemed to work.

As Chris continued to employ all of the options, his fatigue grew, and his eyes became heavier and heavier. Before long, he reluctantly gave in to the pull of sleep's unrelenting pressure. Chris fell into a deep sleep, and one which the apparition had a tough time interrupting: *"Wake up, Chris. You wanted to speak to me. Well, I am here. Wake up. Wake up."* The blurry figure continued to try and wake Chris, but Chris was not easily coming around. The entity spoke louder, being careful not to wake the other occupants of the barracks: *"Chris wake up. I am here. Wake up!"* Finally, Chris stirred and opened his eyes: "Finally, you decided to visit. Thanks for coming around."

"Hey Chris, do I hear a bit of sarcasm? I hope not, because even when we speak, and I try to direct you in the best way I

know how, you ignore my advice. What could be so important now that you spent almost an hour trying to contact me? Unfortunately, I have other obligations, and I couldn't respond as quickly as you would have liked. Tell me what you need."

"It's funny that you know how long I've been trying to get in touch with you. You know that I wanted to speak with you, but you took your sweet time in coming my way."

"Chris, if you have nothing of import to tell me, then there is no reason for me to remain."

"Wait! I guess I reacted without thinking. You must know that I am under a little stress with Melody being in the hospital. In fact, that is why I wanted to speak with you. I don't know if you are able to help, but is there any way that you could assist with Melody's recovery? I know that I am asking a lot, and I know that you advised me to stay away from any relationship with her, but I have strong feelings for Melody, and I only want the best for her."

"If you wanted the best for her, you would not continue your quest for her. However, I understand how you feel, but I cannot guarantee that I can help as much as you want me to."

Chris was surprised by the voice's response. He was sure that this supernatural figure could, if it really wanted to, bring a positive conclusion to Melody's condition. Chris became focused now on the fact that this entity might have known all along that something negative was going to happen to Melody. That was why it gave so many reasons not to continue with his desire to be with her: "You knew all along, and you let it happen. You could have stopped it, but you didn't. Why?"

"You're wrong, Chris. I couldn't have stopped it. It is beyond me to be able to change what is determined by a higher source. In addition, you are forgetting that you all have free will, and that many times that free will decides what will happen."

Chris became incensed: "I don't need you anymore, and I don't want you to come into my life. Stay clear, and you know what you can do with your 'free will.' Now, leave and don't return whoever or whatever you are."

Chris turned his back and closed his eyes as the figure slowly disappeared. Chris had taken out his angst on an entity that up to now had only tried to help. But now, he needed to talk to someone else. He needed some support and good advice. He tried to contact his friend, Danny, through regular channels, but had received no response. He decided to try a different way, one that he was sure would work.

Chapter Twenty-Eight

The Brain

Chris knew that his friend, Danny, would be on the same one-week break if he had started basic training at the same time as Chris. But Danny, because of the accident, had his basic training delayed. He also knew that Danny would not be without his phone, so Chris decided to email his friend. Chris felt that if Danny was still under a doctor's care in the hospital that calling would disrupt the hospital routine, but he was sure that Danny wouldn't have a problem answering an email. Chris was surprised, however, that Danny hadn't already reached out to him. That wasn't like him. Danny had always cared about what Chris was doing and was always there for him. For some reason, it seemed like Danny was avoiding him. Chris was sure that there was a reasonable explanation for Danny's lack of communication, but in the past, he had always found a way to keep in contact. Since Danny's accident occurred over two months ago, Chris was sure that he had to be feeling better and responding to whatever treatment was being prescribed. And if things had taken a turn for the worse, which Chris strongly doubted, he was sure that he would have received some sort of message. That not being the case, Danny should be recovering and able to return an email. Chris emailed his friend.

Bright and early the next morning, Chris was in the shower planning his day with Melody. He still had some paperwork to complete for his advanced training, but that would only take a small part of the day. The doctor had told him that the next forty-eight to seventy-two hours could possibly reveal the extent to which Melody's brain had been damaged, if it had been. However, reading between the lines, it seemed that the doctor was almost certain that Melody had suffered some impairment. The inevitable question was to what degree had her cognitive abilities been altered. The doctor had also mentioned that probably within the next two days, Melody should be conscious and alert.

Chris saw Holly early at the hospital as she worked a day shift. She spent a little time with Chris and Melody before she had to get back to her other duties. She tried to reinforce to Chris that Melody had received treatment quickly and that, many times, it is one of the determining factors that can affect the amount of damage that the brain suffers from swelling. Chris acknowledged Holly's comments and thanked her for what he thought was an attempt at encouragement.

As Chris sat by Melody's bed, he checked his emails and was disappointed in not seeing any response from his friend, Danny. He was sure that Danny would answer his email, and now that he didn't, Chris started to worry about what might have happened to his friend. Chris felt that he had exhausted all of his options for contact but one. His only recourse now was to contact Danny's family to see if they had any contact with him. He had the family number and decided to call the family later on in the day. Presently, he wanted to direct his attention to Melody and the forthcoming results of additional tests that she had taken.

Chris couldn't believe that he was sitting and watching a young woman who just a short time ago was so vibrant and full of life. This was a woman with whom Chris wanted a relationship, and a woman he hoped would have the same feelings as he. Unfortunately, he couldn't even let her know how important she was to him. Just watching her and hoping that she would awake was taken its toll on him. But this might be the day she regained consciousness, and he wanted to be there when she did. So, he watched and waited.

At noon, Holly once again came to Melody's room and stayed with Chris. To her chagrin, there had been no new developments, and the doctor had not yet visited. This was the toughest part of the whole ordeal. It was the "not knowing" that caused the most anxiety and stress. The waiting was brutal emotional torture. Melody's condition could run the gamut from "no damage" to, at least, "moderate damage." Although in their heart of hearts, they both assumed that Melody would suffer some effects from her medical event, they were hopeful that Melody would come through this medical roller coaster almost unscathed.

Just before Holly was about to leave to resume her duties, the doctor came into the room and advised them about the results. He mentioned that the prescribed diuretic medicine was working but suggested that he administer a Mengy Injection to assist with the reduction of the swelling. He explained that the injection is a combination of two medicines: Glycerin plus Mannitol which also acted as a diuretic. The doctor further explained that the combination draws water out of tissues in the brain and assists in decreasing the swelling around the brain. Holly listened carefully and understood, for the most part, what the doctor was explaining; however, Chris didn't understand as well as Holly, but realized that the additional medicine would help in reducing brain swelling. He felt that it was good that Melody would be getting additional medication that would help with her recovery, but it also brought to light that she had a serious condition.

For a good portion of his stay in Melody's room, Chris was distracted thinking about his friend, Danny Ferguson. Chris just couldn't understand why Danny had not contacted him with a response to his messages or emails. It just wasn't like Danny to have disregarded Chris' attempts at communication. Chris really started to worry that it wasn't a matter of choice, but maybe,

Danny could not communicate with him. If that was the case, then Chris had totally underestimated the severity of his friend's injuries. For Danny, who was always there to support Chris, not to respond could only mean that he was incapable of doing so, and if that was the case, Danny's health could be in jeopardy.

Chris couldn't sit in the chair any longer, so he started to pace. Just as his pacing began, he thought he saw eye movement from Melody. He stopped and looked closer, and in fact, Melody's eyes were beginning to open. Chris ran into the hallway to find a doctor. He yelled so loud that all movement in the corridor ceased as everyone just turned toward Chris and stared. Melody's doctor her the scream and quickly responded to Chris who couldn't get the words out quick enough that Melody was waking. The doctor looked on as Melody slowly opened her eyes. He gently spoke to her as she awakened and informed her that she was in a hospital and that everything was going to be all right. There was little or no response from Melody.

Some of the possible effects resulting from an injury like the one Melody had suffered were: difficulty in moving and/or speaking, in addition to the possibility of vision loss as well as other negative symptoms. The doctor could not yet evaluate if Melody was suffering from any of these disabilities because patients just awakening from a coma-like episode usually are disoriented and not totally functional. He would have to be patient and carefully coax her into full consciousness.

The nurse and the doctor blocked Chris' view, so he tried to maneuver so that he could see her, and so she could see him.

Chris reached his goal of being the first one there when Melody opened her eyes, but he wasn't sure if she even saw him. His efforts to see and be seen were furthered hampered as an additional doctor and nurse came into the room to assist. He was more or less shuffled back to the doorway where there was no chance that Melody would see him.

Apparently, Holly had heard the good news, and Chris saw her hurriedly making her way toward him and the room. As she passed him and entered the room, she patted his shoulder as an indicator that things were going to be okay. Holly got close to the bed and heard the doctor speaking to Melody. However, Melody was not responding. Holly felt that, at this time, there was no reason for alarm because some patients take longer than others regaining their total conscious state. Her friend, however, was taking longer than usual and seemed not to be moving or speaking. Additionally, Melody was looking at everyone with a distinctly puzzled look. The doctor kept repeating information that he thought she would want to know, but that also seemed to have no effect on Melody's state.

Holly saw her friend weakly attempt to move her lips, but she was not yet capable of speaking. Holly began to worry because now it was definitely longer than it should have been for her friend to start talking and moving. But she did neither. Melody seemed to be looking right through the people at her bedside with no recognition at all. The more the doctor tried, the more Holly became concerned. She had seen similar reactions or lack thereof, when a patient suffered some degree of brain damage. Tears started to well up in Holly's eyes as it became apparent to her that Melody had suffered some level of cognitive disability. She turned away from the bed, forgetting that Chris was standing in the doorway. Chris noticed that Holly's eyes were filled with tears, and his heart almost stopped beating. She motioned to him to step out into the corridor so that they could talk and not disturb the doctors.

"Holly, what's the matter? Is Melody going to be all right? What did the doctor say?"

Holly tried, for Chris' sake, to regain her composure. She took a few deep breaths and spoke to him: "Chris, I don't know for sure, but it looks like Melody might have suffered some brain damage. Hopefully, it might just be temporary, but I just don't know. We have to be prepared for the worst, however, and celebrate when we find out that we worried for nothing, and that she's okay."

"Holly, how do you know that she might have some damage?"

"She didn't move. She could not speak, and I believe that she didn't recall anything. But again, I am hoping that these are only temporary effects. We just have to wait and see."

Chris was beside himself. His whole world was crumbling before him. Outside of his family, the two people who he most cared about were in potential jeopardy. The woman whose good looks and personality had awakened feelings in him that he didn't even know he had, was lying in a hospital bed with possible brain damage, and the main pillar of support throughout his life, his friend, Danny, was nowhere to be found.

He couldn't imagine the worst-case scenario: a brain damaged girlfriend and a dead best friend. No, that was not going to be the case, he wouldn't be able to handle that. He wanted to speak to the entity again. He desperately needed to seek its help. He regretted the way he left off with the voice and hoped that he hadn't ruined his chances of getting supernatural help.

Chapter Twenty-Nine
A Setback

The doctor recommended that Melody be left alone for a while. According to him, it might be confusing and retard Melody's mental recovery. Chris was not happy leaving Melody, but he definitely didn't want to do anything that would hinder her potential recovery. Shortly after the doctor left, Chris went to the bedside and whispered that he would see her soon. As usual, he kissed her forehead, looked longingly at her, and left.

It was going to be a very long day for Chris, so he decided to focus on the paperwork that had to be completed for the advanced training. He needed something to take his mind off of Melody's fight toward total recovery. For lack of something else, the paperwork would have to do. Surprisingly, as he got into it, his mind began focusing on the training and the details of what he would soon encounter.

As Chris came towards the end of the specifics involved with the application, the effects of exhausting emotional turmoil began to take effect. He felt tired, and he could hardly keep his eyes open. He didn't fight the impulse. He stayed on his bed and closed his eyes for what he thought would be a short catnap. Chris fell asleep almost immediately and stayed asleep for about three hours. Apparently, his body needed rest.

When Chris awoke it was late afternoon, and he immediately thought about Melody. He wondered if he should chance visiting her again. He was leery about going back to the hospital, especially since the doctor thought it best if he stayed away for a while. He pondered this predicament as he walked toward the hospital. As he approached the entrance, he hesitated and rethought what the doctor had said. Chris turned around and left the entrance to sit on the bench in front of the hospital. He needed time to really consider the best thing to do, not for him, but for Melody.

As Chris rehashed everything that had recently occurred, he felt a tap on his shoulder. Holly had finished her shift and was on her way to her apartment. She told Chris that she had stopped by Melody's room, and that nothing had really changed. She also said that she spoke again to the doctor who told her that he was patiently waiting to see if Melody regained some of the cognitive abilities that seemed to be lacking. He also mentioned that he had administered the Mengy Injection and was waiting to see some encouraging results.

"Chris, the doctor seemed like he thought the injection would yield better positive effects. But since he only injected her today, he said that we will have to wait for the results. He seemed more positive today than he did yesterday. Let's focus on that."

"Holly, it's so hard just sitting and waiting. I'm going crazy. I want to see her, but I don't want to do anything that may negatively affect her recovery. When do you think I can see her?"

"For now, let's follow the doctor's orders. He knows best. I'm sure before long, you'll be able to visit Melody and maybe be pleasantly surprised at her improvement."

Chris couldn't hold back any longer, as tears started to well up in his eyes: "I feel so bad for her, Holly, and there's nothing that I can do. I feel so helpless. I have such strong feelings for her, and I can't even tell her."

"Chris, I believe she knows that you have those feelings, but you have to be strong for her. I know it's difficult, but she needs both of us to be her strong support as she might go through some very trying times. You can't do anything just sitting outside of the hospital. Why don't you come with me to my apartment? I'm sure that you probably haven't eaten anything today. I am no great chef, but I can throw something together. Besides, I can use some help boxing some of the items that I will be taking with me to the new apartment."

Although he really wanted to stay close to the hospital in case anything new developed, Chris reluctantly agreed to go with Holly to her apartment. On the way there, Chris asked how the lieutenant was doing.

"He's coming along slowly, and I visit him every day, but I don't believe I feel the same way about him anymore. Knowing now about his past actions revealed a part of his personality that I just can't accept. A leopard doesn't change its spots, and I fear that there is more to Bill Harley that I do not want to discover. Of course, I will not tell him anything now when he is trying to get better, but I will have a discussion with him soon enough."

Chris was surprised that Holly had made such a decision, but he couldn't say that he blamed her. Things had definitely taken a one-hundred-eighty-degree turn. There was uncomfortable silence in the car after Holly's revelation, and in an effort to end the deafening pause in conversation, Chris told Holly that he was planning to contact the family of his best friend, Danny Ferguson: "Holly, I believe you know about my friend, Danny. I have been trying to get in touch with him, but all my efforts have failed, so I am going to call his family to see if they have heard anything from him. He was in an accident involving a military transport bus and a trailer. He survived the crash but suffered some serious injuries. I have not heard from him since I found out about the accident. In fact, it was Lieutenant Harley who relayed a message about Danny to me. I don't think the lieutenant was so happy acting as a messenger boy, but he did tell me that Danny had been the lone survivor. Unfortunately, I've heard nothing since."

Holly was taken aback by Chris' comments. She was hoping that her face didn't express what she was thinking. She just nodded her head and confirmed that she had been listening.

"Chris, why don't you give it a little more time? Do you think contacting his family is the right thing to do? You might unnecessarily alarm them. You don't want to do that!"

"Holly, I've given it the entire ten weeks of basic training. Don't you think that ten weeks is enough time? I'm really concerned about him. He was always there for me, and it's not like him to ignore my communications. I am really concerned."

Thankfully, they had arrived at Holly's apartment, and she could change the subject. Holly even toyed with the idea of telling Chris the truth. Danny Ferguson had passed. She just didn't know if it was her place, or if it was the right thing to do. She really didn't want Chris to call Danny's family and bring the grief of his death to the forefront again. Additionally, she didn't want Chris to find out about Danny from a grieving parent. That would hit him in the face like a ton of bricks.

Holly didn't say anything else about Danny. She was just happy to change the subject and asked if Chris had any preferences about dinner.

"Well, I am in the mood for filet mignon and potatoes au gratin but fearing that you might not have that on the menu, I will take anything that is available. In fact, I really wouldn't mind bringing something in. I am really not that hungry anyway."

"Not at all, Chris. I'm sure I have some combination that will just make your mouth water."

This friendly bantering was helpful in taking their minds off of the ever-present serious situations in each of their lives. They settled on pasta and salad. It was easy and substantial. Following dinner and while sipping coffee, Chris asked if Holly could contact the hospital and check on Melody's condition. She was pretty sure that nothing had changed, but in effort to satisfy Chris' obvious nervous concern, she dialed the nurses' station and talked with the head nurse whom she knew quite well: "Hi this is Holly Fisher. I am just calling to see if there's any update on Melody Johnson's condition. I wanted to check one last time before I call it a night."

"Hi Holly. We just got through attending to Melody. She had a seizure that lasted for a brief time, and now she is asleep. I don't think she suffered any additional physical harm because a nurse was in the room when the seizure came on. However, in her unstable mental condition, the doctor does not know if there was any further damage to her cognitive abilities or if the seizure set back her recovery. I'm sorry about that, Holly, but rest assured, we are watching her carefully."

"I'm sure you are. Thank you."

Chris saw the look of concern on Holly's face and was almost frightened to hear what she had to say.

"Okay, Holly. What did they say? Did something else happen?"

"Yeah, it did, Chris. Melody suffered a seizure. She didn't hurt herself physically because a nurse was in the room when it came on. However, it remains to be seen, what the seizure might have done to her recovery. She's asleep right now, and the nurses are giving her extra special attention. There's nothing more they can do."

"Holly, I can't take it anymore. I have to go to the hospital. I just have a bad feeling about things. I have to see her, and no doctor is going to stop me!"

Chapter Thirty

The Doctor's Advice

Holly attempted to stop Chris from leaving and going to the hospital. In her mind, nothing good could come from his trying to see Melody, at this point. Holly made a decision to call the hospital and warn them that Chris was on his way. She did this for two reasons: one, she wanted to protect Melody from any further potential complications, and two, she wanted to stop Chris from acting in a way that might cause the hospital staff to call for the military police who would unfortunately effect Chris' arrest.

Having hailed a taxi, Chris arrived at the hospital. He was still very intent on seeing Melody; however, he noticed a military police vehicle parked in front of the entrance. He was certain that this was not a coincidence knowing that Holly probably called the hospital to let them know that he was on his way. Chris decided to enter anyway. When he got to Melody's room, he saw two Military Police Officers, M. P.'s, standing at the entrance door to Melody's room. The mere sight of these officers did not deter Chris' determination to visit Melody. As he approached her room, the officers closed ranks and informed him that no visitors were allowed to visit at the present time. Chris tried to persuade the officers that he needed to see her, and that he would only stay for a brief time.

"Private, I am telling you that no one is allowed in the room, at this time. You will have to check with the doctor when you will be able to visit. For now, you will have to leave."

Chris hesitated, weighing his options. They were few, but he did not want to just leave. Once again, he tried to talk his way into the room. This time the officers were more demonstrative: "Private, we are ordering you out of the hospital. This is our last warning. If you do not leave, you will be placed 'under arrest.' Do you understand? Don't be foolish. Leave while you can."

The officers' remarks incensed Chris even more. They were not going to stop him. Who were they to tell him that he couldn't see this very special person for whom he had such strong feelings? He didn't care what happened after he got into the room, but he was going to get by the cops and see Melody. He decided that he would turn away from the officers as if he was about to leave, and then turn back quickly and crash through the officers' barrier. He felt that he would take them by surprise, and his effort would be successful even for just a few moments while he saw Melody.

Chris turned to walk away, and just as he was about to turn back and crash into the officers, he felt a hand on his shoulder and heard someone call his name: "Hello Chris, how are you doing?"

Chris stopped cold and turned to see Dr. Chance, who had given him a ride to the Lawton Indian Hospital where Melody was originally taken.

"Hello, Dr. Chance. I am doing fine, but my friend has had some complications. I came to see her, but I have been stopped by the M.P.'s. I hate to ask for a favor again but is there anything you can do for me?"

"Let me talk to the doctor, and I will get right back to you. Just wait here while I find him."

"Thanks, Doc. You may have saved me from a fate that would surely have had negative ramifications." Apparently, just the fact that someone was working for him calmed Chris to the point that he rethought his original plan of crashing the police barrier. Waiting for Dr. Chance gave Chris time to settle down and consider what might be best for Melody instead of his selfish desire to ease his concern. He waited for about fifteen minutes and saw Dr. Chance approaching.

"Chris, I spoke with her doctor, and he feels very strongly about what might cause problems for his patient. He said that she needs to slowly recover from her latest episode, and that visitors might only retard that recovery. I mentioned how concerned you were, and he said that he would let Nurse Holly Fisher know as soon as he felt that the patient was ready. So, for the sake of her recovery, it is best that you wait until the doctor approves visitation. I would never go against the doctor's orders, and neither should you. If you need anything else, don't hesitate to contact me. If I can help, I will. Take care, Chris."

Chris wasn't exactly happy with Dr. Chance's comments, but he had calmed down enough to follow the doctor's orders. He turned and stared at the M.P.'s as if he wanted to kill them, but he also realized that if he attempted to crash through their barrier, that he would have gotten the short end of the stick. He probably would have been physically hurt, and then arrested. That would have only served to prohibit him from seeing Melody at any time in the near future. The brief interlude with Doctor Chance had allowed Chris to think with a much clearer head, one which was not immersed in overflowing emotions.

Chris reluctantly left the hospital and headed back to Holly's apartment. He had promised to help her pack for the move. He also felt that he should thank her because if he had gotten into Melody's room, he wouldn't have wanted to leave. He probably would have fought the doctor who ultimately would have called the M.P.'s. Long story short, he realized that the obvious result of his actions would have been arrest and incarceration. So, as he rode in a taxi back to Holly's apartment, he couldn't wait to thank her for saving him from potential jail time.

Holly wondered how Chris was making out. She didn't want to call again so soon, but she was worried that Chris might have gotten himself into something that he couldn't get out of. She was beginning to question her initial action of calling the hospital. She thought that maybe she reacted too quickly, and that she should have just let things play out. As she continued doubting herself, the doorbell rang. She quickly went to the peep hole and was relieved to see Private First-Class Chris Martin standing there. Holly hurriedly opened the door and hugged the surprised visitor.

"Chris, I am so glad to see you. I didn't know what to do, and I thought the worst. I hope you understand that when I called the hospital, I was thinking of both you and Melody. I didn't want anything to interfere with Melody's potential recovery, and I didn't want you to get in any trouble. I was so worried afterwards that I might have done the wrong thing, but you're here and okay."

"Holly, I have to thank you for what you did. I wasn't thinking straight, and all I wanted to do was to get into Melody's room to see her. When I arrived at the hospital, the first thing I saw was a military police car parked in front. I wasn't sure if it was there because of my intention to visit Melody. So, I went inside, and as I approached her room, I saw two M.P.'s standing in front of her room. They were big guys, and they were standing like statues in front of her door. That didn't deter me, however, so I headed to her room when the officers told me that Melody's room was off-limits. I tried to persuade them that it was important that I see her, but they didn't want to hear it."

"Thank goodness that just the sight of them stopped you from disregarding the doctor's orders."

"Holly, the mere sight of the M.P.'s did not deter my determination to get in to see Melody. I devised a plan to break through their ranks and get into the room, and just as I was about to implement my suicidal plan, Dr. Chance, who had originally given me a ride to the Indian Hospital, arrived on the scene. He convinced me to let him find her doctor and find out what could be done, if anything. He returned in about fifteen minutes and advised me that it would be best for Melody if I followed the doctor's orders. I had calmed down by that time, and I decided that fighting with the M.P.'s wouldn't benefit either me or Melody. So, I left and here I am to help you pack."

"Chris, I couldn't be happier that you're here for a number of reasons, not the least of which is that I need help packing."

Holly was happy for other reasons also. She wouldn't be able to take the fact that Chris had been arrested, and she didn't want to jeopardize her friend's recovery. But in addition to those, the focus on the hospital and the visit to see Melody apparently took Chris' mind away from the idea of contacting Danny Ferguson's family. She was on the fence about telling Chris the truth regarding his friend. She didn't want him to hear the news from Danny's grieving family, and she didn't want Chris to renew the hurt that the family had already suffered. So, right now, things worked out in Holly's favor, but before long, Chris would have to be told the truth. She just didn't know when the time was right to turn his world upside down and bring it crushing down on him.

Chapter Thirty-One

Not Weird at All

Holly and Chris worked on packing 'till almost midnight when Holly said that they had done enough. Holly had to work a day shift the next morning, and Chris was just plain tired. They both welcomed the break, and before Chris left, they shared some wine. Holly said that wine helped one sleep, and Chris had replied that he definitely did not need any help sleeping. Holly thanked Chris for the help, and once again, Chris thanked Holly for saving his hide. He left with the promise that he would help again as soon as she was ready. Holly said "good-bye" with the comment that she would let him know as soon as Melody's doctor contacted her. Chris was satisfied, and he went out to meet the cab that he had called.

The barracks were very quiet except for the constant hum of snoring. But having been in the barracks for such a long time, Chris had gotten used to the annoying drone. Nothing was going to keep him from falling asleep this night. He was tired and emotionally spent. Before his head hit the pillow, Chris was out like a light. Although he wanted to beckon his spiritual friend to appear, he couldn't muster enough strength to stay awake and appeal for its visit. He would have to do that the next day. He also remembered that he wanted to contact Danny Ferguson's family and find out what was going on with his friend. That too would have to wait until tomorrow.

Chris did not have to wait to speak with his apparition. At four o'clock in the morning, it was calling out his name. As had been on other occasions when the spirit wanted to speak with Chris, Private First-Class Martin was dead to the world. It seemed like even an explosion would not wake Chris from his slumber, but the voice was persistent, and finally the groggy-eyed soldier rose from the dead. He slowly opened his eyes and tried to focus on the blurry figure before him. When he realized that his otherworldly acquaintance was present, he perked up with interest.

"I was going to see if I could get you to visit me this evening, but I was so tired that I fell asleep before even trying. I am glad you decided to come around. I would have been happier if you could have waited a few more hours so I could get some additional shuteye, but I am glad you're here."

"What was it, Chris, that you wanted to speak to me about? You didn't seem so happy with me the last time we met. What can I do for you?"

"The last time we spoke you gave me many reasons why a relationship with Melody Johnson was not a good idea. I think that you knew all along that something horrible was going to happen to her, and you were trying to save me from the hurt. I appreciate your looking out for me, but I am a big boy, and I can take care of myself. That being said, as you probably know, Melody is not in a good way. I need your help, whatever that may be, to help her get back on her feet. I know that I didn't heed your advice, but we are passed that now. I need your help. You've actually come to replace my good friend, Danny, with whom I would normally bounce everything off. He was always there for advice and suggestion and was very rarely wrong. I wish I had him here now."

"You do, Chris. Think of me as him. Imagine that you're speaking directly to Danny because our advice most likely would be the same. Picture him as you look at the foggy, blurry figure you see before you. Now close your eyes and see him. He's speaking directly to you. Besides Melody, I feel that there is something else also bothering you. Tell me what it is. Let me see if I can help with that too."

"It's odd that you mention Danny in the way that you have because he is my other problem. I have tried to contact him a number of times, but I haven't received anything in return. I am at the point of contacting his family to find out what has happened. My friend, Holly, has discouraged me from making any contact with the family, but I don't see any other way of getting information about him. You probably know the right thing to do, or what Danny would advise me to do. So, tell me if I have any other options."

For an extended period of time, there was only silence. It was to the point that Chris thought the voice had gone, however, he still saw the outline of the blurry figure. Chris waited patiently for his spirit-friend to respond, and finally, it did: "*Chris, let me start with Melody. As I mentioned the last time we spoke, there is little that I can do for her. I can only tell you that she is a strong individual, and that she is trying her best to recover. Whether she totally recovers is something that remains to be seen. I believe that your friendship and concern for her can only help, but she has a tough, long, road ahead of her. You cannot allow yourself to be devastated if ultimately, she does not reflect the Melody that you once knew. She would still be the same person, but with some limitations. Do not misunderstand. That is not a prediction, but a situation that you may possibly face.*"

Chris remained quiet and pondered what he had just heard. He couldn't bear to think of Melody in any other way than what he knew. She was perfect, and even if things changed, he knew that he would still feel the same way about her. He understood that she had suffered from some possible damage, and after hearing what the voice had said, he was almost sure that she would have to work through some potential disabilities. All his spirit friend did was to prepare him for a less than total recovery. He understood and appreciated the "warning" of what he might have to face sometime in the future. Chris now wanted to hear the advice about his friend, Danny: "I understand what you've said, but anything that you can do to facilitate Melody's recovery would be greatly appreciated. I would also like to hear what you, and you as Danny, would advise on finding out about my friend. As I said, I've tried on a number of occasions to contact him or find out about his condition, but I failed on every attempt. Let me ask you: 'What would Danny advise'?"

"This is a tough one, Chris, because I believe that you know what has happened to Danny."

"What do you mean? I have no idea what's going on with Danny. That's why I've been trying anything and everything to initiate contact or at least find out some information. You're not making sense."

"No, Chris. You can't see the forest for the trees. I am the essence of what Danny was."

"Wait, what do you mean 'was'?"

"Exactly what you are thinking, Chris. Danny is living in me. He is quite alive and, as always, looking out for you. Accept the fact that you have contacted him and react to him as you always have. I do not advise that you attempt to contact his family. That would only prove to intensify the pain that they already feel. You do not need to know anything more than what I am telling you. As I have been your entire life, I will be that support that you might need from time to time, and I will never steer you wrong. I can say no more, so, for now, you should lie back down and get

the sleep that you sorely need. I am sure things will be clearer for
you in the morning. Good-bye, Chris."

With that, the fog and the figure disappeared, and with the spirit's influence, Chris fell back asleep. He stayed asleep 'till late in the morning, and when he awoke, he felt that he had a night filled with dreams. Dreams that were very specific and which he remembered quite well. Did he have a visit from his spirit-friend? Did it give him advice on the things that Chris had wanted to ask him? If the voice did visit, this was the only time that Chris wasn't sure if it was real or imagined. He was confused, and if he did have a visit, there was surely a lot to think about.

Chris got dressed and headed toward the hospital. He was hoping to catch Holly on her lunch break. Although he knew that Holly would contact him if there was any news about Melody, he felt better just being there at the hospital. His mental framework told him that even if he was just sitting on the bench outside of the hospital entrance, he was mentally able to let Melody know that he was there and thinking about her. He kept looking inside the entrance hoping to see Holly. Fortunately for him, Holly appeared at the door and saw him on the bench. She had a few more minutes before her lunch hour expired, so she came out to join him on the bench.

"Hey Chris, what are you doing here? I thought that after the day you had yesterday, that you might still be sleeping."

"Hi Holly. I did sleep in a bit, but I thought that I'd take a walk to the hospital just to see if anything changed or if you had any news for me."

"No, nothing yet, but it should be soon. I see the doctor every day and he knows that we are anxious to see Melody. Chris, I told you that as soon as I know something, you will know. You have my word on that."

"Thanks, Holly. By the way, I think I'm going to put my idea of contacting Danny's family on the back burner. I had a dream last night, and, to say the least, it had an effect on my thinking. I dreamt that a spirit apparition was actually Danny, and that he advised me not to contact his family. Weird right?"

"No, Chris. Not weird at all."

Chapter Thirty-Two

Waiting For the Transfer

Two weeks had passed, and finally, the doctor told Holly that it was okay to visit her friend, Melody. Holly immediately informed Chris who, after spending his entire day in advanced training, hurriedly headed to the hospital. When he arrived at Melody's room, Holly was already there. She stopped him at the doorway and tried to let him know that Melody was still not fully recovered. There were some obvious disabilities that she was still trying to work through. Chris didn't care. He just wanted to see her, to hold her hand, and maybe even kiss her.

"Hi Melody. I can't tell you how much I missed you. I thought about you every day, and I'm so glad that I can visit you now. How are you feeling?"

Melody didn't answer. Much to Chris' disappointment, all she did was manage a diminutive smile. He let that slide and continued with whatever small talk came to his mind. But no matter what he said, Melody didn't say anything in return. It was then that Holly stepped in and told Chris that the doctor asked them to stay for only a brief time since Melody had been extremely tired. Holly motioned Chris away from the bed as she noticed his sense of bewilderment. As soon as they reached the corridor, Holly began speaking to Chris who just listened as though he was in some sort of trance. Even though Holly continued speaking, he still tried to look into the room and stare at Melody.

"Chris, please pay attention to me. Let me explain what is going on with Melody." Chris still looked over Holly's shoulder in an effort to look at Melody. Holly spoke louder and actually shook Chris in an effort to get him to pay attention to her. Finally, his gaze left Melody's room, and he focused his eyes on Holly. She realized that she now had his attention, and she began to tell him what had befallen their mutual friend: "Chris, understand that Melody is going through a process that may take a long time. She's having trouble concentrating and is having a rough time verbalizing her thoughts. Additionally, the doctor has told me that her memory is not as strong as it might be."

"Holly, what does all that mean? Is she going to recover or not? Be straight with me."

"She's going to recover, Chris, but no one knows to what degree. Also, according to the doctor, the recovery could take longer than expected. It seems that the second concussion might have done more damage than originally anticipated, and the whole process of recovery will be a slow and tedious one for both the patient and for those who want to see her whole again. Lastly Chris, there is a possibility that Melody will never be the person who she once was. I am not saying this is fact, but bear in mind that there remains the possibility that Melody will have to live in a limited lifestyle with her disabilities."

Chris just stood there staring at Holly. He heard what she said but just didn't want to accept it. It was too much for him to mentally digest, so he nodded his head at Holly and without saying a word, just walked out of the hospital. Holly looked after him but didn't try to call him back. She knew that he needed time to adjust to what she had told him. He was devastated and physically shaken by the news, but Holly felt that he needed some time alone to think about Melody and the future. She would contact him in a day or so to make sure that he was okay. Holly had to deal with her own concerns and disappointment. Her friend, who was lying in a hospital bed, had not only come to visit her, but was there to break some sad news to somebody who one of her patients cared for very much. Because of her close relationship with this patient, Melody had made it her business to deliver the sad news in person and try to soften the blow. The irony of the situation lay in the fact that Melody never got the chance to relay the sad news, and now she was the recipient of what might turn out to be some very sad news.

Chris was beside himself. He walked and walked what seemed like miles, but he stayed within the confines of the base. He still had weeks to go before he completed his advanced training which would lead to a transfer to another station. He was sure that there would not be enough time for him to see a fully recovered Melody. He did not want to accept the possibility of anything but a full recovery. He didn't care what the doctor said. Melody was too good of a person for God to allow anything to stop her from fully recovering. But just as he thought about that, the question of "If she was such a good person, why did God allow her to be so injured in the first place?" came into mind. He quickly dismissed doubting God's will; he didn't need anything else to weigh him down. There had to be a good reason; he just wasn't aware of what it was. He was going to discipline himself to deal with the present and do his best to aid in Melody's well-being.

Private First-Class Chris Martin had already completed eight weeks of his now extended fourteen weeks of Field Artillery Training. He only had six weeks left to be with her and help with her comeback. It was going to be very difficult for him to leave once his training ended, but there was no way that he was going to be able to change what the army had in store for him. He would have to rely on Holly to continue working with Melody, as she has been, but also depend on Holly to keep him updated on any and all progress. He and Holly had gotten very close, and they both welcomed the support that each gave to the other. It had worked out well for Holly since Lieutenant Bill Harley had been transferred to a hospital that specialized in burn treatment and recovery. And because of that, the break between the two of them was facilitated. Holly had made up her mind long before the transfer, but the two of them being geographically separated helped ease the pain and chagrin of Holly's decision. Holly hadn't known how she was going to break the news to her boyfriend, so the introduction of a mandated transfer greased the rails for her announcement.

By the time Chis was in his twelfth week, Melody seemed to, at least, recognize Chris as someone who she had cared for. Prior to that time, Holly and Chris both felt that Melody's memory did not include any type of relationship or liking for Chris Martin, but, as of late, she started reacting in a different way toward him. They weren't sure if it was a new affection that she had or a recollection of the feelings she once had for him. But no matter what, Chris was just glad that she was showing this attitude toward him. She seemed to have no problem relating to Holly. In fact, she treated her as an old friend. That was one less disappointment that Holly had to deal with.

Nurse Holly Fischer now lived in a development of modern apartments and couldn't be happier. Chris had helped her move, and he spent a lot of time in the apartment helping Holly get adjusted. The whole move and the rearrangement of necessities acted as a catharsis for both of them. It took their minds away from a situation that was both trying and depressing and brought them into a world of new expectations and happiness for at least one of them. Chris found himself eating dinner there quite often, and Holly enjoyed the company. Although Holly was not an accomplished chef, she was able to experiment with food combinations which, for the most part, came out well. When she couldn't cook or just needed a break, Chris was more than happy to take her to dinner or order in. They got along well.

Time passed quickly, and Chris had only one week left before his transfer. He began to feel the pressure and stress of the upcoming mandated separation. He tried to spend whatever free time he had with Melody. That cut into the time he used to spend with Holly, but she was more than understanding. Holly spent time with Melody during the day, and Chris stayed with her at night. Between the two of them, they had it covered.

Although Melody seemed to understand whenever a person spoke to her, she still had a difficult time verbalizing her thoughts. She attempted to speak on a number of occasions but became frustrated when she couldn't get her thoughts out. Her pronunciation also suffered. In fact, whenever she would call out Chris' name it would come out as "Ris." She had a difficult time with many combinations, and apparently, "ch" was one of them. Chris did not feel any pity or sorrow for Melody when this happened. No, he looked at it as something that was unique just to him. He cherished hearing her say his name in a way that only she could. Yes, he was making lemonade out of lemons, but it worked for him.

The time was close for his transfer, so he decided to tell Melody that he would soon not be able to visit with her. What he didn't know was that Holly had already prepared her friend for the inevitable news. So, Melody's reaction wasn't one of devastation, but more of concern. She smiled her little smile, squeezed his hand and said: "I know." Chris surmised that Holly had done the right thing, so Melody's reaction was well-calculated. It didn't make Chris feel any better about his leaving, but it eased the tension for the moment.

Chris was graduating in one week from advanced training, and he had one week after that before he shipped out to his new station. So, in the two weeks he had left, he was determined to make sure that Melody knew how he felt. The doctors were right, and the road to whatever recovery Melody was going to achieve was a long and arduous one. He hated to leave knowing that Melody had not yet fully recovered, but in the back of his mind, as the days and weeks passed, he had become more and more convinced that total recovery might be out of reach. That possibility now being closer to a real life situation, Chris accepted whatever her final condition would be. Whatever it was, would not lessen his feelings for her, in any way. And before he left, he would make sure she knew it.

Chapter Thirty-Three

Tough Advice

The night before advanced training completion, Chris was tossing and turning in anticipation of the transfer orders he would soon receive. He knew that he most likely would be heading abroad, but abroad was a mighty big place. However, things were both explosive and tenuous in the Middle East, so it was there that he thought he would be going.

With everything going on about Melody's recovery, Holly's move, and the advanced training classroom and field exercise program, Chris hadn't had much time to think about his friend, Danny, or his "here and gone" entity friend. Not being able to calm down and relax, sleep was evading him. He lay in bed with his eyes wide open, and now he had time to think about everything. Some good, some not so good. As he pondered both his military and personal futures, the "voice" saw a perfect time to appear. Chris saw the mist and the fog as the blurry figure took hold. Since it had been weeks since the spirit voice visited, and since sleep wasn't coming, Chris welcomed the visit. As Chris tried to look through the fog to finally get a more detailed look at his personal apparition, he wondered if this would be the last time that it would appear to him. Since Chris was leaving in a week or so, he wondered if this unknown entity would appear to him wherever he went. He doubted that this supernatural, otherworldly being would follow him abroad to such places like Iran, Syria, or Afghanistan. Chris was more than sure that the Middle East was going to be his next stop, and why would anyone or anything want to follow him there. So, Chris treated this visit as its last.

"Hello, Chris. Haven't spoken in a while, and I just wanted to catch up. I know that you've been quite busy with training and visiting Melody. I also see that you have struck up quite a strong friendship with Nurse Fisher. All good things, but you know that all good things come to an end. Are you prepared for that?"

"You know, whoever you are, you are very apt at pointing out the negatives. I think I am going to refer to you as the 'spirit of doom.' I should have thought of that a long time ago. However, I am not going to focus on your negativity since this might be our last or one of our last meetings. I doubt very much that you would want to follow me to whatever God forsaken place the army is sending me to. So, while I have the opportunity to question you, have you heard anything further about my friend, Danny?"

"Chris, I thought we reconciled that the last time I spoke with you. I told you to treat me as if I were Danny. Did you forget?"

"No, I didn't forget anything. I just can't substitute you for Danny. It's okay though because I may be going home for a short while since I have some time off after advanced training graduation and the transfer to my new station. I will split the seven to ten days off between visiting Melody and going home. I am sure once I am home, I can find out all about my friend. In fact, I will probably go to Danny's house and visit his family. On another subject, can you tell me anything about Melody's potential recovery?"

"Why are you insistent on getting Danny's family involved. I told you that, in due time, you will know everything. Isn't that sufficient for you?"

"No, it's not. Why are you so negative about my finding out about Danny? He's my friend, and I am concerned. I don't want to be rude since this may be one of our last meetings, but who are you to dictate what 'due time' will be? Danny is my friend, and I am going to do what I want to do. How about Melody?"

"I think you already know a lot about Melody and her recovery. I am sure you know that Melody will not totally recover from her episode. She will definitely have some cognitive

disabilities, and down the road, there is a possibility that those disabilities can get worse."

"Wait. What do you mean by 'worse'?"

"Just that, Chris. I don't have a crystal ball, but from what I can see, her life is not going to be an easy one, and therefore, yours' will also be difficult. I am aware that you want to make your relationship with Melody a permanent one, but I can only reinforce the unknown aspect of such a relationship. It might be unfair for you saddle her with the possibility of your never returning, and to be frank, it is unfair for you to be saddled with the potential ultimate outcome of her not recovering at all."

"Wow, I guess the label I gave you of 'spirit of doom' definitely fits. Why not think positively; that I will return and that a fully recovered Melody will be there to greet me?"

"Chris, because I can't. You know that nothing I tell you is cemented in fact, but you also know that my inklings are pretty close to ultimate reality. Think about it. Give yourself and Melody time to adjust to an ever-changing situation. When and if you return, there will be plenty of time to formalize a relationship. Don't rush into something that could possibly result in hurt which could last a lifetime."

"One time, you told me to think of you as if you were my friend, Danny. It's very hard to do that because he would never have given me the advice that you want me to follow. He would understand, and if I know Danny as I'm sure I do, he would tell me to 'go for it'."

"Chris, you've labeled me the 'spirit of doom,' but a more accurate label might be the 'spirit of reality'. Just like Danny, I only want the best for you. The 'best' might not sit well with you, but I assure you that I only have your best interests at heart. Reality is sometimes a hard pill to swallow, but if you refuse to accept it, you allow uncertain possibilities to exist which ultimately can cause devastating damage."

"Enough with your philosophizing. I don't want to debate the issues with you anymore. I would like this to be a pleasant 'good-bye,' and one which we will both remember as a friendly 'till we meet again'."

"Of course, Chris. I cherish the times we have spoken and 'who knows,' we may very well meet again."

"The odd thing about this whole experience is that I don't know if it's really true or that I may have lost my mind. Unfortunately, if it is real, I can't tell too many people about it without them calling for the men in the white suits. Who is going to believe that a foggy, blurred figure appears to me so that we can discuss problems and concerns about the present and possible events in the future. Even as I say it, it is difficult to believe that I am a part of this absurd happening."

"You would be surprised, Chris. I am telling you that there are a number of people who do believe you, and who would believe you. What has happened between us is not such a rare occurrence. You will learn that as you go through life."

"I'll take you at your word, for now, but I think it's time for me to get some sleep. Thanks for all your efforts. Good-bye for now, and maybe, we'll meet again."

"You can count on it, Chris."

Chris laid his head on the pillow as the apparition slowly faded. He wondered, however, how this unknown entity, this apparition, could be so sure that they would meet again. He was too tired, now, to think about an answer, so he closed his eyes and quickly fell asleep.

When Chris awoke the following morning, he already had a message from Holly on his cell phone. According to the message, Holly wanted to meet Chris for lunch to discuss some important concerns that had arisen. Chris was still tired from a debate-filled night with his spirit-friend, but he dragged himself out of bed and got ready to meet Holly at the hospital. He was a little worried about what Holly had said in her message. He didn't need any more problems or concerns to think about, but he wanted to help with whatever was on Holly's mind.

As he walked to the hospital, Chris thought to himself that he only had one day left before graduation, and he didn't want to deal with any SNAFU's before then. He got to the hospital just as Holly was getting out for her lunch break.

"Hi Holly. Hope everything is okay. I got a little worried when I saw your message. What's up?"

"Chris, it's about your graduation."

Private Chris Martin froze! He couldn't move.

Chapter Thirty-Four

A Cheating Connection

Holly had spoken at length with Melody who was insisting on attending Chris' graduation from advanced training school. However, Melody was still not as stable as the doctor would have wanted her to be. She still experienced moments of debilitating dizziness which caused her to feel nauseous on occasion, and she still had not regained the vision that she once had. Holly explained the situation to Chris who gave a sigh of relief that the message was not about a failure to graduate or stumbling blocks to graduation, like disciplinary procedures which would negatively affect his next step.

Holly wanted Chris to convince Melody that her attendance, although surely welcomed, was not the best move for her overall health. Chris was gratified that Melody wanted to be in attendance at graduation, but if the doctor thought it best for her not to overextend herself, then that's what Chris would try to insist upon.

When Chris went in to see Melody, he went in with a heavy and conflicted heart. He wanted her at graduation, but he had to convince her that, for her own sake, he didn't want her to attend. She listened carefully to Chris' warning, but for all intents and purposes, his admonitions fell on deaf ears.

"I've worked too hard to get to this point. My goal, although you may not have known it, was to get healthy enough so that I could be there for you when you graduated. I may not be as well as I would have liked, but I am still able to attend graduation." Chris looked at her and saw a determination that he wasn't going to be able to fight. He looked at her and recalled what Holly had said about the dizziness, nausea and vision problems. In conflict, he heard Melody's convincing pleas through the impaired speech that her injuries had burdened her with. He loved her even more now, if that was possible. Even with all these negatives, Chris couldn't find the heart to tell her not to attend. Her sincerity and determination had worn him down. Much to Holly's chagrin, Chris agreed to make plans to have her attend graduation.

Although not in full agreement, Holly ultimately understood the situation and told Chris that she would help him get Melody there. Chris and Melody both thanked Holly as she left to continue with her shift. However, before she left the room, she told Chris to come over for dinner so that they could discuss what they would need to make Melody's trip to graduation as comfortable as possible. They needed to think about what they would employ when the "what if's" showed their face. In addition to getting a good meal, Chris readily agreed to go to Holly's to get their thoughts together. Holly left, and Chris stayed with Melody for a good part of the day. But before Chris left to go complete some errands and ultimately head to Holly's, he explained to Melody how he felt about their relationship, and to his great relief and joy, she said that she felt the same way.

Chris was elated when Melody echoed his own feelings, and he felt that it was the right time to formalize, in a small way, a relationship that he wanted to last forever. Pins, ribbons, and patches are dear to the hearts of military personnel. In many cases, it signifies to what branch or unit of the military a soldier is assigned or has chosen. In the case of Private First-Class Chris Martin, he was assigned to the Field Artillery Unit of the army. The pin for this unit is a pair of crossed field guns (19th century-style cannons) cast in gold. Chris had this pin with him, and he took it with him for a specific purpose. He was hoping that Melody would feel the same as he about their relationship, and if she did, he was prepared to "pin" her, which signified a relationship that was more than just girlfriend and boyfriend, and a step just below engagement.

Melody was aware of what accepting his pin meant. With tears in her eyes, and love in her heart, she clutched the pin and drew Chris in close for a kiss to seal the deal. At this point, Melody was feeling no pain, just the invigorating endorphins of excessive joy. Chris, amplifying that, was drunk with affection that he had never felt before. He held Melody close and hugged her tight to the point that she began to feel some pressure and pain, but she held her breath and said nothing. She enjoyed every moment and wished that she could stay that way forever.

After an elongated and reluctant "good-bye," Chris left to complete his final tasks before graduation. He stayed with these tedious undertakings for the rest of the day. Before he realized it, the time had arrived for him to make his way to Holly's apartment. He was both hungry and ready to facilitate plans to make Melody's attendance at graduation as comfortable and memorable as possible.

As Chris arrived at Holly's and exited the taxi, he saw Holly's landlord's wife leaving the complex. She had always looked familiar to him, but he could never place the face. Her blond hair was flowing over an outfit that he had seen before and one that now sparked his memory. Chris had seen this woman for just a brief moment, but long enough to recognize her again. This was the same blond-haired woman who he saw with Sergeant Brown in the restaurant the night he went to dinner with Melody. It was the night that the sergeant stopped at Chris' table and greeted him and Melody. Although Chris only caught a glimpse of the woman's face as she exited the restaurant, the outfit, the hair, and the slight but significant facial recognition couldn't be denied. It was the same woman who hung on the sergeant's arm. Chris stared as she got in her car and drove away.

When Chris knocked on Holly's door, his mind was working overtime. Holly opened the door and welcomed Chris into the apartment. Apparently, Chris had an unusual look on his face, and Holly asked him if everything was okay. Chris didn't know where to start, but he had always been straight with Holly, and he wasn't going to change now. He explained that he saw the landlord's wife leaving the complex, and that she had looked familiar to him. He had mentioned the familiarity factor before to Holly, but now he added more emphasis to the scenario. Relating the whole restaurant story to Holly, Chris was surprised by her reaction, or lack thereof. Holly didn't seem surprised or shocked at Chris' revelation. As a matter of fact, she acted as if it was business as usual. Chris couldn't let it go: "Holly, you don't seem surprised at all. Did you know what was apparently going on between the landlord's wife and Sergeant Brown?"

"I never knew for sure, but after speaking with Harmon Brown's wife, I drew the conclusion that she was closer to the landlord than anyone suspected. When she guaranteed that I would get the apartment and get it at a rental price that fell well within my budget, I assumed that she had a definite influence over the landlord's actions. I further assumed that Mrs. Brown was aware of the connection between the landlord's wife and her own husband, so she decided to get back at the sergeant the only way she knew how, and in a way that would hurt more than anything else. Mrs. Brown went ahead and entertained her landlord."

Chris just stood there stunned at what he was hearing. Holly had described a tangled web that was hard for him to accept. He heard that people played games with the feelings of others and sometimes sought to hurt them as much as they could. But that was not Chris nor was that what Chris was used to. He couldn't understand how a husband and wife could turn on each other. He could only relate to his own family, and something like cheating and revenge didn't exist in that world. So, he was taken aback, but he couldn't argue with Holly's logic or knowledge. Unfortunately, and maybe due to Chris' lack of life experience, he didn't realize that what Holly had related to him was not an oddity, but more or less, a phenomenon that occurs all too often.

"It's hard for me to believe that people would do that to each other, but the facts remain. There was no love lost between the sergeant and his wife since the subject of separation and divorce had been discussed, and you did get Mrs. Brown's apartment when I'm sure others were interested in it. You also got it for a monetary contract agreement that probably would have been doubled if anyone else took the apartment. It's hard to dispute those happenings, so I have to concede that you know what you're talking about." "Believe me, Chris. I am not one to spread rumors. Take what I have told you as fact. But that's enough about past history that no longer concerns us, let's have some dinner and talk about Melody and tomorrow."

"That's okay with me because, in addition to graduation, I have another item that I want to discuss with you. It's something very significant." "Chris, I already know. I had a visit!"

Chapter Thirty-Five

And That's That

During dinner, Holly and Chris just shared some small talk. They both knew that this was a prelude to a more significant conversation as soon as dinner was completed. Chris couldn't wait to share the good news about the formalized relationship between him and Melody. Holly had mentioned that she already knew because of some visit, but it couldn't be that the information that she had was the same as what he was going to share. It had just happened, and he had strongly doubted that Melody would have been able to contact Holly in such a short amount of time. However, it wasn't impossible. As he continued to think about it, maybe Melody was able to contact Holly and give her the good news. However, Chris was going to assume that Holly had some other news to tell him. He couldn't wait to let her know that he and Melody were a couple.

Dinner having been completed, Holly and Chris got down to business. Chris started the conversation because he wanted to give her the good news before he burst: "Holly, when I visited with Melody today, I brought something very special with me. I didn't know if I was going to give it to Melody, but I was hoping that things would go my way, and that I would be able to surprise her. Fate was kind, and I was able to present Melody with my Field Artillery Unit pin. She seemed to be as happy as I was at that moment. So, we are now 'pinned.' I don't know if you know what that means, but it's significant in a relationship."

"Hey Chris. I have been a nurse in a military hospital for quite a while, and it's not the first time that I heard someone got "pinned." However, your news is not a surprise to me. This may sound crazy, but believe it or not, I had a visit from a spirit who told me what you did. Follow me on this. This spirit seemed to be well informed, and it had a strong opinion against what you've done. I know it sounds nuts, but this spirit was very real and asked for my cooperation in persuading you, for your own sake, not to formalize your relationship with Melody. You know that I don't have to be persuaded to discourage you because we already had a conversation about the whole scenario. The spirit mentioned a lot of negative possibilities that could arise in the future. I also agree with its concern regarding the hurt that either one of you or both could suffer from unexpected events. I am telling you this because it is just another reminder that you are treading on a foundation that could be very weak."

"Wow, Holly. That was a mouthful. And no, I don't believe that you are crazy because if I did, I would have to assume that I too would have lost my mind. As you may or may not know, I have had these same visits. It is a spirit that has strong opinions, and one that is constantly offering calculated advice. It warned me too about the pitfalls that I might face if I entered into a serious relationship with Melody. Holly, I took all that into consideration, but in my opinion, the 'pros' outweigh the 'cons.' We both know what we may have to face, but we are willing to work together to conquer any obstacles that might come our way. And sometime in the near future when I come home on leave, I'm going to ask Melody to marry me. I'll save for an engagement ring and make it a formal proposal. Our minds are made up, and you would be wasting your time trying to convince either one of us to rethink our decision. Please be happy for us. Now, let's figure out what we are going to do to make Melody's attendance at graduation as comfortable as possible for her."

Holly was frustrated but agreed to drop the conversation that focused on Chis and Melody's relationship. She asked for Chris' suggestions and ideas that he felt would facilitate her friend's attendance at the event. She noted that although Melody would probably want to walk to the event, a wheelchair should be available just in case. Holly felt that her friend could not walk the whole way, and that she was too weak and possibly too dizzy to stay for the entire commencement. Chris agreed that they should have a wheelchair available. He also felt that oxygen should be readily on hand. They both agreed that all of her medications should be taken before she left for the event.

Chris also suggested to Holly that she meet with the doctor right before she attempted to get Melody to graduation. Holly mentioned that she had already informed the doctor that Melody had insisted on attending the event. Although the doctor was adamant in his opinion, he offered to assist Holly with medications and medical paraphernalia that she might need. Chris and Holly discussed some of the other tangential concerns that they might have to deal with. They concluded their meeting and hugged each other before separating for the night.

Holly had asked Chris if he wanted to borrow her newly repaired car. He refused for two reasons: he didn't want to risk the possibility of damaging her vehicle again, and coming back in the morning to pick her up would be too much of a hassle with everything he had to do in preparation for graduation. He thanked her and left to wait for the taxi that he had called. On his way back to the barracks, he thought about the evening with Holly. It had started on shaky grounds, but with Holly actually understanding how he and Melody felt, the meeting turned out to be a good and productive one. He also thought about the visit that Holly had experienced. Chris was really perturbed that his spirit-friend went behind his back to get Holly's cooperation. He hoped that the voice would appear tonight just so he could give it a piece of his mind. The more he thought about it, the more upset he became. When he finally got back to the barracks, his anger was overflowing.

When Chris left Holly's apartment, even though it was late, Holly decided to contact the nurses' station that was responsible for the care and well-being of her friend, Melody.

When the nurse on duty answered the phone, Holly was gratified that it was a person with whom she had a good friendship. This facilitated obtaining all the information that Holly wanted about Melody's present condition. After some brief small talk, Holly got right to the subject of Melody's condition. Unfortunately, she was disappointed with what the duty nurse related. Although Melody was in no obvious critical danger, the cumulative effect of the smaller attacks and abnormalities were having their way in delaying her recovery. In fact, the nurse mentioned to Holly that, once again, Melody suffered a seizure attack. Each time she had one of these, it took a while for her to come back to the level of strength which she had previously attained.

Holly was taken aback by the news but was gratified that the doctors and nurses were keeping a watchful eye on her friend's condition. She thanked the nurse for her help and asked that she be notified if Melody suffered any additional setbacks. The duty nurse assured Holly that she would contact her if Melody was further impacted. Upon hanging up with the duty nurse, Holly contemplated contacting Chris. The news about Melody might be a downer on taking her to the commencement exercises. Whether it affected his decision to take Melody or not, Holly felt that Chris should know about the recent setback. He was just as concerned about Melody's health as she was. Holly dialed Chris' number.

Chris was wide awake when his phone rang. His raging anger at the "voice" kept him from embracing the throes of sleep. So, the phone ringing did not startle him at all. However, seeing that the caller was Holly alarmed him.

"Hello, Holly. Is everything okay? Do you need anything?"

"Sorry to call so late, Chris, and everything is all right with me. When you left, I had the inkling to call the hospital just to make sure that Melody was doing okay. A feeling came out of nowhere, so I wanted to satisfy my nerves and curiosity and I called the hospital. Lucky for me, the nurse on duty is a personal friend, so she leveled with me."

"Okay, Holly. You sound like you don't have good news. Tell me what's happening. Is Melody okay?"

"Chris it's not devastating news, but it is not good news. The nurse told me that Melody suffered another seizure. The seizure itself wasn't massive, but you have to realize, Chris, that the culmination of these smaller incidents lead to setbacks for her recovery. I am sure you realize that now the doctor will be even more emphatic with his order not to take her to graduation. And, Chris, I can understand his concern. As a result of the news that I got from the nurse, I am also very concerned about moving her to the event. Maybe we should rethink our decision. She may be disappointed, but in the long road, we have to think about her overall health and recovery. It might be harmful for her to leave the hospital. What happens if she experiences a seizure while we are at graduation? What do we do?"

"Holly, it's killing me not to have her there. However, I don't want her condition to get worse or to be negatively affected. And I don't know what I'd do if she did have a seizure during the commencement exercise. Unfortunately, it would all fall on you. That's not fair to you. Tell me what you want to do."

"I know it's difficult, but we'll have to tell her tomorrow morning before you go to graduation. We should do it together, so she sees a united front. And no matter what she says or how she pleads, we have to be strong."

"Holly, I'd rather not graduate than to disappoint her, but I know it's for the best. In fact, I'll tell her that there is no other option. I will convince her even though my heart isn't in it. It's not the best way to start a relationship."

"Chris be thankful that she's alive, and hopefully she'll stay that way so you can have a relationship."

"You're right. What would I do if I caused her death? I can't even think about it."

Chris practiced: "Melody, you're not coming and that's that!"

Chapter Thirty-Six

A Plan for Recovery

To Chris' surprise, he didn't have to practice at all. Melody was waiting for Holly and Chris, and she understood that, in addition to it being a great imposition on both of them, she knew that she wasn't up for attendance at graduation. When Chris approached her bed, he saw the crossed cannons clutched in her hands, and tears in her eyes. It killed Chris to see her like this. She looked like a little child disappointed that she couldn't go out to play. It was the first time that he really felt sorry for her. It was pitiful. She didn't have to say anything; it was understood that she accepted the fact that she was not going to see Chris graduate from the Advanced Training School.

Holly came closer to Melody and told her that she was doing the right thing. Holly tried to ease the emotional pain by telling her that soon enough things would be different, and that she wouldn't miss anything. Then, in an attempt to change the subject and the mood of disappointment and despair, Holly congratulated her friend on her "pinning." Melody smiled a "thank you" and looked lovingly at Chris. She didn't say anything at all, and Chris wondered if she had a setback with her speech. He was relieved, however, when he asked her if she was okay, and she answered that she was fine. The response was weak but audible enough to make out what she was saying. It was like a strong whisper, which both Holly and Chris realized was a degrading of her speech. Not to bring attention to her setback, Chris told her that he had to leave in preparation for the ceremony. He told her that he would return as soon as it was over, and by that time, he would know where he was going to be stationed. As usual, he kissed on the forehead and left.

Holly wished Chris "good luck" and turned her attention to Melody.

"So, you're in a relationship. Well, I can't say that I am surprised even though I thought that it might not be the right way for you to go. However, the more that I interact with Chris, the more I like him. He seems to be a serious, mature man who really cares for you. In fact, you are all he talks about."

That brought a smile to Melody's face, and she clutched her crossed cannons even tighter.

"I couldn't be happier for you, Melody. You and Chris will make a beautiful couple, but you have to do what's best for you so that you can recover as quickly as possible. You did the right thing today. Going to graduation might have put too great a strain on your body, and you don't want to retard your progress."

It was obvious to Holly that Melody strained when she attempted to speak, so Holly told her not to try. However, as was witnessed many times before, Melody had a mind of her own. So, in whispered tones she spoke: "Thank you for staying with me, but it's really not necessary. I am okay."

"No Melody, you're not okay, and I really don't mind staying here with you. In fact, I can see the graduation ceremony from the window, and I can give you a blow-by-blow account."

As Holly rose from her chair to look out of the window, Melody grabbed her hand and stopped her. She actually pulled her hard so that Holly sat back down. Melody stared at her friend, Holly, and it looked like she wanted to say something but didn't know where to start. Holly patiently waited for Melody to get her thoughts together and garner the strength to speak. However, Melody said nothing for an inordinate amount of time. Holly looked at her friend and decided to start the conversation: "What's the matter, Melody. I was only going to the window to see if the ceremony had started. Don't you want my progress reports? And I'll give them to you at no charge. What's the matter?" Finally, Melody whispered: "Holly, I know that I am not okay. I feel like I am getting worse, and I can't do anything about it. I keep getting seizures, and I take one step forward and two backward. I don't know if I can beat this thing. I'm having trouble remembering; I can hardly speak, and I am constantly nauseous and dizzy. You know that I have to be feeling really bad for me to agree not to go to Chris' graduation ceremony. I really love him, Holly. I don't want to become an anchor around his neck. It's just not fair to him."

"Hold on, Melody. First of all, you're not giving yourself enough credit. You're a young, strong woman who can beat anything, and you will get better. Sure, it may take a while, but you will get there. Secondly, do you really think that Chris is just going to throw his arms up in the air and say you're right and just leave? That man is in love with you, the same way you are with him. I don't think he would leave if you turned into a vampire and wanted to suck his blood."

Melody laughed at the last statement, and thanked Holly for the "one-for-the-Gipper" speech. She knew that Holly was a good friend, but she wondered if Holly really believed what she had said. But no matter how hard Holly tried, Melody knew her body and how it was reacting. She did not have half the confidence that Holly seemed to have because she was the one who felt every pain, nausea and dizziness attack and the inability to recall at will. Also, she knew that no one could understand the depression and despair that permeated her consciousness every day and which brought her to the lowest level of hopelessness. She didn't tell Holly, but there were times that she thought that death might be better than living the way she was.

"Holly, I am certain about Chris' feelings for me, but I don't want him to waste his time on something that may never be. I do not know if I will be here tomorrow, let alone sometime in the future. He is young and has his whole life ahead of him, and all I am doing is stopping him from moving on. He is a good man, and he deserves much better than I can give. I need your help in persuading him to direct his time and affection to someone who will be able to return those same things to him. That person is not me. I do not believe that I will be around long enough for either one of us to totally enjoy the other's company. Please help me persuade him that I am not the one for him. I can't do it alone."

"Wait a minute. Let me understand this. You want me to help you persuade Chris that you are not the right person for him. Do you really think at this point that anyone could persuade him to cease and desist? Melody, that young man is in love with you, and there is no way that anyone is going to tell him that it would be better for him to leave. No Melody. There are not too many things that I would not do for you, but if you want Chris to look elsewhere, you will have to be the one to tell him and break his heart. And that will not be such an easy task."

"Holly, I can't do it alone. I need your help. I don't want him to waste his time on something that can never be. I love him too much for that."

Holly just started pacing the floor. She was at a loss for words and for the next move. Melody was talking like she wasn't going to be around much longer, and that was something that

Holly couldn't accept. No, what Holly decided to do was to become more involved in her friend's recovery so that Melody would be around for a long time.

"Hey Melody. I've decided to become your drill instructor. Together we are going to get you back on your feet and hopefully better than ever. First, I need you to understand everything I direct you to do is for your own good. And I'm telling you from the get-go, it's not going to be such an easy journey back to full recovery, but we are going to give it our best shot. You are going to be as healthy as ever for Chris when he returns from his tour of duty. He deserves it, and you deserve it even more. So, do I have your full cooperation?"

"Holly, I will do what I can whenever I can. I just hope that you aren't wasting your time or effort on something that may be impossible."

"Wrong attitude, Melody. There is no wasting time. You just have to put it in your head that you're going to get better and be the woman that Chris deserves. And if you don't do it for him, do it for you. Life is just too short, and you are just too young to throw away whatever chance you may have to make this life as beneficial and worthwhile as you can. And I will be here to make sure that you toe the line. Will it be easy? Hell no. But whatever you put into making your life better will come back to you in spades. I don't know what that means, but I've heard it used that way before."

They both looked at each other and began to laugh. They both knew that the road ahead was going to be difficult, but they both committed to getting as much as possible out of a positive approach to recovery. Just as Holly finished her "one-for-the-Gipper" speech, she heard applause coming from the assembly field where Chris' graduation was being held. She was sure that before long, Chris would be coming to the hospital to visit Melody to tell her where he was going to be stationed.

Holly was right on the money. It was only about fifteen minutes after the ceremony ended that Holly and Melody heard Chris' footsteps approaching the room. It seemed that Chris could not get to Melody's room and bedside fast enough.

"Well, it's over. I am a full-fledged field artillery soldier. I am glad that it is over, and the faster I transfer to my new unit and location, the faster that I will be able to return. I wasn't surprised by the assignment, and I will have a lot of company. About fifty of the guys who were in advanced training will be going to the same place as I. We will be going to Camp Vance in Kabul. And just so you know, I am part of the B Battery, 2nd Battalion, 4th Field Artillery Unit. By the way, that's the address where you will be sending all of my letters. Before you know it, I will be back here bothering you."

Melody forced a smile, but deep down she was more than worried about Chris' safety. Both Holly and Melody congratulated him on his completion of the advanced training course, and they suggested that they would celebrate later on that same evening. They knew that Chris had a lot to take care of before he would be ready to board the military transport plane that would take him to Khost Province in Afghanistan. He told them that this would be his first stop before he traveled on to his final destination which was going to be Camp Chapman. He further informed both Holly and Melody that this camp was named for Sergeant First Class Nathan Chapman who was the first United States soldier killed by enemy fire during the Afghanistan war. Chris took some pride in telling them a bit of military history.

Chris followed up his history lesson with the fact that he still had some time off before he would have to ship out, and he told Melody that he would be bothering her as much as he could. Although he dreaded leaving Melody, he felt that the quicker he reached his new station, the quicker he would be able to make it home and to her. He was filled with mixed emotions. He hated living Melody, but he was somewhat enthusiastic about this new chapter in his life. He knew that there would be danger, but there was a certain amount of excitement being a part of a military operation. Unfortunately, Private First Class Chris Martin did not know what was in store for him!

Chapter Thirty-Seven

A Visit Home

Chris hadn't been home in a while, and there wasn't that much communication during both his basic training and the advanced training, so he decided to arrange for a brief trip home. Sure, it would take valuable time away from his visits with Melody, but he also missed his family. Additionally, he would be able to visit Danny's family and get the real story about his friend. He decided that he wanted to surprise them and not let his family know that he was coming home.

The first thing he had to do was to make arrangements for a flight from Fort Sill Lawton Airport to JFK Airport in New York City. He found out that he could get a direct flight to JFK Airport on one of the major airlines. He also found out that the ticket would only be about two hundred dollars. He was happy about that. What he dreaded more than anything else was telling Melody that he would be gone for a while. He really wanted to spend as much time as possible with her since he would soon be leaving for the Middle East, but he did miss his family, and he was sure that they would want to see him before he left for the desert. He also wanted to let Holly know that he would be gone for a few days, and that she wouldn't be able to depend on him for any help until he got back. He was sure that she would understand.

The next day following graduation, Chris made all of the arrangements for his trip back home. Of course, he had mixed emotions about leaving, but in addition to seeing his family and finding out about his friend, Danny, this would set the stage for both Melody and him to experience life without each other. Sure, it would only be a short time before they saw each other again, but it would give them a small taste of what was to come.

Having arranged for his trip, Chris headed over to the hospital. He knew Holly would probably be there even though it was the weekend, and she had the day off. She was just as concerned as he when it came to Melody's health and well-being. As he walked toward the hospital, he thought about how he would tell Melody that he would be gone for a short time. He also wondered if she would be upset that he left when she wasn't at her best. However, he quickly focused on the type of person his girlfriend was. She would probably encourage him to go home to see his family with total disregard as to how she was feeling. That's who she was, and the more he thought about it, the more he knew that he didn't have to think about it.

Chris was right on the money about Holly. She was right there at Melody's bedside. She was really a good friend, and now that her former boyfriend had been transferred to another hospital, she had plenty of time to spend with Melody. This, of course, made Chris' leaving somewhat easier.

"Hi Holly. How is our star patient doing?"

"Hi Chris, but don't ask me. Why not get it right from the horse's mouth? Tell him, Melody, how you are doing."

This was part of the recovery program that Holly had initiated. She was forcing her friend to speak, to exercise those muscles that she needed to build up. It also forced Melody to overcome her shyness and embarrassment that was caused by her incorrect pronunciation of some words. Holly had become a taskmaster, but for Melody's own good, and Chris knew it. Chris looked directly at Melody in a way that she knew he expected her to answer. She struggled through the response, but let Chris know that she was doing fine. Following her strained response, Chris immediately went over to her and kissed her "hello."

"I have some news for both of you. It has good and bad elements, however. I am going to go home for a short time to see my family before I am transferred to my station in Afghanistan. As you know, I haven't seen them since I started training, and I miss them. I am sure that they also miss me, so I am going to surprise them and arrive unannounced. The visit will also allow me to find out more about my friend, Danny, since his family lives right across the street. They should have all the information that I need."

As far as Chris could see, both Holly and Melody took the news of Chris' family visit as expected. They were encouraging the visit to his family. However, what Chris didn't know was that they simultaneously flinched when he said that he was going to visit Danny's family. They quickly looked at each other in what could only be described as an 'oh no' moment. They didn't make it obvious, but the concern was felt by both. How were they going to convince Chris not to visit his friend's family? Holly and Melody needed to talk privately. They needed an excuse to send Chris someplace so that they could get their heads together and discuss the next step in preventing Chris from finding out the truth.

Suddenly, it came to Holly, and without letting Melody know her plan, she said: "Chris, I wonder if you could do me a big favor? Melody is going to have a therapy session with the doctor in a few moments, and I have to take care of a work report that is overdue. Would it be possible for you to take my car to the repair shop? They need to adjust something that they failed to do when the car was there for repairs. They notified me yesterday that today would be a good day for them. Melody is going to be unavailable, so you won't be taking time away from her, and I would be more than grateful if you could get that done for me."

Chris was taken by surprise. He didn't know about Melody's therapy session and was unaware that Holly was having problems with her car. He looked at Melody who nodded in the affirmative, and looked back at Holly who was waiting for an answer. After all that Holly had done for him, there was no way that Chris could refuse her request.

"Sure Holly. Just let me know what the problem is and the location of the repair shop, and I'll get it done."

Holly took out a piece of paper that itemized the necessary adjustment, and the location address of the repair shop. She handed it to Chris, and he looked it over. The repair shop wasn't far from the base, and the adjustment would probably only take a short time. It wasn't that big of a favor, and Melody wouldn't be available for a while. So, he bent over and kissed Melody and said "goodbye" to them both. He took the keys from Holly's hand and smiled as he left the room.

"Wow, Holly that was quick thinking, but then again, you could always think on your feet."

Although her speech was garbled, Holly understood what Melody said. She had gotten used to the various mispronunciations and inflexions in her friend's affected speech.

"Okay, Melody. Do you have a plan because I am at a loss? Maybe we should tell him before he leaves so, he isn't shocked when he gets home."

"If we tell him now, Holly, he will know that we knew all along and just kept it from him. I don't know if I want to do that."

"Well, we have to do something, Melody, or he will definitely find out when he arrives home. Thinking more about it, maybe it would be better if he found out at home having the support of his family right around him. Or am I suggesting the coward's way out?"

Just as Holly finished her comments, and although it was midafternoon, the room suddenly darkened, and the all too familiar fog and mist of the spirit entity began to fill the room. They looked at each other, and then stared at the blurred figure that was developing. The only sound they heard was similar to the sound of rustling leaves in the wind. Finally, they heard the voice: *"I was not planning to visit with the two of you today, but necessity warranted my appearance. It is my understanding that Chris Martin has made arrangements for a trip home. I also understand that you may be contemplating a plan to tell him about his friend, Danny, before he leaves. In my strong opinion, that is not a good idea. There is no need for anyone to disclose information about his friend. As I told him, I will now tell you: there will be ample time ahead for him to find out about what has happened to Danny. There will only be hurt for you to reveal anything to him now. Also, Chris would then know that both of you knew about Danny and chose not to tell him. Again, in my opinion, that would cause major strife among the three of you. Take my word, there will not be a problem for Chris when he returns home. He will know nothing more than he knows right now. Nothing negative will come from his visit home. Take my advice and say nothing."*

As quickly as it appeared, the entity was gone. Holly and Melody said nothing. They just looked at each other and wondered if they could depend on the advice and information that this otherworldly apparition just offered. If it was true, it was an easy way out. But if the entity was wrong, irreparable damage might be done. Either way, the risk was great. The apparition hadn't been wrong in the past, so they decided that they would toss the dice and hope that it was right again. They would have to deal with the ramifications if it was wrong, and if in some way, Chris found out that they had both known about Danny Ferguson.

Chapter Thirty-Eight

Chris' Announcement

Chris returned from his errand for Holly and stayed with Melody for the rest of the day. When evening came, he headed to the barracks to prepare for his trip home the next day. He wasn't looking forward to the approximately three-and-one-half-hour flight, but he wanted to visit his parents, and there was no other way. His leaving Melody was not an easy task, but she made it bearable. She mentioned how good it was for him to be thinking about his parents. It showed her the strong family bond that existed, and that impressed her. For Melody, it was just another reason to cherish their relationship. So, leaving Melody was not as bad as he thought it would be.

Chris arrived at the airport in plenty of time to check in. Since Lawton-Fort Sill is not an international airport, it wasn't a situation where there were wall-to-wall people. Following a relatively easy "check-in," Chris found a coffee shop where he ate some early morning breakfast. It also gave him time to think about a myriad of things presently affecting his life. It had gone from high school graduation, applying and going to college, to enlisting in the military, completing basic and advanced training, meeting the love of his life, flying home and then leaving for the desert in Afghanistan. There was an awful lot to ponder. It was a good distraction, however, from the fear of flying.

His life had twisted and turned at an incredible rate, but, for the most part, he was happy with the way it was developing. One of the only things that persisted in bothering him was the fact that he couldn't find out about his friend, Danny. But he was consoled, now, knowing that in a short time, he would be speaking with Danny's family. He closed his eyes as he thought about the reunion with his family and before he knew it, he was landing at JFK airport.

Unlike Fort Sill-Lawton, JFK was always crowded. He exited the plane and was immersed in the ever-present hoard of people. To him, it was like bumper cars, bouncing off of one person just to be pushed into another. He never liked crowds, and JFK specialized in crowded conditions. He made his way to the taxi line and waited patiently for an available cab. Fortunately, the line went more quickly than he thought it would, and before long, he was well on his way to his home in Brooklyn. Just as JFK airport is always crowded so are the roadways in every borough of New York City. Chris found himself in a taxi that was experiencing bumper-to-bumper traffic. It was exacerbating but nothing new. The only saving grace was the fact that he wasn't driving. There was nothing he could do about it, so he sat back and tried to relax.

Finally, the taxi turned on to Chris' tree-lined street in Brooklyn, and he couldn't wait to surprise his parents. As the taxi approached his house, Chris looked across the street to Danny's house and was surprised to see a "For Sale" sign propped on the front lawn. His surprise quickly turned into concern as many different thoughts flooded his mind. He would find out about the "For Sale" sign from his parents as soon as he spoke with them. The cab stopped, and Chris jumped out with the enthusiasm of a child on Christmas morning. He hadn't realized how much he missed his parents. As he walked up the front path, he noticed that the family car was not in the driveway. Unfortunately, that was a sign that his parents could be out.

Chris did not have his house keys with him, so he rang the doorbell and waited. There was no response, so he rang it again. To his disappointment, no one came to the front door. Just as he was about to turn away from the door, he heard his name being called. When he turned, he saw his mother yelling from the car window as his dad pulled into the driveway. So, the surprise that Chris had planned backfired, and he was the one surprised by his parents. Chris' mom jumped out of the car with the same enthusiasm that Chris had shown just a few moments ago. Following the hugs and kisses from his mom and dad, they all went into the house.

Catching up on all the latest news covering the past few weeks, Chris inquired about his friend's house. Chris told his parents that he had a tough time finding out anything about Danny. He mentioned that he left messages for him but received no response. He explained that the only message he had received was one relayed to him by his squad lieutenant, and that was at the very beginning of basic training. He asked his parents if they knew anything about Danny. They told him that they had heard about the accident that his friend had been involved in, but that they heard very little after that because Danny's parents put the house up for sale and moved away.

"Did you speak to his parents about Danny or the move?"

Chris' mom took the lead and responded: "No Chris. We didn't even get a chance to speak with them before they moved. It was quite odd. They were there one day, then the "For Sale" sign went up, and they were gone. There were no "good-byes," and no information on why or where they were going. They were just gone. We never even saw a moving truck. It was one big mystery, and no one knew anything about their quick exit."

"Wow, that's quite the story, mom. As you know, Danny and I are real good friends, and the two of you were close with Danny's parents. I don't understand why they would do something like that and not say anything to you. Were you able to talk to the real estate agent who is selling the house for them?"

"No Chris. If you look closely at the "For Sale" sign, it says "By Owner," but we haven't seen either one of Danny's parents since the sign went up. If they did move, I don't know how they expect to sell the house. They are never around. It's just weird."

Chris was beside himself. One of the things that he was looking forward to on his return home was visiting Danny's parents to find out about his friend. Now, that seemed like an impossibility. He couldn't believe that all avenues to gaining information about his friend were closed. It was crazy that he couldn't find out about his best friend. There had to be a way to get information on Danny. He just couldn't think of it. He even thought about trying to contact his spirit-friend. It, for sure, could find out. However, what would he tell his parents if they knew that he was in contact with some otherworldly entity? That would be another whole dilemma.

Chris had been so involved in finding out about his friend that he forgot to mention to his parents that he had a girlfriend. The fact that he was heavily involved with someone never even came to his mind. That's how concerned he was about his friend. He thought, however, that he shouldn't put off the news any longer. He was sure that his parents, especially his mom, would have a barrage of questions. After giving it some careful thought, however, Chris decided to wait until after dinner when they would all be more relaxed.

It was usually the custom for them to have coffee after dinner and discuss some of the day's current events. That would be the perfect time for Chris to talk about a very current event. He couldn't wait to tell them about how he found the perfect woman for him. He was sure about what his father's reaction would be, but his mother would be a different story. She would be worried that he was still too young to be in a serious relationship, and that he would leave a girlfriend behind when he was ultimately transferred. There, no doubt, would be additional questions and concerns, but Chris felt that he was ready for the onslaught. He also knew that when the inquisition was over, his mom would wish him the best.

There is nothing like a home cooked meal, and Chris' mom was an excellent cook. She prepared his favorite dish of beef stew and gave him his requested second serving. Chris hadn't been full like he was in a very long time. Although, if he could have fitted it in, he would have had one more bowl. He just couldn't do it. He knew he would regret not having that extra bowl when he was overseas eating army food, but there was nothing he could do about that now.

The family took an extended break between the main course and coffee time. They were all pretty full, and there was still some stew left over. Chris was happy about that. It meant that he could have it again tomorrow. But it was time to get into the thick of things. There wouldn't be a better time, so Chris opened his comments: "Hey Guys, I have an announcement to make. I met a beautiful young woman, and we are committed to each other. In fact, we are "pinned," which is a step away from engagement." He expected the awe and surprise by both his parents and prepared himself for the unending questions that were sure to come, at least from his mother.

"Chris, where did you meet her? Is she also in the army? How long have you been seeing her? How old is she?"

"Mom, hold on. You've asked four questions in a row, and I haven't even gotten to the first one yet. Let me tell you all about her, and then if you have any additional questions, I will be happy to answer them for you."

They both answered "okay," and Chris began from the beginning and brought them up to date. Contrary to what Chris thought would happen, they both remained quiet and uninterrupting, waiting for Chris to finish speaking. When he stopped and took a breath, the questions and concerns began. His mother was mostly concerned with two things: Melody being older than he, and her apparent ill-health. Chris explained that she was only a little older and that age didn't seem to be a barrier to how well they got along. His mother's second concern was the more serious one for her. Melody's poor health could put an unfair burden on him. Chris was prepared for that problem also. He told them both that a nurse friend of his was working every day with Melody to hasten her recovery. He also told them, although he wasn't as sure as he wanted to be, that there was an excellent chance that Melody would make a total recovery. He saw the doubt on their faces and started to regret that he might have told them too much.

"Chris, you are going to leave a very ill woman not knowing what the outcome will be. Are you certain that is what you want."

"Mom, I couldn't be more certain. Beside the two of you, there is no one I care for more. I will ultimately return, and one day marry her."

His parents both saw their son's determination and realized how futile it would be to try to convince him that he might be making a mistake. So, being parent-wise, they just told him that they wished for Melody's recovery and his safety abroad. He had told them where he was going to be stationed, and it came as no surprise. Many of the enlisted personnel were going to the Middle East.

The conversation finally slanted its way to the local goings-on, and they stayed talking 'till late in the night. Chris was glad that his parents didn't bring up the incident with Tim Jenkins, but they have to had known what happened. He guessed that they felt that it was better for everyone to keep it in the past.

Before retiring for the night, Chris called Holly to find out how Melody was doing. Although she said that everything was okay, he didn't like the sound of her voice. She wasn't very convincing. He asked her again, and this time she sounded more sincere in her answer. Chris didn't know if she was being as truthful as she could be. He went to sleep that night praying extra hard for his girlfriend's recovery. Things just didn't seem right.

Chapter Thirty-Nine

An Unsolved Mystery

Chris' stay at home was comforting and uneventful. He saw some of the guys that he went to school with and some of his neighborhood friends. But since he wouldn't be home for quite a while, he tried to spend as much time as he could with his parents at home. He knew they appreciated it, and he knew that leaving wasn't going to be easy for them or for him. The time they spent together was filled with talk about good memories and future plans. And by the fourth day, they seemed to be all talked out.

Chris had been calling Holly each day, and she seemed better on the phone than she had that first day. He spoke with Melody each time he called, but he didn't keep her on the phone for any length of time so she wouldn't have to strain. She also seemed to be in good spirits. He was very glad that he came home, but he couldn't wait to get back to base so that he could spend more time with Melody. His leave was quickly coming to an end, and in less than a week, he would be traveling to the other side of the world – a world in which there were no parents, no girlfriend, and probably, no happy times.

On his final day home, Chris promised his parents that he would write to them every chance he got, and he asked them to write as much as they could. Being in a strange place where you don't know who is friendly or who might be your enemy is a terrifying and lonely spot. So, any word from home is more than welcome. Before he left, Chris walked over to Danny's house and just stood there staring and remembering all the good times he and his friend had. He was frustrated because he couldn't find out anything definite about his friend. He hated not knowing, and he promised himself that he would not give up until he found out the facts. Again, he thought about his spirit-friend. Although Chris had tried on a number of occasions to solicit help from the entity, he felt that one last plea might sway it to disclose whatever it knew. As he further thought about it, he realized that he had no other option but to question his apparition.

At one point, Chris had thought about actually journeying to Lakehurst General Hospital to find out from the source about his friend. However, he was not a relative or immediate family member, so there was no guarantee that he would gain any insight into Danny's condition or whereabouts. Additionally, he was fighting time constraints. He had to spend time with his family, and he wanted and needed to get back to Melody. He hadn't set aside a block of time for him to travel to New Jersey where he could have inquired from the hospital staff about Danny. But again, he would not be given any information if he was not a relative or immediate family member. So, a trip to Lakehurst General just might have been a wasted effort.

Chris' parents saw him looking at the Ferguson house and called to him. He had been standing in the middle of the street as if in a trance. His mom got his attention and told him to come back into the house. His mom's voice brought him back to the present, and he walked over to his house. His parents realized how upset Chris was about his friend, but there was little they could do to console him. His parents had been close to the Fergusons, and they were also saddened by the way their friendship ended. They too had no idea what had happened to have their friends leave on such short notice and without even a "good-bye." They had asked other neighbors if they knew anything about the unorthodox exit, but they too had no idea what influenced the Fergusons to leave as if they were fleeing the police. Even the mailman was surprised as they left no forwarding address. No one knew if they were gone for just a short while or if they planned to return at a later date. All these questions and concerns did nothing to help Chris find out about his friend.

The day before Chris was to leave, he decided to visit some of the haunts where he and his friends often frequented. He wanted to see some of his friends but more so, he was hoping that one of them could shed some light on what was happening with the Fergusons and Danny. Although they were all out of high school and going to college, many of them were creatures of habit, and so Chris found a number of them "hanging out" at the same old place. He received a raucous greeting and was overwhelmed with the man-hugs from the guys and the kisses from the girls.

As soon as everyone recovered from the over-ambitious "hello," Chris asked the group about Danny Ferguson. They all agreed that that they had heard that he was in a bad accident in New Jersey. They mentioned that he was recovering in a hospital in Lakehurst. This was the same information that Chris had, so he learned nothing new. He then asked about the "For Sale" sign on the Fergusons' front lawn. Once again, it was as much a mystery to them as it was to him. He stayed for a while with the group and shared drinks and memories. It was good catching up, but Chris was leaving in the morning, and he wanted to spend some more time with his parents on the night before he left. He left his friends in early evening with the promise that they would all keep in contact. It was a promise that they all knew would never be kept. Life interfered with that.

He got home relatively early, and his parents were there waiting for him. They knew that he would come home early enough to spend some of his last evening with them. It was a melancholy atmosphere, but one that he and his parents relished. They stayed up talking 'till late in the evening because no one wanted the time to end. However, Chris had to wake early in the morning to catch his flight back to Fort Sill, so he told them how much he loved them and promised to write as soon as he reached his new station. They exchanged kisses and hugs again, but this time filled with teary eyes. They went to their bedrooms and cried some more, Chris included.

It was late, but he wanted to get a progress report on Melody. He couldn't call Melody because of the hour, but he figured that Holly would still be up. He was right and Holly answered on the second ring.

"Hi Holly. It's Chris. Sorry for calling so late, but I really needed to know how things were going. I miss you guys. What can you tell me?"

"Hi Chris. You don't have to apologize for the time. I was cleaning up a bit. I've had problems sleeping lately, anyway."

"Is everything all right? What's keeping you up?"

"Chris, things are going as well as I thought they would."

"What do you mean? Is it about Melody?"

"Yeah, Chris. She is trying very hard, but she takes two steps forward and three backward. She's been having mini-seizures, I forget the medical term for them, but they keep impeding her progress. It is frustrating for me and her."

"What does the doctor say? Does he know what's causing these little seizures? There's got to be some medication that can stop them from occurring."

"The doctor has given her several medications, but nothing has seemed to work. And Chris, the seizures are not something you want to see. Although they are not massive, her body still twists and contorts in a very disturbing manner. It's something you don't forget."

"Holly, does that mean that her speech and stability are still impacted the way they were. Is there any improvement, at all?"

"For the past four days, it has been a roller coaster with Melody's condition. One day she's okay, and the next she's contorting. Like I said though, they are not massive seizures and maybe, in time, they'll stop by themselves. The doctor said that there is a possibility that they can stop on their own if the brain develops a defense system against them."

"I will be flying back to Fort Sill early tomorrow morning. If you're working, please let Melody know that I'll be seeing her later in the day. Is there anything that she needs or wants?"

"No, Chris. Other than wanting to see you, she doesn't need anything else. I am sure that your coming to visit her will lift her spirits and put her back on track again. You know what they say about the power of love!"

"Okay, Holly, but please tell her when you see her in the morning that I will be there later."

Holly agreed to Chris' request, and she would definitely tell Melody that he was coming. The problem that Holly faced, however, was the fact that her friend might not remember that she told her about Chris, or possibly worse, not even remember Chris!

Chapter Forty

A Dose of Reality

The night was a restless one for Chris. How could he sleep with the fact that he would be leaving in the morning not knowing the next time he would see his family; leaving in the morning not having learned anything new about his friend, Danny; leaving in the morning knowing that his girlfriend was not doing as well as he thought she would; and leaving in the morning knowing his next stop was somewhere in the Afghanistan desert?

Although he left at an ungodly early time in the morning, both his parents were up and there to send him off. Another soulful and tearful "goodbye," and Chris was on his way. He sure had a lot to think about as he traveled back to Fort Sill. In one respect, he was glad that his mind would be occupied trying to make sense of all the incongruities affecting his life. Because of that, he could give very little thought to the fact that he was flying approximately thirty thousand feet above Terra Ferma.

Racking his brain over potential solutions to the problems facing him, Chris heard the unexpected announcement that they were on their final approach to Fort Sill-Lawton Airport. As he surmised, time flew because of his congested stream of consciousness. He was happy to be out of a metal can flooded with combustible liquids. Chris was not an advocate for plane travel.

He was so anxious to get to the hospital to see Melody that the taxi ride back to the base seemed longer than the plane ride. Finally, he arrived at Fort Sill and went directly to see Melody. As a result of Holly's employment and influence at the hospital, Chris had carte blanche when it came to visiting hours. When he got to Melody's bedside, she was asleep. He didn't want to wake her, so he gently kissed her on the forehead and sat quietly waiting for her to awake. It didn't take long when Melody stirred and opened her eyes. She made eye contact with him and smiled, but immediately following that friendly acknowledgement, Melody began twisting and turning in a way that was foreign to Chris. He hadn't seen anything like that and was alarmed by Melody's apparently involuntary movement. Because of the unfamiliarity with seizures, Chris didn't immediately react. Finally, when it dawned on him that his girlfriend was experiencing something that a doctor should be handling, he ran to the hall and yelled for help.

When the doctor and nurses arrived in Melody's room, they immediately attended to her while shooing him out of the room. Their main concern was to secure the patient so that she wouldn't involuntarily do harm to herself. As is hospital routine, they do not want anyone other than the medical team present when they are handling any type of emergency situation. Chris understood the policy but strained to see what was happening.

To Chris' satisfaction and relief, the medical team finished their immediate application and follow-up within a relatively short time. However, it was long enough for Holly to have been notified that her friend had suffered another "petit seizure." As the doctors were leaving Melody's room, Holly arrived to greet Chris: "Hi Chris. I didn't know you had arrived. This is what I was telling you about. She seems to be vulnerable to these seizure attacks, and each time she experiences one of these, it sets her back a pace in her recovery. It's almost like swimming upstream. You may get there, but the effort is sometimes overwhelming, and in some cases, the tide is too great for a person to reach shore. I hope you understand what I am saying, Chris. Do not think for a minute, however, that I am giving up on my friend. I am just trying to tell you how difficult the routine is becoming."

"Holly, I know that you are trying your best, and I'm sure that Melody, as well as I, appreciate everything that you have been doing. I'm just disappointed with what I see. When I got back, I foolishly assumed that Melody would be well on her way to getting around to the woman we knew. Maybe, it was wishful thinking, but I really thought that I would see a sharper, more alert Melody when I returned. I know when we spoke, you warned me that her recovery was not progressing as well as it should have been, but I didn't want to accept that, and my refusal didn't prepare me for what I just saw. You know that I am leaving in a few days. Do you think that she might be somewhat better by then?"

"Chris, I want to say 'yes,' but I truly don't know. If she continues to be impacted by these seizures, I can't see her making any significant progress. Also, not to add to the distress, I wonder what the cumulative effect has been as she suffers one seizure after another. It can't be good!"

Private First-Class Chris Martin read between the lines. His thinking focused on the fact that the "piling-on" effect of the seizures could ultimately lead to a point where her mental acuity was so damaged that it sent signals to her body to just give up. Holly was implying that Melody could very well die if the condition persisted. He stared at Holly, not with hate or anger, but with the understanding that she was begrudgingly dealing with potential reality. Saying nothing, he nodded to her and turned to go into Melody's room. Holly followed.

Once again, Melody was asleep. Holly mentioned that the seizure attacks take everything out of her, and that she sleeps after each attack. Holly emphasized that seizures have an exhausting effect on the body. So, it takes time for the body to refuel. She explained to Chris that Melody could be sleeping for a few hours, but he didn't care. He was going to be there when his girlfriend awoke from her seizure induced sleep. Holly understood Chris' determination and dedication to her friend, and that it was commendable and heartwarming, but she worried, once again, that the possibility of Melody not recognizing him could raise its ugly head.

She couldn't imagine Chris' disappointment and despair if that were to occur. It would be devastatingly cruel for that to happen, but it had already happened to Holly. It was not easy for Holly to accept it, and she was only a friend. Chris was her loving partner. Someone who had committed to sharing a future together. It would be so much more catastrophic for Chris not to be recognized by his "pinned" girlfriend. It would be a jolt of reality from which one does not easily recover. But Holly, roundaboutly, had been hinting at this raw possibility. So, if it did occur, Holly hoped that her implications would soften any unexpected calamity.

Holly had to go back on shift, so she left Chris at Melody's bedside. Once again, he thanked her for all of her efforts, and she responded that although Melody might be his girlfriend, she was still, in fact, Holly's good friend. So, the implication was that "thanks" was not necessary. Chris understood that but was grateful that Holly was around and so caring for Melody. Even more so, he was ecstatic that she would be there for his girlfriend when he was pounding sand in Afghanistan. He wasn't even there yet and wondered when he would be able to come home to see Melody.

Chris waited patiently in Melody's room. It had already been, at least, two hours, and his girlfriend was still sleeping it off. Finally, two-and-a-half hours after her recent attack by the invisible and unpredictable enemy, Melody stirred and awakened from her deep sleep. He was glad that he waited for her to come back to the conscious world, because her smile was well worth the wait.

"Hi beautiful. How are you doing? I could not wait to get back from New York so that I could see you again."

In a struggling, half-whispering, sleep-affected voice, she said how happy she was to see him. He bent down and stroked her face as he kissed her "hello."

"I kept in contact with Holly every day when I was away. Even if I couldn't get to speak with you, I spoke with her to find out how you were doing. I can't tell you how glad I am to be back here with you. Sure, it was nice to visit with my parents. I missed them too, but even as I went through the days with my family and some of my friends, there wasn't a moment when I wasn't thinking about you, and the next time that I would see you. And now I'm here. Tell me how your therapy sessions with Holly have been going."

"Well, I don't know if Holly mentioned that every once in a while, I sneak out of the picture. The doctor tells me that my brain is reacting to my injury. He mentioned that it could very well be that my brain is formulating a new way for the cells to recognize and organize my thought patterns in an alternate manner. So, instead of a negative event, it could very well be a positive move to getting better."

Chris smiled at her to let her know that he was happy to hear that such a possibility existed, but this was not the same story that Holly had relayed. He didn't know if Melody was grasping at straws and trying to make lemonade out of lemons, or if she was actually given the slightest hint that there was a positive possibility afoot. No matter, Chris was going to encourage her positive thinking. What harm could it do? It also helped him to deal with the unspoken potential of a disastrous reality.

Chris stayed with Melody long after Holly had paid her final visit and left for the day. She said that she would be in contact with him, and that before he went off to play soldier, she wanted to have him over for dinner one last time. He thanked her and said good-bye.

It was already late in the evening, and Chris could see that Melody was struggling to keep her eyes open. He took the hint and told her that he would see her in the morning. She smiled and told him that it was a date.

He left the hospital and prayed as he walked. He really loved that girl, and he wanted, more than anything else, to see her back on her feet again. He knew, however, that he could not do it alone, thus the prayers. When he finally got back to the barracks, he sat on his bed, put his head in his hands, and cried.

Chapter Forty-One

The Alarming Odds

Early the next morning, Chris had to report to the transport center to find out about the specifics of his transfer abroad. By the time he got all of the details and finished the paperwork, it was early afternoon. He wanted to get to the hospital and visit Melody because the time was getting closer when he wouldn't have that option. So, to him every minute counted, and he didn't want to waste it on continuous paperwork.

He reached the hospital just as Holly was taking her lunch break. They both went into Melody's room only to find her asleep. Entering right behind them was the doctor who attended to her. The doctor looked at them and then at her. He mentioned that he was not surprised that she was still sleeping. He then relayed what had occurred throughout the night. Melody had suffered two more seizures: one minor attack early in the morning hours, and one about two hours later. He said that the latter one was more severe and left her totally exhausted. So, the fact that Melody was still asleep was to be expected. The doctor also mentioned that the fact that the seizures seemed to be coming more frequently and apparently were more serious was not a good sign for recovery. This news was devastating for Holly and Chris who had hoped for a positive reaction from the doctor. It was not what Melody had relayed to Chris about the possibility that brain cells were formulating a pattern to become part of an alternate transmission route for thought processing. According to the doctor, the seizures continued to cause damage and delayed the potential for recovery.

Holly and Chris had a number of questions for the doctor, but before they could ask him anything, a nurse entered the room and told the doctor that he was needed for an emergency situation. He left with the promise that he would return as soon as possible and answer whatever questions they had. Apparently, he had seen the concerned and questioned look on their faces.

They were alone now, except for their sleeping friend. They looked at each other with what could only be described as desperation, despair and real concern. They were both thinking the worst, but neither one wanted to verbalize the possible ultimate outcome of Melody's condition. Tears welled up in both of their eyes and they simultaneously hugged each other as they silently sobbed.

Their moment of consolation was interrupted by a stirring from Melody's bed. They turned to see their friend waking from her seizure-induced slumber.

"Hi Melody. Glad you could join us." Holly was the first to greet her friend. Chris followed with his salutation: "Hi beautiful. I'm glad you're awake so that I can tell you how much I missed you. When I was away, I was alone in a crowd, but now that I am back, everything is right with the world."

Melody said nothing. She smiled just a bit, but looked utterly confused as to whom these two people were. Holly and Chris looked at one another realizing that Melody was having problems recognizing them. They were at a loss for words but were saved as the doctor came back into the room: "Just a small problem that was easily solved. Sorry, I had to leave so abruptly, but these things do come up." He turned his attention to Melody and spoke directly to her: "Hi Melody. How are you feeling? You had a rough night, and we didn't want to disturb your well-deserved sleep."

Whether it was the bedside manner that he had, or the fact that he was wearing a white medical jacket with a stethoscope hanging around his neck, Melody apparently realized that the man standing in front of her and asking questions was a doctor. Melody answered in a garbled almost undecipherable speech: "I have a bit of a headache, but other than that, I feel okay."

"I am sure that your headache will go away as the day wears on, but I will prescribe something that will help with the pain."

Melody nodded, and then briefly looked at the two people standing next to her bed. She turned to the doctor in such a manner as to ask: "Who are they?" The doctor picked up on this and proceeded to tell his patient that her two friends had been waiting patiently for her to wake up. She looked at them again and offered the same gentle smile, not indicating any sign of recognition.

Chris couldn't take it anymore: "Hey Melody. I am back from my visit home. I told my parents about us, and they can't wait to meet you. So, the quicker you get better, the quicker we can relieve their curiosity. You have to realize that I am their one and only child, so they want to make sure that you are going treat me right." He smiled after his comment, but just saw a blank stare in return.

Holly picked up after Chris' attempt to break down the wall of unfamiliarity: "Hey Melody. Glad to see that you're ready for more hard work. We have to get you better so that you can prove to Chris' parents that he hit the lottery when he met you. We'll start where we left off. It shouldn't be hard to get back on track, and with a little dedication to the routine, you should be back to yourself in no time." Holly wasn't sure she was saying what she said for Melody's benefit or her own, but she was convinced, now, that Melody would never be the Melody she once knew.

Chris gingerly picked up Melody's hand to see if he could help her start the process of recollection; however, as gently as he clutched her hand, she gently disengaged. It was obvious that in Melody's mind she was speaking to strangers. The seizures had taken their toll on her memory, and it was taking a very long time for her to recognize these two people as her friends. Nothing seemed to jog her memory. It became more and more disturbing to Holly, and devastatingly disturbing to Chris. This was the girl who he was in love with and the girl who was in love with him. It truly bothered him to believe that the love they shared wasn't strong enough to break down any barrier that prevented recognition. He was going to leave in two days, and he couldn't stand to go with the knowledge that his girlfriend didn't know who he was. Chris was at a loss, and all he could do was to look at her in disbelief.

Holly noticed how affected Chris was with the present situation, so she whispered and tried to lessen the blow: "Chris, it's probably only a temporary setback. She will come around to being herself before you know it." Trying even harder and attempting to make light of the problem, she said: "Your good looks and charm alone will bolt her into recognition. Just stay strong!"

"It better bolt her into some sort of recognition real soon. I ship out in two days, and I don't want to leave with her not knowing that we are a couple. Holly, it seems that we are going backwards instead of progressing. I am really beginning to worry that we are swimming against the tide."

There was silence in the room. The whole conversation between Holly and Chris had taken place out of the earshot of Melody. The doctor, who had gravitated to the back of the room, asked them both to step into the hallway so that they could talk about Melody's condition. They moved with heavy steps and an even heavier heart. Whatever the news was, they both felt that it was not going to be good.

When all three got together in the hall, the doctor suggested that they follow him to his office where they could speak more privately. They went to his office where he addressed them both: "I do not want to sugarcoat my comments about Melody's condition. That would be unfair, and I don't believe that you would want me to do that. It probably has become obvious to you that her condition has worsened. Unfortunately, the reoccurring seizures are not giving the brain a chance to heal. The attacks are impeding any substantial progress. It doesn't mean, however, that all hope is lost. No, if Melody experiences any elongated period where seizures do not raise their ugly head, she could possibly regain some of her mental stability, and progress towards recovery. However, in my opinion, no matter how much progress she makes, Melody will never fully recover."

The doctor's remarks hit Holly hard but drove a stake through Chris' heart. The harsh reality of Melody not making a full recovery was almost more than Chris could take. He had to know more: "Doc, you're telling us that you don't believe that Melody will ever be herself again. Is there any way that you could predict, percentage wise, the amount of recovery we could expect?"

"That's real hard to say, son. It depends on how long she can go without another seizure and the seriousness of that seizure. I cannot give you a degree of recovery now, but down the road, if she remains stable, I will be able to more accurately formulate a prediction. For now, it is a waiting game, but I recommend that both of you continue to stimulate her toward whatever progress she may make."

Just as the doctor was finishing his comments and before either Holly or Chris could ask any more questions, the hospital's in-house intercom system requested the doctor's appearance "stat" in one of the rooms on the floor. The doctor quickly rose out of his chair and excused himself with the caveat that they could wait for him in his office. As he hurriedly left the office, the two friends grabbed hands and looked at each other, but could say nothing. The hospital intercom system had called for the doctor to respond to a room with which they were all too familiar. The doctor was responding to Melody Johnson's room, and the odds for her recovery decreased again.

Chapter Forty-Two

The M.P. Threat

As a result of the most recent emergency involving Melody Johnson, the doctor ordered that she have no visitors for the rest of the day. This destroyed Chris who only had two days left before he boarded a military transport to parts unknown in the Middle East. The doctor had taken away valuable minutes from Chris' visiting time, but the doctor was adamant about his order. Holly understood this and explained to Chris the necessity of keeping Melody calm and quiet. Chris understood too, but he was under different time constraints than Holly. She could wait and visit her friend whenever the doctor okayed visitors, but he wasn't going to be around. This bothered him to the point that he began thinking of different ways he could sneak in to see his girlfriend. Even if she wasn't awake, he could at least be there and in her company.

Holly was attuned to Chris' way of thinking, and she just knew that he was weighing the possible options for sneaking into Melody's room. She tapped his shoulder to get his attention, and then she warned him against any measure that would jeopardize her friend's health or his freedom. Getting caught disregarding the doctor's orders could lead to a call to the base M. P.'s, and that could ultimately lead to an arrest situation. That's the last thing that Holly wanted to see, but Chris wasn't thinking with a clear head. All Chris was interested in was time with his girlfriend.

"Chris, I know what you're thinking. Just forget about it. You may succeed in circumventing the rules, but in the long run you are jeopardizing your career, and any future you may have with Melody. If you are caught by the M.P.'s, you will not only face charges, but I venture to say that you may never get the chance to see Melody. Don't go for the initial gratification of a one-time visit and cast aside plans that you can develop for a potential future relationship that could last a lifetime." Holly continued pleading with Chris, but she could almost see that her pleas were falling on deaf ears. He wanted to see his girlfriend before he left, and there was no convincing him otherwise.

"Holly, I know what you're saying, but you have to realize that I may not be back this way for quite a while. I could be gone for eighteen months or even two years. That's a long time to not see your girlfriend. That's why I want to get as much time in as possible now while I can."

"But Chris, you're missing the point, you can't. Do you really think that you can get away with sneaking into her room and not getting caught. Sure, you may be able to get in initially, but ultimately you will be seen. Once that happens, you are screwed. Also, you're thinking about Chris Martin. Are you thinking about Melody Johnson? The doctor is saying that visitors may not be good for Melody's health and recovery. Why would you put Melody's wellbeing in jeopardy?"

"Holly, you and I know that the doctor is being overly cautious. I am sure that my visit would not present any problems for Melody."

"Chris, let me ask. From which college did you receive your medical degree? Who are you to decide if the doctor is being overly cautious or not? He knows what's best for Melody, not you."

Holly's remarks were pointed and demonstrative. She needed to convince Chris that he was only thinking of himself. He wanted to be there no matter what. He wanted to see Melody before he left for Afghanistan. He wanted to make sure that she knew that he was committed to returning to her. Everything was for him, totally disregarding what it could do to her.

"Chris, I understand where you're coming from, but I am a nurse, and I know the doctor is looking out for Melody's health. Listen carefully. If you violate his orders, I will contact the M.P.'s.

I feel for you, but I'm not going to allow you to hurt my friend. Also, you don't even know if Melody will be awake from now until the time you leave. After her last attack, she could very well be out of it for the whole time. And ironically, if she does wake up, we don't even know if she will recognize us. I would say that most likely she won't."

Chris was taken aback by Holly's comments and especially by her threatening tone, but maybe that was what he needed to start thinking clearly. He looked at her for a long time, and then finally spoke: "I'm sorry Holly. You are right. I am thinking only of myself. It's just that I'll be gone for a long time, and I won't have the luxury of seeing her. I wanted to get in as much as I could while I still can. I know it is selfish, and the last thing I want to do is prolong Melody's possible recovery. You don't have to worry about me, Holly. I've come to my senses. By the way, would you really have called the M.P.'s?"

"I like you, Chris, but I am not going to let anyone, or anything interfere with my friend's good health. I am glad that you're seeing it the right way, and yes, if I thought that you were hindering Melody's recovery in any way, I would take her health over your freedom. Sorry about that."

"You're a good friend, Holly, and I guess I already knew what you would do to secure her recovery. I think I'll go back to the barracks now and continue preparing for my transfer. I still have a number of things that I have to do including a call to my parents. I know they are worried, and I want to let them know that everything will be okay. Please call me if anything changes, including the doctor's orders."

"Of course, Chris. As soon as I know anything, you will know. Take care of what you need to do. I will be here. You have enough to think about."

Chris hugged and thanked Holly. He left the hospital and headed for the barracks where he wanted to pack some last-minute items. Tomorrow would be a day that he would be dealing with his new squad sergeant, the other soldiers who would be flying out with him, and the ordeal of leaving both Holly and the love of his life, Melody. So, he wasn't going to have a whole lot of free time. He was also scheduled to attend a preliminary orientation which would take the better part of tomorrow afternoon. It was a busy time for him, but his mind always came back to the hospital and the possibility of his seeing Melody one last time before he left.

When he got to the barracks, he realized how tired he was. In addition to preparing for his new station, he was emotionally exhausted because of the hospital situation. Emotional stress, many times, can be more exhausting than physical strain, and that was what he was feeling. He laid back on his bed and tried to get in a few minutes of relaxation. He tried to clear his mind and just rest. He almost succeeded when the thought of his friend, Danny Ferguson, came to mind. He was still very concerned about Danny. He was unsuccessful in finding out where Danny was or what condition he was in. This bothered him to no end, and now he would have to put any effort regarding Danny on hold. He wouldn't be able to initiate any plan to find out about Danny when he was going to be digging out sand from his combat boots in Afghanistan.

Chris only planned to lie down for a short while. He underestimated how tired he was and how much his body needed some rest time. It was nine thirty in the evening and the barracks were empty. He figured that most of the guys went out for one last fling. He wasn't in a party mood, so he just laid there trying to wrestle himself from the effects of sleep. He blinked his eyes to get a clearer picture of his surroundings, but no matter how he tried, it was still blurry.

"Hello, Chris. How are you doing? I was in the neighborhood, so I thought I'd drop in."

It wasn't Chris' eyes that needed clearing, the blurry, foggy figure of his entity friend was there before him. The apparition hadn't visited in a while, but it was here now.

"Well, I haven't seen you for some time. To what do I owe this unscheduled appearance? Do you have news for me? Are you here to help me with some of my problems, or are you just here to offer some of your sage advice, once again? Understand, I can't spend much time with you because, as you probably know, I have to get ready for my station transfer. So, tell me why you're here."

"If I didn't know better, Chris, I would say that your comments are filled with sarcasm. I don't understand why. I have always tried to help, even though at times, you disregard my

counsel. I am going to assume, however, that you are not being sarcastic, but are influenced by the problems that you are facing. I am sorry to hear about Melody and her struggles, but I did mention to you that a relationship with her may involve some overwhelming hurdles. But on a positive note, I do believe that you will be finding out a lot more about Danny when you arrive at your station in Afghanistan. That's all I can tell you right now, but I will probably see you again sometime soon."

"Hey before you do your disappearing act, can you tell me any more about Danny. Is he okay? He can't be in Afghanistan, so why would I find out more about him there? Once again, you're not making a whole lot of sense. And while we're exchanging predictions and/or revelations, why haven't you helped at all with Melody? You have to know that she is struggling to keep her head above water. She could use some supernatural help."

*"I have to be on my way, but I will leave you with this thought. I am almost certain that you will see Melody again, and this time you will really **see** her. Good-bye, Chris."*

"Wait! As usual, you're talking in riddles. What the hell does 'really see her' mean? Also, how can I find out about Danny in Afghanistan. He didn't even complete basic training. What the hell are you talking about?"

Before Chris could finish his questions, the apparition was gone, but one of the soldiers assigned to his barracks walked in as Chris was raising his voice and asking questions. The soldier asked Chris if he was okay, and Chris just smiled and said that he was yelling at his ghost friend. There was a pause, and they both just laughed. The soldier just assumed it was nerves. He couldn't be more wrong.

Chapter Forty-Three

Time to Leave

The next day saw Chris rushing through the scheduled tasks that he had to complete. The faster they were done, the quicker he might be able to see Melody. He hated that orientation was scheduled for a good part of the afternoon, but he was sure that there would be time for a quick visit, if he was allowed. He hadn't heard anything from Holly, so he assumed that the doctor's orders were still in effect. Today would really be the only time he would get to visit. Tomorrow would be launch day, and there would be no wiggle room for personal errands.

As the day rolled on, Chris became more and more concerned that he was not going to be able to see his girlfriend.

So, on a break from the orientation training, he reached out for Holly. He told her about his concern, and she said that she would check with the doctor. It took about twenty minutes before Holly got back to him, and he had to leave the orientation to answer the call. The news was good, however. After Holly explained to the doctor that Chris was about to ship out, the doctor told Holly that Chris could visit for a short while in the evening. The doctor was direct in his instruction that there was to be no excitement or distress. He also emphasized that if the patient was sleeping that she is not to be awakened. He mentioned that Melody needed as much rest as possible, no matter the circumstances. He understood the underlying emotions, but his concern had to focus on the medical progress of his patient.

Chris understood everything that Holly told him, and he let her know that he would abide by the doctor's orders. Chris was just happy to be able to see Melody, and maybe hold her hand. Also, there was a possibility that Melody would be awake and alert. He could only hope. Chris went back to the orientation with a big smile on his face. He couldn't wait for it to be over so that he could race to the hospital. He prayed a silent prayer that Melody would be feeling okay and that she would be awake to see him. Leaving was never going to be easy, but it would be tolerable if he was able to personally say good-bye.

Unfortunately for Private First-Class Chris Martin, because of the barrage of questions, the orientation session went longer than he anticipated. It was evening by the time he was able to leave orientation. He still hadn't called his parents, which he needed to do, but he decided to visit the hospital first. His plan was simple. If Melody was sleeping when he arrived, he would then leave to contact his parents. That diversion would give Melody more time to wake up. However, he would make sure that the doctor knew that the first brief "look-in" didn't count as a visit. If Melody was awake when he first arrived, then he would stay with her for as long as he could. When the doctor ultimately ushered him out, he would contact his parents. Upon examination, he had all options covered.

When Chris arrived at the hospital, his anticipation was through the roof. He saw the doctor as he approached Melody's room and explained to him what he had planned. The doctor was okay with what he heard but emphasized that no matter when he was going to visit, it had to be brief. Chris nodded, and he entered the room. Melody was lying peacefully in her bed with her eyes closed. He approached quietly and realized that he had to employ plan "B." He gently touched her hand and bent over to kiss her forehead when she started to stir. He stepped back and saw her settle into another sleeping position. With that, he smiled and left the room, letting the doctor know that he would be back later.

He tried to think of a way to make light of his imminent departure to the combat zone known as Afghanistan. Because of his involvement in the military, Chris' parents had become as well informed as possible on the combative missions of the U.S. military in Afghanistan. So, his conversation with his parents was not going to be an easy one. They knew a lot about what he was going to experience. He dreaded the call, but he wanted to speak with them. No one knows what can happen in combat.

"Hi Mom. How are you doing? Is dad there with you?"

"Hello Chris. We're both here, and we were waiting for your call. Are you all prepared for your trip?"

"Yeah, Mom. It's funny that you call it a trip. I never thought of it that way. I guess it sounds better."

"Hi, son. As a dad, I couldn't be prouder of what you are doing. But also, as a dad, it is hard not to worry about your only son. We both know that you are more than capable of taking care of yourself, but you are going to be doing things that you haven't done before, seeing things that you haven't seen before, and facing things that you haven't faced before. So, putting that all together, stay as safe as you possibly can."

"Well, dad. If that was a "one for the Gipper" speech, it didn't fall short. You don't have to worry about me. I am not a hero, and I will make every effort to come back in one piece. I am a little nervous, but the sergeant says that being nervous is a natural thing, and that being nervous can save your life. But again, you don't have to worry about that. I will volunteer for 'k.p.' (kitchen police) duty whenever I can. I might be peeling potatoes for my whole time in Afghanistan." They all laughed at that, but you could tell that it was a nervous laugh. They stayed on the phone a while longer, and Chris promised his parents that he would write whenever he could. His parents told him that they loved him, made him promise to stay safe, and blessed him before they hung up. Chris told them not to worry, and that he would be home before they knew it. He hung up with an "I love you both."

It was a difficult phone call, and he was glad that he had the best parents in the world. He expected some of their comments, and he could tell that there were tears as they spoke. But he wasn't going to dwell on that. It was difficult enough to leave all those things that are so familiar to you and to enter into a world that is completely unknown. He felt it, and so did his parents. The call could have been a lot more troublesome, but both his mom and dad were on their best behavior, not making a bad thing worse. Thank God for little favors.

Chris was still a little saddened after the call to his parents, but his sadness slowly dissipated as he approached the hospital to visit Melody. With just a bit of luck, his girlfriend would be up and wide awake. As he thought about his visit, his pace increased, and by the time he reached the hospital entrance, he was almost at a full sprint. He stopped and waited for a few seconds so that his breathing returned to normal and entered the hospital.

As he approached Melody's room, he saw a nurse exiting. He asked the nurse how Melody was doing and if everything was all right. The nurse smiled and told Chris that the patient was doing as well as could be expected. It wasn't exactly what he was hoping for, but it was better than a negative response. He turned into the room and to his extremely happy delight, Melody was awake and sitting up in bed. He approached slowly offering a mellow "hello." He wasn't sure if she was still having problems with recognition. She smiled, but it wasn't a smile that told Chris that she knew who he was. At this point, he didn't care. He was just happy to be able to see her and talk a bit with her.

Unfortunately, because of her difficulty with speech, the conversation was mostly one-sided. He spoke about his advanced training, his visit home, and ultimately about his scheduled transfer to Afghanistan. She listened attentively, but Chris didn't know how much she understood. She attempted to speak a couple of times, but had trouble getting her words out, so she stopped trying. He explained to her that he cared very much for her, and he hoped to get together with her when he returned. Again, she just smiled. He was able to hold her left hand without her pulling it away. To him, that was a great sign. It was a step up.

Before long, the doctor came into Melody's room, and Chris knew that his time was up. It had passed quickly, but, at least, he had been able to spend some time with her. Without the doctor saying anything, Chris rose from his chair and prepared to leave. He grabbed her left hand again and kissed it. He had noticed that while her left hand remained flexible and open, her right hand stayed tightly closed throughout the visit. He just assumed that she was experiencing some difficulties from the seizure attacks, and that her right hand was negatively affected by the episodes.

He told her that he would write to her, and that he would also stay in contact with Holly who would let him know about the continuing progress. Melody, once again, smiled in a confirming way. It was quite difficult for Chris to leave, but the doctor had been quite cooperative in allowing him the time, so he started walking out. As he approached the doorway of her room, he thought he heard her say his name. When he turned around, she smiled and lifted her right arm, opened her right hand and displayed a pair of gold, crossed, field cannons which she had been clutching the whole time.

Chris gazed at the cannons through tear-filled eyes.

Chapter Forty-Four

Welcome to Camp Vance

The day had finally come for Private First-Class Chris Martin to board a military transport plane with his fellow soldiers and begin a journey to defend against the aggression of rebel factions in the Middle East. There was the natural surge of nerves mixed with the enthusiasm of finally getting a chance to serve. Each soldier was leaving a wife or husband, a girlfriend or boyfriend, and a family or friends. So, although the anxiety level was very high, there was little conversation taking place.

For Chris, he was leaving the person with whom he wanted to spend the rest of his life, and who unfortunately was fighting her own battle. He knew that, for the most part, he would have to depend on Holly for any progress reports. He regretted that he did not set some time aside the past week to take Holly up on her offer for dinner. He was just too busy getting ready for the transfer, and he wanted to spend as much time as he could with Melody. He was sure that Holly understood because she said so when he briefly met with her to say "good-bye." She mentioned that she would let him know all about Melody's recovery. He had no choice but to depend on her, and he was more than happy that she would be there for Melody. It made his leaving a little less worrisome.

Chris Martin was leaving his family, his girlfriend, a neighborhood that he knew like the back of his hand, and a culture that nurtured him into a respectable, God-fearing, patriot. He was sitting in a plane with approximately fifty other men who were willing to sacrifice all for the betterment of others. Although doubtful about what was to come, it was awe-inspiring to be among so many who were ready, willing and able to defeat those who would threaten democracy. He felt that it would be soldiers like himself who would ensure that no one would ever dare attack Americans on the homeland soil again. Their efforts were also going to show the world that those who would dare attack us would never be free from pursuit. No matter how long it took, he and the soldiers with him would ensure that the aggressors would ultimately face the consequences of their actions.

It was these recurring thoughts that helped dampen the anguish of leaving all behind. However, no matter how hard he tried, Melody and her fate permeated his every thought. The memory of Melody clutching the crossed cannons tugged at his heart. He knew that he would carry the memory of that moment with him forever, wherever he went. He was more determined than ever to serve his country as well as he could, but also to serve it while making every effort to return home safe and sound.

Traveling on a military transport is quite different from flying on a commercial aircraft. There were no comfortable, body-conforming seats. The soldiers were sitting on metal, bench-like formations that ran the length of the fuselage. There were no shock absorbers, so there was no doubt that you felt every change in altitude and any unexpected turbulent displacement of air. The whole situation served as a prelude to the fact that luxurious living was giving way to the raw elements of military survival.

The flight to their first stop, Kuwait, was approximately fifteen hours long. To distract from the boredom, the squad sergeant reviewed elements of the orientation program that were important to one's survival in the Afghan desert. Some of the soldiers listened while others tried to get some additional sleep. However, no matter how tired or sleep deprived one was, sleeping wasn't easily attained. The combination of the rough ride, the extremely uncomfortable seats, and the intermittent loud gestures of the squad sergeant didn't make for palatable accommodations.

In addition to the long, uncomfortable ride, the guys were going for fifteen hours without an offering of the usual food and beverage items that a commercial airline carried. Instead, these defenders of democracy were subjected to unknown fare wrapped in aluminum foil. They were also treated to bottles of water that tasted like they had been in the plane since it rolled out of the production plant. Chris guessed that it was the army's way of introducing one and all to the rigors of combat survival. If that was the idea, they were slowly but surely succeeding.

Following the fifteen-hour non-stop flight to Kuwait, the schedule included a five-hour layover thereat. This delay allowed the brass to assign soldiers to their individual stations. Kuwait seemed to serve as a distribution point for station assignments. The fifty or so soldiers who Chris had flown with were being separated and assigned to different areas. When the station assignments were finally completed, Private First-Class Chris Martin was traveling with twenty other soldiers to Camp Vance, Bagram Afghanistan. The camp was established in 2002 and was situated approximately threequarters of a mile from Bagram Air Base. Camp Vance was about two and one-half hours by plane from Kuwait. So, after additional information and orientation, and having remained for approximately five hours in Kuwait, twenty soldiers boarded another military transport for the trip to Bagram Air Base and the final truck ride to Camp Vance.

Reacting to the original plane ride from Fort Sill, the secondary plane ride from Kuwait, and the final transport to the camp, Chris felt like he had been in a ten round boxing match and lost. He was physically hurting and emotionally strung out, but there wasn't going to be anyone there to make things go away. Private First-Class Chris Martin, the soldier, had arrived.

Chris was surprised to see how large the camp was. There was a combination of buildings and makeshift huts that served as living quarters, meeting areas and supply warehouses. It was a lot bigger than Chris imagined, and it seemed like there was a large contingent of soldiers. He was now going to be part of this military complex. He also learned that he was going to be involved in a continuing mission deemed: "Village Stability Operations." This was a patrol operation where U.S. soldiers helped stabilize local villages against terrorist attacks.

Soon after settling in his quarters, he was called to a mission detail session. He was in the thick of things. In addition to information and procedures regarding the patrol missions, the newly assigned soldiers were warned that periodically, the camp experienced mortar fire. The camp "safe" areas were noted, and the proper course of safety procedures were also related. Chris, being a novice to such military routines, was surprised to hear that the camp was not a secure location. Once again, it was his unfamiliarity with army maneuvers that caused him some consternation. Following this briefing, Chris looked at Camp Vance in a different light.

The lieutenant and sergeant didn't take long to indoctrinate Chris to the tasks associated with the "Village Stability Operations" mission. He was told that he would be part of the unit going out first thing in the morning. He was scheduled to get his baptism by fire. However, Chris felt that it was better to get the first tour out of the way so the aura of the unknown could be dissolved.

Back in his quarters, as he thought about his current situation, it seemed almost surreal. He was a soldier who was going out on a patrol where he might have to enter into combat against rebels who want to kill him. Although his thoughts about his station in life were definitely serious and troubling, they did not prevent him from thinking about home and the love of his life, Melody Johnson. It was a double-edged sword. He felt some comfort thinking about her and the relationship they would have, but he also felt a conflicting sadness that he would not be able to see her for many months. He tried to anchor his thoughts, however, on the last time he saw Melody. The thought of her clutching the crossed cannons was a significant indicator to him that his girlfriend was not just clutching his pin, but she was solidifying a relationship which they both wanted to share, a lifetime commitment.

Chris realized that there were hurdles that they both had to overcome, but he was naively confident that their love and determination would conquer all. An objective observer might shake his head and say: "It's nice to be young."

Chapter Forty-Five

An Unexpected Reunion

For a number of reasons, it was difficult to get any sleep that first night, not the least of which was mortar shells landing in the camp. It was a nerve-racking experience for everyone, but especially for the new transfers who hadn't experienced anything like this before. For the most part, Chris slept with one eye open as intermittent shelling occurred throughout the night. Morning came much too soon, and it seemed to Chris that he was going from the frying pan into the fire. Not only was the patrol going to clear out certain villages, but now they were also looking for the mortar nest that shelled the camp throughout the night.

Chris was tired as he donned his gear, but the adrenaline rush kept him on point. Before the fifteen-man patrol left the camp, the sergeant checked the equipment and especially the gear of the newly assigned men. Everything having checked out, the patrol began their search and destroy mission. It was early in the day, but it was still hot and muggy. Some of the more experienced patrol members gave as much encouragement to Chris and the other new transfers as they could. And Chris felt a wave of relief that they were going to take him under their wing. He realized that the time would come when he would be the one offering encouragement and comfort to the newly assigned soldiers, but for now, he was the one who needed the pat on the back and words that told him that everything was going to be okay.

The patrol entered and cleared two villages without much resistance. In fact, it seemed quite routine to Chris, and it closely resembled the routine procedures that he went through during training. The whole experience was encouraging to Chris, but he was warned by the others that this was not always the case. Chris realized the obvious but was just thankful that today was a mission that was not risk-filled. Although the patrol had been successful in furthering the "Village Stability Operations" mission, the soldiers had not located the mortar nest that had been firing shells into the confines of the camp. This meant that there would probably be more attacks later today and into the evening. Most of the guys were used to it, if one could really get used to being bombed; but for the new guys, it meant that they were in store for another sleepless night.

Chris' patrol returned to the camp late in the afternoon, and it couldn't be too soon for Chris and the others who were suffering from fatigue that finally caught up with them. Even though the possibility of mortar attacks existed, the guys were just too tired for their nerves to have an adverse effect on sleep. So, most of the fifteen soldiers, but especially the newcomers, went to their quarters to take advantage of the down time. Chris closed his eyes, and in minutes, he was asleep.

Just as dusk came upon Camp Vance, so did the mortar fire. Chris was rudely awakened by the warning siren and although groggy from sleep, headed to one of the "safe" locations in the camp. If he was asleep a few moments ago, he was wide awake now. Shelling, apparently, had that effect on people. He watched as his fellow camp members scurried for cover. The attack only lasted for a short time, but to him, it seemed like an eternity. Fortunately, none of his fellow soldiers were injured, but a few of the buildings suffered some damage. It was nothing that couldn't be quickly repaired, but sooner or later, luck could run out. The quicker the nest was located and destroyed, the safer the camp would be, at least for a while. Chris found out that, unfortunately, as soon as one mortar location was put out of commission, another one cropped up in a different area. This was how the Afghan war was being fought.

In the relatively short time that Private First-Class Chris Martin was an active soldier at Camp Vance, he had been a part of a directed patrol and experienced the frightening moments of a bombing. He couldn't wait to see what else awaited him. He hadn't had too much time to get acquainted with many of the other guys who were assigned to the camp that hosted Army Special Forces, infantry, a Marine Special Operations Battalion, and a Navy Seal Team. It also headquartered the Combined Joint Special Operations Task Force. In fact, Chris had learned that the camp was named for Gene Arden Vance Jr., a member of the United States Special Forces, who was killed saving others during the hunt for Osama Ben Laden. Camp Vance was a significant asset for the combined forces of the United States, and the more Chris learned about his new home, the prouder he was to be a part of its operation.

Following the mortar bombardment, the camp went back to normal operations. Chris now had some free time, so he decided to familiarize himself more thoroughly with the outlay of the fortification. It was a large complex. It had to be to house so many different units. As he walked, he saw the different uniform patches signifying specific units. He was a small part of a much larger operation, but everyone had to do their bit to ensure success.

Chris was on his way back to his quarters when someone rushed up behind him, grabbed him by the shoulder and spun him around. To say the least, Chris was startled until he recognized the aggressor: "Aaron Obutu. I can't believe it's you." They hugged each other like they hadn't seen each other for years. It was more of a comfort greeting than anything else. In reality, it had only been a short while since they were together at Fort Sill.

Chris continued the conversation: "When did you get here, and did you come with anyone else?"

"Actually Chris, I got here just a little before you. I thought I saw you yesterday, but I got sidetracked, and when I finished with what I had to do, you were gone on patrol. But now when I saw you again, I was going to make sure you knew I was here. I am really glad to see you. It makes things a whole lot easier when there is a friendly face among a whole lot of strangers. Although I can't complain about the guys that I am working with, there is nothing like seeing an old friend."

"You could say that again. So, you are assigned to the infantry contingent in the camp?"

"Yeah, but apparently, we hook up with a lot of different units for escort support. It's different, and it surely doesn't get boring. So, tell me: how did you leave off with that young lady that you had your eye on? Did she come to her senses and dump you?"

"No, and as a matter of fact, she's wearing my unit pin. She knows when she has something good. Unfortunately, though, she's had some health problems that she is working to overcome, but she has her good friend, Holly, to help her out."

"Sounds good, Chris. Well, I have to get back to my unit. I think we're going out on assignment shortly. Let's make sure we run into each other again. We sure do have a lot that we can discuss."

"Absolutely, Aaron. Just make sure you keep your head down. However, after the last mortar barrage, we could be in just as much danger here as we are on patrol. Stay safe, and hopefully we'll get together soon."

"Take care, Chris, and I promise I won't sneak up on you the next time. I wouldn't want the others to see how frightened I can make you."

They laughed and went their separate ways. It was a pleasant surprise for Chris, and he welcomed the camaraderie. It served to lighten the heavy heart that he was silently carrying.

Chapter Forty-Six

Eternal Friends

The next week or so was repetitive with patrol assignments and periodic mortar attacks at Camp Vance. Chris had seen Aaron a few more times, and just like their first meeting in the camp, the conversations were stress relievers and even funny at times. Both Chris and Aaron had gone on directed patrols, but they hadn't yet been assigned to the same mission. They exchanged experiences and some concerns, but for the most part, they were involved in the same planned strategies. However, they spoke at length about the imminent dangers of repeated mortar attacks on the camp. It seemed to them that the occupants of Camp Vance depended on dumb luck not to become a casualty of the unpredictable bombing attacks. It wasn't very comforting to hope that you weren't in the wrong place at the wrong time. But unfortunately, that was life at Camp Vance.

Having escaped injury on a number of occasions, the soldiers of Camp Vance were under another bombing attack. Mortar shells were falling all over the camp. It was early evening and Aaron had been catching up on some needed sleep. Chris had been on his way to visit Aaron when the attack began. He was caught out in the open and was running for cover when he saw Aaron stumbling out of his quarters still somewhat under the influence of slumber. Aaron was heading for one of the "safe" bunkers when a mortar shell exploded just a few yards from him. Although still conscious, he was blown to the ground and not moving. Chris changed his route from heading to the "safe" bunker to where his friend had fallen. When Chris got to his friend, a barrage of shells began falling right next to both of them. Chris jumped on top of Aaron to save him from additional injury while exposing himself to the possible effects of exploding mortar shells.

While Chris Martin and Aaron Obutu were experiencing a life-threatening situation, Nurse Holly Fisher, a thousand miles away, was also experiencing a situation that threatened life. However, it was not Holly's life that was in danger, but the life of her friend, Melody. Holly had been called to Melody's room by the attending doctor. Apparently, following the most recent seizure attack, Melody's overall condition had worsened to the point that her life was in jeopardy. Melody knew how she was feeling and realized that she was not going to recover from the attack. It is said that people know when their time on earth was about to expire. Melody looked at Holly and indicated that her time had come. Holly could say nothing. With tears in her eyes, she just looked at her friend as Melody folded her hands across her chest, smiled a faint smile, closed her eyes and expired. Melody's locked right hand opened to reveal the same crossed cannons that she held as Chris left for war.

Holly was distraught with grief. She had lost one of her best friends. As if that loss was not enough, she would now have to inform Chris Martin that the woman he loved, the one with whom he wanted to spend the rest of his life, was no more. She couldn't think straight right now; she just bent her head onto Melody's bed and cried.

Aaron Obutu was lying in a hospital bed with only superficial wounds from which he would soon recover. He owed his life to his friend, Chris. Aaron looked around the large hospital room but didn't see Chris anywhere. He wondered if Chris had suffered more severe injuries which had necessitated surgery. He hoped that he would soon see Chris recovering from whatever treatment the doctors saw fit to employ. His concern went farther that hope; however, he prayed and asked God to keep his friend safe.

When Chris Martin finally opened his eyes, he felt no pain and was shockingly surprised to see his long-lost friend, Danny Ferguson, standing right in front of him. He couldn't believe his eyes and was extremely overjoyed to finally catch up with his friend.

"Danny, what are you doing here, and where the heck have you been? I have been trying for months to contact you. How come you didn't answer my messages?"

"Chris, the question isn't 'What am I doing here?' The question is 'What are you doing here'?"

Chris wasn't clear about what Danny meant, but he finally connected the unidentified voice that had been contacting him to his friend, Danny. He also realized that there was no fog, no blurry figure. Danny was standing in front of him and was clear as day. As if struck by a bolt of lightning, Chris Martin understood that he was no longer lying on the ground at Camp Vance, no longer in a hospital room, and shockingly no longer on the same plane as others who were alive on Earth. He had entered this other world where Danny Ferguson had resided for all this time. It was surreal, but as he slowly accepted his surroundings and what fate had dictated, he became saddened with the realization that he would never again be able to see his soul mate, Melody. He would never be able to tell her again how much he loved her, and how sorry he was that he broke his promise to return. Chris looked at Danny and said*: "I hope my efforts saved Aaron, but I realize, now, that I didn't make it. Don't get me wrong, I'm glad to see you, but I left the love of my life behind. It's heartbreaking for me to never see her or be with her again. Eternity is a long time to hurt."*

From behind Chris, he heard a voice: *"Stop feeling sorry for yourself. Did you think I would let you go just like that?"*

Chris turned to see Melody Johnson right there: *"Melody, don't tell me."* Melody interrupted: *"Yep. The seizures finally won the battle, and I left just a short while ago. I am here with you, and 'yes' for all eternity."*

"I couldn't be happier, but how is Holly doing? I am sure she's not taking it well."

"Don't worry, Chris, I will appear to her soon and relieve some of her grief. I'll let her know how happy I am, and that, from time to time, I will contact her."

"That sounds good, Melody. But my parents just came to mind and how the military was going to notify my parents that I have been killed in action. That news will destroy them both."

Danny heard Chris and interjected: *"I wouldn't worry too much about that, Chris. In our world, things have a way of working themselves out. Give it time."*

Holly was having a tough time dealing with the loss of her friend, and she hadn't thought of a way to let Chris know about it. She was alone one early evening in her bedroom when the familiar fog appeared with the outline of a blurred figure. She immediately assumed that it was the apparition that had appeared to her before and had visited Chris many times. However, this time she was surprised to hear a different voice: *"Hi Holly. I hope you are feeling better. I am sorry that I had to leave you like that, but, as you probably know, I didn't have much of a choice."*

In a quivering almost undetectable voice, Holly whispered: "Melody, is that you? It sounds like you, but I can't really see through the fog."

"Oh, I'm sorry, Holly." And the fog disappeared. The blurry figure was clear, and Holly saw her best friend.

"Melody, I can't believe it's you. You sound great. I'm happy for you except for the fact that you and Chris can now never be. And as you probably know, I haven't found the right way to tell him about you. Do you have any ideas?"

Another figure appeared and answered Holly's question: *"No need to worry about telling me anything. As you can see, I already know."*

Holly was flabbergasted: "Chris, what happened? Why are you there?"

"It's no big deal. I happened to be in the wrong place at the wrong time. So, your worries about giving me the bad news are no longer a concern."

Holly just couldn't believe what was going on in her bedroom, and neither could her guest who heard her speaking aloud. Before he entered the room, however, Holly mentioned that she would be going to New York with her guest, and if Chris wanted, she would stop by and see his parents. She would also break the news that they shouldn't be surprised if their son appeared to them, like in a dream. She was sure that the appearances would greatly soften the blow from their loss. Chris thanked Holly for thinking about his parents and agreed to have Holly visit them.

Just as the figures became foggy and began to disappear, Chris noticed a familiar person enter Holly's bedroom to inquire about the apparent conversation he heard.

"Holly, I heard you talking to someone. I didn't know that anyone else was here."

"There isn't. Do you think I would have someone else in the room and jeopardize a trip to New York with the one and only, Dr. Jason Chance. No way!"

"I could only imagine that after the circumstances that took your friend, Melody, and knowing you, that you might have been repeating the mantra that "life's a bitch and then you ..." Holly stopped him before he was able to finish, and then she continued: "Life's a bitch and then you LIVE!"

Jason Chance looked at her in bewilderment. She said nothing else. She reached up and kissed him, and they left the bedroom. However, they had stayed long enough for Chris to recognize his friend, Dr. Chance. Chris turned to Melody to let her know about his association with the doctor, but she just hushed him with an: "I know. I know."

Chris wondered what else she knew that she wasn't telling him, but he wasn't concerned about it because he had an eternity to find out!

Epilogue

One Year Later

Holly had been true to her word, and although there was a lot of sadness, Holly felt that her visit to Chris Martin's parents served its purpose. Chris' parents didn't truly understand everything that they were told, but they were willing to accept anything that would lighten their burden of grief. They were told that they would see and hear from their son again in the near future. It was difficult, at first, to convince them that this was a real possibility and even harder for them to conceptualize the framework of an apparition. However, Holly was very patient with both of them and even asked her friend, Dr. Chance, to weigh in on the possibility of an appearance by their son. His credentials added to the veracity of Holly's prediction, and if the doctor was saying it, it had to be true. Over the past year, although Jason Chance had never seen the apparition that Holly spoke so often about, he was convinced, because of her dogmatic sincerity, that such an entity existed, and such appearances occurred.

The year had been a difficult one for Holly. She lost her best friend, her former boyfriend, and a soldier who she had come to really like and respect. That having been said, however, she was more than happy about how things were going with Dr. Jason Chance. They had gotten very close, and the possibility of making their relationship a permanent one had come up a couple of times. Neither one of them had been married before, so marriage was a big step for both of them. Their discussions about matrimony were becoming more and more detailed and, as time passed, they both were convinced that the sanctity of marriage was in their future.

Melody had not forgotten her friend, Holly. In fact, when Melody made an unexpected appearance, Holly was excited to discuss her future plans. Although Melody couldn't be happier for Holly, she regretted that she was not available to be Holly's Maid of Honor. But Melody did not allow that disappointment to dampen the enthusiasm that she felt for her friend. She would help Holly in any way that she could.

In addition to visiting his shocked parents, Chris made it a point to appear to his friend, Aaron Obutu, who was suffering from the guilt related to the fact that Chris Martin had sacrificed himself to save Aaron's life. Aaron was having a terrible time justifying Chris death in exchange for his own life. He had gone over the scenario a thousand times and wondered how he could have done things differently. Chris had learned that his friend, Aaron, was laboring every day under the weight of this unjustified conviction. So, Chris decided to set Aaron straight and release the anchor of guilt that laid on Aaron's shoulders.

One night after Aaron had returned from a patrol mission, the fog of a supernatural apparition appeared at the foot of Aaron's bunk. At first, just like all the others, Aaron was shocked at what he was seeing. He was even more surprised when he heard the familiar voice of Chris Martin. Chris tried to ease Aaron into the experience of speaking to an otherworldly individual, but it took Aaron a while before he accepted the fact that he was speaking with the spirit of his friend. Once that was realized, Chris told Aaron how he was not responsible for Chris' demise. Chris emphasized that he would have done it for any other soldier who was in harm's way. After what seemed like an eternity, Aaron finally accepted Chris' pointed and persuasive argument and was able to discard the jacket of guilt that he had been wearing since Chris' death.

It was imperative that Chris Martin get to Aaron when he did. He wanted Aaron to enjoy the freedom of a guilt-free existence, for as long as it lasted. The anchor of guilt had weighed down heavily on everything that Aaron did. It was extremely difficult for him to perform well or even live a comfortable life with the face of guilt always there. So, for a good twelve hours, Aaron was free from the chains that guilt had placed on his body. On a patrol mission the following day, however, Aaron Obutu became the successful target of a suicide bomber. Two soldiers were critically wounded and Private First Class Aaron Obutu was counted as one of those who made the ultimate sacrifice. He had been free of a guilt-ridden conscience for far too short a period of time.

Chris continued to visit his parents whenever he could. With each visit, the aura of disbelief decreased. The shock of the appearances was no longer apparent. The ability to speak to their son far outweighed any of the misgivings that the Martins may have been internally harboring. Danny Ferguson also made it his business to meet with his parents who, long ago, had been notified of Danny's demise. They also were comforted by the fact that they could speak with their son.

On one of Melody's visits to her friend, Holly, she was told that a date had been set for Jason Chance and Holly Fisher to exchange marital vows. Melody was not surprised and couldn't be happier for her friend. For the entire length of the visit, all they spoke about were the arrangements for the marriage ceremony. However, all during their conversation, a distressing cloud hovered above their heads. It was the fact that Holly's good friends (Melody, Chris and also Danny) could not be there to share in the celebration. It was a tough pill for all to swallow, but Holly knew that her friends, whether they were there or not, wished her the best.

It wasn't long before the wedding day had arrived. Dr. Chance and Nurse Fisher were getting married at the outdoor chapel on the base. There were doctors, nurses, staff and soldiers attending the ceremony. The only people missing were the friends that Holly knew couldn't be there.

It was an overcast day, and although the sun tried to peek through the clouds, the day remained gray for both the weather, and for the absence of Holly's friends. Holly looked beautiful and tried to hide her disappointment as she exchanged vows with her new husband. The weather continued to evolve into an even darker overcast when one of the guests in the audience yelled and pointed to the altar. There, above the newly wedded couple, was a bright, glowing, semicircle as brilliant as the sun itself. It engulfed the couple, and its rays lit the entire event. All that the people saw was this huge, brilliant halo like light above the couple, but as Holly looked more closely, she saw the specific images of three people who she had hoped wouldn't forget about her wedding day. As they circled above the couple, the images smiled and gave the "O.K." and good luck signs. Then as quickly as they appeared, they waved "good-bye" and vanished leaving the brilliant glow behind.

The attendees were at a loss to explain the phenomenon that they had just witnessed, but Holly couldn't contain her happiness upon seeing her friends. Jason Chance, who had not been privy to any of the previous apparitions, finally experienced what his wife had described to him on other occasions. Holly was about to clarify what had just occurred, but Jason raised his hand like a traffic cop and stopped her before she started to speak. He looked at her, smiled and said: "Life's a bitch, and then you LIVE."

Acknowledgments

I want to thank my wife who is always available as a sounding board for me. The astonishing amount of patience that she exhibits is nothing short of amazing. Many of her ideas and suggestions are incorporated into this work, and it's with her encouragement that I push on to complete each book. Thank you, **Lisa**. I have also picked the brain of my son, **Marty**, who is always there with a suggestion, viewpoint or correction. Thank you, Marty, for your keen insight. One of the few people who closely follows whatever progress I may make in my attempt at being an author is my cousin, **Carol**, who continues to encourage my putting "pen to paper." I also have to thank her for always making sure that my book appears on whatever social media platform to which she subscribes. Thank you, Carol, for all your help and remaining one of my greatest fans. As with my other novels, I want to thank **Dave** Manzolillo for his fantastic work in making the book come alive as he applies his graphic artist talents to the cover. Once again, Dave, you outdid yourself. Thank you. I also wish to thank all the young men and women who are willing to sacrifice all that they have to ensure that we are safe. It is their unselfish dedication to others that has truly inspired me to write about the two young men who decide to change their lives for the betterment of people they will never know. Thank you for the courage that enables you to look at potentially harmful and possibly deadly situations and still carry on. You are my heroes! Finally, I want to thank Mr. **Avi** Gvili and Ms. **Aliyah** Manuel for, once again, having the patience and confidence to advance the publication of my work through Boulevard Books.